Forced Family Fun

God Bless the Whitesides

Life is good among those joyfully residing above dirt. I am the last surviving family elder. Guess there is something to be said about this. Gratitude for one. I am no longer one of those young whippersnapper octogenarians. The eighties are in my rearview mirror by some seventeen years. I am now what they have dubbed a centenarian. At the ripe old age of ninety-seven I have experienced what many can never lay claim to in these modern times of living for the moment. I will turn ninety-eight in a few months if God wills me the opportunity. My driver's license expires then. I suppose I will have to take those tests, written and driving, to prove to the naysayers that I am no threat to their safety. The best truck I have ever owned bit the dust last month. She had nearly 400,000 miles under her belt before throwing a rod. I reckon buying one of those new ones is not so intriguing to me being long in the tooth as I am. Store bought, but teeth just the same. I am thinking about undertaking one of those leases they advertise. It would be a hoot seeing the look on one of those car salesmen's faces when I say I am gambling I run the table and make it to the end of the lease agreement. Taking baby bites seems the way to go now, one year at a time. Or in my case one day at a time might be more appropriate even though I feel fit as anyone has reason to be at my age.

I am blessed with good health and a dementia free mind as best I can recollect. I am not bragging. My old body is not that of an eighty-year-old, but I can get around without the use of a cane or walker. I live by my lonesome. I shop and do my own cooking. What I cook is not half bad, but I am the only critic, and I am not that hard to please. I manage my bills and have never been late on a payment a single time. I attend church regularly and volunteer more than most of those younger folks with a perception that their life is more important that serving the Lord. I always pay my church tithes, often giving more than my ten percent. Not a braggart just a man who lives by the golden rule and has respect and love for God Almighty.

I have occupied widower's man status twice. My last bride, Annie passed twenty years ago at the age of seventy-three. Died peacefully in her sleep of what the doctor called natural causes. Never saw it coming. It just arrived out of the blue and to my heartfelt shock. Bessy was the best for sure. My first wife of forty-three years, Bessy passed of that awful cancer, and she was not spared the suffering. Times were hard back then but we persevered. Neither of us was aquitter nor complainer. We played the cards we were dealt. Most were far from winning hands. The Lord delivered me a special one with that Bessy and he gathered her back by His side when the time suited Him. I cannot begrudge Him for taking her. He knows what is right for us and when it is right for Him. We don't have the ability to choose when we go. Some think that by committing suicide that it takes the plan out of His hands. I say that He knew the plan all along regardless of the outcome.

Thinking and rambling is an old man's rite of passage. Reckon I capitalize on mine more so than some do. It is a blessing to be of sound mind when I have seen so many of my peers go the rough way with that dreaded Alzheimer's curse. It is a tough thing to think on which is the worst, a failing body or a failing mind. Again, I try not to dwell on it. I am too old for one and thankfully have dodged both bullets so far. Secondly, it gets back to it being His plan. Two incidences you have no say so in, when you are born and when you die. They both just happen. Best you can do is manage the in between and be thankful for everything else. And by thankful, I mean thanking the Lord for your beginning, your in between and the end when it arrives.

By the sound of it I just received a text alert on my smart phone. That dang contraption is a lot smarter than me. Just because I am old doesn't mean the old dog can't be a trick pony, if that makes any sense. I like modern technology. It makes life mostly easier than back in the way yonder when we did not have all the creature comforts that we have today. I text. I email. I twitter a little and I even Google when googling helps me figure out something either I have forgotten or have a hankering to know. YouTube is a life saver too sometimes, a video better than a thousand words. Reckon I ought to check that text. Gut tells me it is probably that great grandson of mine. He has this notion that he wants to learn all the family business. By family business I mean the history of our family, the good, bad, and ugly of it. He wishes to document it, to preserve it for generations to come. I guess I cannot blame him for wanting to do this because I am the one responsible for baiting and setting the hook. I have often shared stories with him from my fondest memories of growing up in a time long forgotten. I told him when old people die so do the stories and precious memories. He thought on that a spell and it resonated with him something powerful like. He has gathered the pail and plans to milk this old cow for what it is worth. No bull just fact as best I can recall which is quite easy. Seems I can forget what happened just yesterday or even today, but I can visualize those long-ago yesterdays like they were frozen in time. If he is ready to do this for preservation purposes, I am willing to make sure he gets his money's worth. Proud to do so.

Yep, the text was from him. He will be here shortly. It is Saturday according to the calendar hanging on the fridge. One day is about the same as the next to me except Sundays. For him though, the weekends are nonworking days so I will adapt to his schedule to get it done. I hope he can write fast because I am not a slow talker when I get all fired up over something like this. Might be we should hire one of those court stenographers to do this properly. No need chancing on leaving something out if we are going to do this the right way. While I enjoy repeating memorable stories, we have way too much to cover to spend time on telling it twice.

Hope he arrives with an appetite. I have got speckled butterbeans in the Dutch oven, seasoned with fatback, BBQ short ribs dripping with my special sauce recipe and black skillet cornbread. When I say cornbread, I mean cornbread not the Jiffy stuff in a box or what some of those northerners like to rustle up that taste like a dessert muffin. Sliced tomatoes and spring onions will provide proper garnishing. Nothing is complete without an ice-cold pitcher of sweet tea. I even made my mama's old fashion banana pudding, a recipe passed down for generations. This is not the store-bought junk in a box. He will have to pack up some leftovers to take home for sure. The boy is not hitched yet and I am not convinced he can cook worth a lick. When I visit him, we always go out to eat. Might be that he will learn some cooking sense from me during this nostalgic journey. I will be sure to include some of the best hand me down recipes. After all they are an important piece of our family tradition and history. I just hope he enjoys hearing my ramblings as much I enjoy letting them rip.

Chapter 1

I hear his car on the crush run making its way up the drive. Funny little vehicle he drives, that Prius. Runs on electricity not gasoline. He must plug it in with an electrical cord to recharge it. I enjoy the perks of the modern world, but I reckon I have not warmed up to this innovation. Makes me feel like I am driving a toy. I worry about what you are supposed to do when the battery runs low or are drained completely, and you are out in the middle of nowhere without a plugin outlet or maybe a long enough extension cord. For the record, I have never run my engine dry of gasoline nor got stranded on the roadside. Never been much of a gambler trying to squeeze out that last drop in the tank. Had plenty of friends growing up that did though. My Annie played with fire too much for my comfort, seeing that gas tank light come on, claiming she could drive another thirty miles. I, for one, do not need a warning light to warn me. I don't trust it for one thing. Quarter tank left on the gauge means you fill up then and not later.

"Come on in David, no need to knock like a common stranger. I reckon you are here to slay old Goliath this afternoon."

"Grandfather Nelson, I do appreciate that you are willing to do this."

Not one to bruise his ego, I let it slide that I had planted the seed in his head. "Got nothing more important to do. I am proud of you for taking on this by your lonesome. It is a wonderful thing that you are doing for our family and any family that follows us. You won't find most of this in any history book, especially in a time when people are trying to rewrite or erase our country's history with all the senseless wokeness and cancel nonsense. They are ruining this great country for which we have always stood. I hope you stay clear of the indoctrination brainwashing."

"Not to fear Grandfather, you and my parents have instilled wonderful values and a solid foundation for me. I never did like Kool-Aid of any flavor. Give me sweet tea and the honest truth."

"That's my boy. You just stick to those values, and you will go far. Hope you are hungry."

"Smelled your vittles when I exited my car. Bet you left the windows open and fanned it just for my benefit, didn't you?"

"Mere coincidence. House needed airing out a bit on a beautiful day like today. Hope the neighbors did not catch a whiff. This is supposed to be a two man endeavor today. We'll eat first, just in case."

"Am I still your favorite, Grandfather Nelson?"

"Today you are my favorite, David."

"Spoken like a true politician."

"Fighting words if ever they were any. Most politicians are scallywags, not to be trusted any further than you can throw them. All promise and no delivery. During my life seventeen presidents have held office. Up until this year, none have been more incompetent and untrustworthy than Carter. Biden makes old Jimmy look like an Eagle Scout. These elected officials are supposed to work for us not the other way around. Enough on this subject, we don't need anything upsetting our digestive system, do we? Today is a day to embrace our past not dwell on the present and scary future if things don't get back on the rightful American way track. Let's partake of the prepared meal and pay our thanks and ask forgiveness for our sins and trespassing."

Wonderful chit chat ensued during the meal, David and I reminiscing over fond recent and past memories. Today he was indeed my favorite great grand of seven so far. It pleased me to watch him enjoy every crumb and morsel the meal had to offer. He frequently complemented the cook and inflated my centenarian ego. Breaking bread around the table has always been a family tradition whether it is two at the table or twenty-two. Sadly, it is a lost art. Fast food, busy schedules, smart phones, and other gadget distractions have all but destroyed this sacred practice. Kids and adults alike are drawn to their cell phones while sitting at the table and have forgotten how to carry on normal conversations. In my home I ban these devices during a meal. Family nor friends take too kindly to me telling them to deposit their distractions in the basket in the den before breaking bread at my table. Mostly it works to elevate the conversation but too often there are those who scarf down their meals quickly so they might excuse themselves to retrieve what holds them prisoner. I do embrace modern technology but with applicable controls and restrictions. Overusing anything can be an addiction and obsession. Smart phones have become the new alcohol dependency, a drug that destroys a social existence. Kids are losing the ability to communicate one on one and converse without these handheld distractions. I think and act like an old fool, critiquing the new fangled like I am clinging to the old ways. Far from it, like I have already said, I embrace technology, but I do so in moderation. I remain the captain of my ship and refuse to allow those gadgets to take control of my vessel.

"Dishes washed, food put away, leftovers packaged for you, I reckon it is time for us to get down to business, David."

"Ready when you are, Grandfather Nelson."

"How do we proceed then?"

"Let's start from the beginning or as far back as you can remember and wish to share."

"I am worried I will outpace you, taking all this down with my lightning speed of gifted gab."

"Not to worry, I have this and will record the sessions." David held out a tiny black device in the palm of his hand saying it was a voice activated recorder.

"Hope that thing has enough memory to pace mine."

"It has more than enough memory to record what you have to share. Let's start by you saying your name, age, and today's date. Then I will ask questions where appropriate. Fire when ready, Grandfather Nelson."

"My name is Nelson Rutherford Whiteside, ninety-seven years young, to be ninety eight April first when I will require a renewal of an automobile operational driver's license. Today is January 19th of the year 2021, less than four months from that DMV visit. I don't think I will be purchasing one of those electric cars to replace my old truck once I successfully secure my renewed license. How's that for starters, David?"

"Perfect Grandfather Nelson. What is your first childhood recollection?"

"Well, I must have been four or five as best I can recall. I was birthed in the era of the roaring twenties as they were called, born April 1, 1924. Of course, I don't recall much. I was too young to be one of those rebellious teenagers or remember anything about the women scantily clad in what they called flappers back then. I came along after World War 1 and that deadly Spanish flu had double whammed the population, killing so many people. Reckon it was around 1928 or 1929 and I had come down with something and was deathly sick. My folks took me to the doctor, and they injected me with this newfangled medicine called penicillin. It pert near killed me, according to my folks, what little I remember about being sicker after getting the shot. I always mark down that I am allergic to it on my medical records during doctor visits, what few I have ever had. Thankfully other than that penicillin almost ending it for me I have been as healthy as a horse otherwise. Never spent a day in a hospital, knock on wood."

"You were born April 1, 1924, where?"

"According to my mama, a midwife delivered me at our house. We lived in the country, in the boonies, and there were no towns, doctors nor hospitals nearby. I was born in Tatertown. Wipe that silly grin off your face, David. There once was such a township as Tatertown."

"Why in the world would someone name a town Tatertown?"

"Well, we'll have to back up a little further to reel that one in."

> According to say so, it was the late 1800s and the area was unincorporated. Farms were spread about but there were no stores to speak of. Mercantile was delivered by wagon when ordered or residents had to make the long trek to pick up goods, sometimes the neighboring farms pooling resources for joint ventures to obtain what they needed. Silas McMurtry owned and operated the largest farm and primarily raised sweet potatoes, what some like to refer to as yams. His

10

crop was so huge that none of the other farms included sweet potatoes in their crop rotation. Silas had the market cornered when it came to harvest time. He controlled and set the price of sweet potatoes. Story goes, as time passed, Silas had this notion that he wanted to incorporate the area and establish a post office. Back then the post office had to have a name among all kinds of other requirements. Silas built one that more resembled a one room log cabin and called it the Tatertown Post Office after what he called his farm. Apparently, he eventually met all the other requirements, and the community became known as Tatertown. After the post office laid the foundation, other venues sprung up like a mercantile business, barber shop, a country grocery, an eatery and even a funeral parlor. It was still known as Tatertown when I was brought into this world. It has since dropped that name and has been renamed after one of the first mayors. Money can buy most any recognition.

I was six when the storm struck. And boy what a storm it was. I had one sister and two brothers, all older than me. We were in the field when the sky got dark. Daddy motioned for us to head to the house as the wind picked up and hail began to come down. Daddy said it was pea sized but it felt much larger. He hurried all of us down into the root cellar located behind the barn. That wind roared something louder than I have ever heard. We were all scared. The doors on the root cellar rattled like they were going to be yanked off their hinges. Suddenly everything got deathly quiet. Daddy finally ventured outside making us stay behind. We saw him fall to his knees after he reached the outdoors.

Our house and the barn were gone like they had never been there. Trees were snapped and twisted. I had never seen anything like that. I don't think any of my family had. A tornado had left a path of destruction half mile wide in some places as it zig zagged nearly five miles across the countryside. Three people lost their lives as did three horses, a mule and twenty-seven cattle and no telling how many other animals. Someone named it the Cow Killer Twister.

11

Some of those poor cows were picked up and dropped miles away from their pastures. Henry Wiley claimed his roof was snatched off his house and an angus calf was deposited in his bathroom inside his clawfoot bathtub without a scratch on it, live and mooing. Most did not believe his tale, but he swore it happened. As evidence, he did produce a little heifer that nobody ever claimed.

Unable to afford rebuilding what had been destroyed we moved away and moved in with my mama's parents. Boy is that when the fun began let me tell you. Three generations under one roof makes for challenging times according to Daddy's spin on it. He appreciated the outreach but did not like it for a minute. I was a young'un, what did I know?

Chapter 2

David kind of let me have free rein, telling what I remembered sometimes not in chronological order. Sequence and time references don't always line up when you are viewing the world through a child's eyes and imagination. Snippets and memories come in rushes or in trickles. They can be vivid or vague. Sometimes they make perfectly good sense. Other times they can be murky as the muddiest creek. Ninety something years ago can be a blur or as vivid as yesterday, depending on the memories, good or bad. Back to rite of passage, I am old and deservingly so have earned a pass when remembering and telling it like I think it might have been.

There were five of us living with my grandparents, Juniper and Clarice Barnhart. Counting them there were seven of us in that house. If you included Uncle Rusty, that made eight, but he lived in a little shed behind the barn. He was my mama's brother. I never knew why he lived in that shed. I did not ask, and nobody ever said. It was just the way it had always been, him living there. Looking back now, I guess I never realized just how eccentric thirty-seven-year-old Uncle Rusty was. He was fun to be around as a kid. I learned a lot of stuff by hanging out with him, stuff I would have probably not learned anywhere else. I don't think Mama appreciated the education I was receiving. Daddy just let it be and never said much about anything. He reluctantly accepted the situation for better or worse, mostly worse. He ate his share of humble pie while we lived there. Proud men prefer standing on their own two feet and being the primary family provider. That Cow Killer Twister had changed everything.

Uncle Rusty, what can I say now that I could not comprehend back then? He was the not so perfect man child. He lived for the day every day. For him, the past stayed where it had landed and the future was just another tomorrow, a day that would paint its own picture when it arrived. I don't recall Uncle Rusty ever working a job, not that I ever gave it much thought back then. He was always there just hanging out and ready to do stuff. Uncle Rusty was an expert in doing most anything. Rhyme never had to have reasoning behind it. If it was worth doing, it was worth doing with vigor. He was a regular MacGyver, way ahead of his time. He could make anything out of nothing and improvise when improvision seemed an impossibility. He wowed me like nobody else has ever done. Uncle Rusty could do most anything providing he had a rope, a flashlight and something like a brick or rock. If he didn't have what he needed he would figure on another way to do what needed to be done.

I'm not sure where, but somehow Uncle Rusty had found a discarded fisherman's net. I say discarded but with him you never knew. In his mind he never stole anything. He found the next whatever he had in his possession. Not much more complicated than that, the possession is nine tenths of the law rule, not that he ever claimed the law ruled. So now he has the humongous net more the size of a large tarp. I wondered what in the world he planned to do with it. I liked to fish but he had no boat. He certainly could not cast it into the water by himself and fat chance the two of us could do it either. An imagination will not be denied. He draped it over the top of an old a-frame that used to be a swing set and claimed it would keep the mosquitoes out saying he had seen them use netting in Africa in a National Geographic Magazine. A mosquito would have to be the size of a bird to get caught in the net. No talking him out of it once he had his mind set. He even tried to use it for corralling chickens. It would have sort of worked had he figured a way to secure it properly and a method for convincing the chickens to go inside. Later he did come up with an amazing use for it. The netting could be used to secure items in the back of a truck. I don't remember anyone asking him where he had found it nor anyone coming by to claim it. Like anything in his life, he eventually lost interest in it.

One afternoon I looked for him and could find him nowhere. It was unlike him to wander too far away. Usually all I had to do was call his name and I would then hear that familiar whistle nearby. Uncle Rusty was always whistling a tune, most of which I had never heard before. Whistling tunes had this way of calming him, so said Mama. He never acted uncalm to me, so I did not understand what she meant. I called his name again and again but never heard that familiar whistling. I was becoming worried that something bad had happened to him.

"Up here!"

I heard him but still did not see him.

"Up here!"

"Up where," I yelled back.

"Up here!"

I looked up left and then right but still did not see him not until I saw the huge cedar tree shaking.

"Uncle Rusty are you in the cedar tree?"

"I am."

"Why are you in the cedar tree? Are you on lookout or something?"

"Christmas, I am fixing it."

"It is summer not wintertime. That cedar is too big to be a Christmas tree Uncle Rusty."

"Come over here. I will lower the rope. Tie that hacksaw to the end."

Just then I saw the rope snaking its way out of the cedar tree, but I still could not spot Uncle Rusty among the thick bushy branches. I could hear him whistling a tune though. Sure enough, there was a hacksaw on the ground underneath the cedar tree. I grabbed the rope and then the hacksaw and did what Uncle Rusty asked me to do. I had learned never to question what he had in mind. He never warmed up to questions being asked of him. All you needed to know was that he knew what he was doing. And whatever it was, it would work the way he planned it. If it didn't, you would

15

never know it because he would make like whatever changed or didn't work was the way he had planned it all along. This made perfectly good sense in Uncle Rusty's world whether you agreed or not. Like I said, never question his technique or intent.

Uncle Rusty hoisted the hacksaw up with the rope until it vanished in the thick of things with him. Christmas tree concerns in July, what was all this about I wondered, but dared not ask again. I heard him begin sawing, tree sawdust raining from somewhere up there in that tree. I stepped back far enough to see if I could figure out what he was doing. The top of that giant cedar was swaying and shaking. I was afraid Uncle Rusty was going to fall out of it. The more it shook about, the faster he whistled a tune. Suddenly, the whole top of the tree began leaning and then, with a loud cracking sound, the tree top tumbled to the ground. It was then that I could see Uncle Rusty's head at the top, peeking out like a turtle from a shell with this big grin on his face.

"I am lowering the rope. Untie the hacksaw when it reaches you."

I did what he asked me to do like I always did when he asked me to do anything. After I untied the hacksaw, the rope dropped from the tree followed by Uncle Rusty, noisily climbing through the branches. He patted me on the head once he reached the ground, smiling proudly like he had accomplished whatever he had set out to do. I stared at the treetop on the ground, and it looked to be the perfect size for a Christmas tree we might use in the house. I wanted to ask him what he intended to do with it, but I knew better.

"There! Much better!"

I looked at Uncle Rusty then looked at the treetop on the ground. He then tied the rope to the bottom end of the tree and motioned to me to help him drag it. The grownups were going to have a hissy fit if we dragged that treetop inside the house. I did not want to, but I did what he asked me to do. He was my uncle. I was supposed to do whatever an adult told

16

me to do. Even Uncle Rusty, so we dragged the tree toward the backdoor but then we kept going until we reached the deep gulley behind the house. Uncle Rusty untied the rope and then we pushed the tree into the gulley. Now I was more confused than ever. He coiled up the rope and we walked back to the shed and put the rope away. Uncle Rusty then stepped back outside and said, "See, perfect."

I scratched my head, following his gaze. He was looking at the topless cedar tree. I feared that this was not going to set well with my folks or my grandparents. That tree now looked ugly and out of place near the house. I was a willing accomplice to what he had done, making me as guilty as he. My mouth was dust dry. I did my best to wet my lips, trying to muster up the guts to go against the rules and ask him why he had done it, why we had done it now that I was part of it.

"Runway," he said.

I misunderstood him and thought he was saying run away, thinking the grownups had spotted what had been done.

"That will do it all right," he added and then he just walked back inside the shed.

Well as anticipated my grandfather had that hissy fit when he saw the decapitated cedar tree. He stormed past me and toward the shed. I figured I must be off the hook, too small to have had anything to do with it. I heard plenty of yelling going on inside the shed but could not make out what was being shouted. I was just glad I was no part of it, at least not yet. Grandfather exited the shed still fuming, waving his arms about and kicking up dust. Mama met him about halfway between the shed and the house. I kept my distance and just did my best to eavesdrop.

"Can you believe it? Your idiot brother topped that cedar tree."

"Why would he do something like that, Daddy?"

"He said he was building a runway."

"A runway, I don't get it."

"He said that the tree was too tall and blocking the roof."

"I still don't understand."

"That cedar tree was blocking Santa's landing strip to our rooftop. Now the sleigh could land perfectly for Christmas. That boy, that man is thirty-seven years old, and he is worrying about Santa Clause so much so that he clears the landing trajectory for an imaginary sleigh and reindeer. He ruined that old cedar by giving it a crewcut. Rusty is going to put me in an early grave."

"Hush your mouth, Daddy. If Rusty hears you saying that, he will be out back digging you the perfect one."

"You've got a point. Well, I already gave him what for, not that it means a hill of beans. Rusty does not have a mean bone in his body. I am the one that always comes away from these situations like I have taken the beating."

Let me tell you, I was so glad I had dodged that bullet. Short lived though. After Grandfather went inside, Mama walked over to me and said, 'thank you for helping Rusty drag the tree to the gully.' I had no choice then. I confessed it was me that had tied the hacksaw to the rope that he had hauled up in the tree. Being guilty as charged sometimes guilts you into saying more than you should ever have said. On the bright side, Santa would be able to land his sleigh this Christmas without wrecking it in that cedar tree. Uncle Rusty is to thank for that, with a little help from his accomplice in the crime.

Another thing about Uncle Rusty is that he had this humongous appetite. If anyone might be hungry enough to eat a horse, like they sometimes say, Uncle Rusty would be the very one to give it a shot. Grandmother would never say Uncle Rusty was fat. She referred to him as big boned. She always made sure he had a second helping when we ate. Even with that, Uncle Rusty was always scheming about how he could sneak more. Yep, you got it, he included me on a lot of that scheming. Once an accomplice I was often utilized as the distractor. I would do my best to keep folks from going into the kitchen while he was in there foraging. When successful he usually shared the spoils with me. I didn't always take him up on it because he too often wasn't choosey about what he snuck from any leftovers. This one time he ended up smuggling some macaroni and cheese pie from the Sunday spread. In his haste he had scooped it up in a paper cup and had forgotten to get a spoon or fork. This is the one time I turned down the opportunity to share it with him after I watched him use his tongue to remove chunks from the cup. He then offered it to me, my turn, and I told him it was all his. Rusty must have had the tongue of an anteater. I came up with a little tune that I sang to him, 'He stuck his tongue into the bowl and called it macaroni.' To this very day I still vividly remember that episode, tough to get those images out of my head.

Uncle Rusty would eat directly from the garden. Not an uncommon practice for any of us eating tomatoes, cucumbers or radishes. Rusty took it to another level. He would pluck pods of okra from the stalks and chomp them down with one bite. I couldn't even pick okra because it made my skin sting. Snow peas were my favorite raw vegetable right from the pods. The peas were sweet like candy. Uncle Rusty thought you could eat any beans or peas from the pod. It was hilarious watching him give butter beans or pinkeye purple eye peas a try. I never saw so much spitting and coughing. Short term memory, not one to learn his lesson, he would do it again after we tried the snow peas during our next visit. Banana peppers were a favorite during our raids. Uncle Rusty made the mistake of eating habanera peppers. Those hot peppers did a number on him. Memory jolted he weaned off any type of peppers for good.

Then there was the time he came home with his new pet, a possum. He had found it in a tree in Cook's Woods. I think he thought it was some kind of ugly feral cat. A possum is not usually the petting kind, but somehow, he soothed the critter. It never bit him but Smiley, as he named it, would not allow anyone else to hold it. That thing hissed like there was no tomorrow when anyone else was around. The dang thing slept with him too. It took after Uncle Rusty and would eat about anything. We didn't know it then, but a possum can carry plenty of nasty diseases. I reckon Uncle Rusty possessed an uncanny immunity. The possum never contracted anything from him either. Uncle Rusty and Smiley swapped turns playing dead when a dog or cat threatened them. Uncle Rusty kept that critter for nearly two months before Smiley up and went missing during the night. A neighbor, Pepper Finley, was rumored to have stolen him. Pepper had a fondness for possums and not in a pet sort of way. We could not prove it, but we think Smiley might have ended up on Pepper's dinner table. Uncle Rusty was devasted for about half a day before he found a box turtle that he named Stretch. Go figure, he named it Stretch because of the way it stretched its head from the shell. Uncle Rusty was always bringing home a wayward or stray something whether they were cooperative or not.

Who could ever forget the great snipe hunt? For the record, there really is no such thing as a snipe. Some say it is a bird too smart to be caught. It is really a trick; a prank people enjoy playing on other people. Purely innocent tomfoolery. We had some Georgia kinfolk, what Daddy called Georgia crackers. Cousin Dennis was about my age and if anyone was a bad influence on me, it was him. He enjoyed picking on Uncle Rusty and putting him up to almost anything, more for his enjoyment than poor Uncle Rusty's. He decided that we would take Uncle Rusty on his first snipe hunt. A snipe is supposedly a nocturnal critter. The premise of the snipe hunt goes like this. One poor sole is chosen to wait at the end of a long ditch while holding a croaker sack to catch any snipes that the others flush in his direction. That person is literally left holding the bag while the others leave him there and go home. It didn't feel right doing this to Uncle Rusty, but I did it anyway. Dark arrived on schedule. We positioned Uncle Rusty in the woods at the end of a long winding ditch that used to be a creek bed. We told him to stay put until he caught a snipe.

Hours passed and no Uncle Rusty. Guilt was eating me alive. Dennis was laughing up a storm enjoying every passing minute. We heard a commotion from the heavy brush behind the out shed and out stepped Uncle Rusty still clutching that croaker sack. As he got closer, we could that the sack was moving. Something was inside.

Rusty smiled as he stood there in front of us, "Got a snipe."

Dennis spoke up, "Can't be a snipe, there is no such thing."

Rusty grinned, "No such thing is in my sack, a snipe."

"Something is in that sack Dennis."

"Well, it ain't no snipe. He's just fooling us."

"Uncle Rusty doesn't know how to fool anyone. If he said he caught a snipe, then he believes he caught a snipe."

"Just dump it out and let's get a look at your snipe," said Dennis.

Still smiling, he did as asked setting free a polecat. The skunk didn't take too kindly to being in that sack and let loose a reminder. It took us nearly a week to get that stink off us. Uncle Rusty had not been caught in its sights being the dumper and all.

You would have thought Dennis had learned his lesson. He was more determined than ever to best Uncle Rusty for what he had done to us. What made him even madder was the fact that Uncle Rusty called him 'animal cracker' having overhead Daddy calling them crackers behind their backs. This time Dennis wanted to introduce Uncle Rusty to cow tipping. Cow tipping was no more than another version of snipe hunting. You just need that one naïve and trusting person to pull the wool over their eyes. Uncle Rusty was that target. Supposedly, you sneak in a pasture when the cows are sleeping. Some do sleep standing up. You sneak up on an unsuspecting cow and sort of push it over and it lands on his side and can't get back up...cows tipping.

Old man Davis just down the road had a pasture full of cows. After it got dark, we snuck inside the fence line. Dennis explained to Uncle Rusty to pick out a cow and tip it over. Without so much of a blink or smidgen of hesitation, Uncle Rusty disappeared into the herd of cows. The mooing and bellowing let us know that the cows knew that had unwanted company. Just coming into view, we spotted one heading our way. It was the largest bull I had ever seen. It was none too happy and had us in its crosshairs. We barely made it through the barbed wire, both of us ripping our clothes and bleeding like stuck pigs.

Winded and sitting on the ground we heard the barbed wire creak and looked to see Uncle Rusty crawling through. He shrugged and then said, "That cow didn't want to be tipped."

Uncle Rusty had bested us yet again. The next day out Georgia kinfolk headed home but not before Dennis tried one last time to best Uncle Rusty. The chicken yard was ruled by the meanest Dominicker rooster. Daddy had come close to killing it because it had attacked Mama and us a few times. Dennis convinced Uncle Rusty to go fetch it saying it was going to be readied for dinner. It was in the predawn minutes when Uncle Rusty entered the chicken coop. Just at the crack of dawn he returned holding the rooster by its legs. Dennis was fit to be tied. He didn't know that chickens stayed on the roost until daylight. Uncle Rusty had no problem snatching it up.

"Here," he said, handing the Dominicker devil to Dennis.

Dennis held up his hands saying, "No way."

Uncle Rusty turned that Dominicker loose and the rooster began to flog Dennis like there was no tomorrow. I gave the encounter wide berth and busted a gut laughing. There was no besting Uncle Rusty. I don't recall Dennis and his family returning to our place. I would later overhear Daddy telling

Mama that he was glad the freeloaders were gone. All they had wanted was money, peddling a sad sob story of some kind that he had seen right through from the get-go.

"I wish I could have known Uncle Rusty," remarked David.

"He was indeed one of a kind. I think I was about twelve when he passed. There are so many stories and adventures with Uncle Rusty that I cannot remember them all. If I do, I will be sure to include them."

"I never heard, just how did Uncle Rusty die?"

"As only Uncle Rusty could," I laughed before explaining.

Uncle Rusty would have been in his forties. He no longer lived in the shed and we no longer lived on the farm with my grandparents. Daddy had gotten a new job in the textile mill over in the next county. We lived in what they called back then the mill hill projects. The textile mill had constructed several streets worth of four room houses near the mill for those that worked there. It was affordable and it made sure that the people working at the mill had no excuse for not reporting to work. They even issued coupon books as part of the earned wages that could only been redeemed at a store in the neighborhood, owned and operated by the mill. I guess I am getting a little sidetracked and ahead.

Uncle Rusty, like I said, now resided in one of the spare bedrooms inside. I am not sure why he had not always lived in one. Uncle Rusty never complained about his accommodations. Guess they may have relocated him because the old shed had gotten in bad shape and eventually had to be torn down. Seems a sad situation them having thier son banished to an out shed and only allowing him to live in the family house when the shed had gotten unlivable. One thing for sure, Uncle Rusty could never have made it on his own. My grandparents realized this and never banished him from the homesite.

Uncle Rusty loved to fish. He is responsible for teaching me how to fish, how to bait my hook with red wigglers and how to watch that bobbing cork to know when I had a fish nibbling on my line. Those were wonderful times when we went fishing at the pond on the property. It was a harsh winter in 1937, colder than it had been in many years. A January winter storm blew in and buried the countryside with over fourteen inches of ice and snow. The temperatures dropped into the teens and hung there for nearly a week never getting above freezing. That snow had hardened and was going nowhere anytime soon. Grandfather subscribed to National Geographic magazine. He always passed the copies along to Uncle Rusty when he was finished with them. The January edition had a featured story about ice fishing and how to construct the sheds on the ice and drill open holes for fishing on the Great Lakes. Old Rusty MacGyver, not to be outdone, began planning how he could fish on that frozen over pond. As does Rusty, he is his own drummer and does it his way seldom sharing his plans unless someone stumbles into his little operation. In this case nobody did.

It took him the better part of the week to construct his masterpiece out on the middle of that pond. It was no more than a lean-to built from leftover boards from the dilapidated shed that had once been his home. Somehow, he successfully drilled a series of small holes with grandfather's handheld cork drill. In true Uncle Rusty fashion, he had not thought everything through. While he could drop a hook and a line through the holes, it was impossible to retrieve his fish through the tiny holes. Not to be outdone, he used a pickax and began widening his fishing spot by basically connecting the dots from tiny hole to tiny hole until he had enlarged the opening. It was nearly dark by the time he dropped his first line, but his ingenuity had paid off. He landed his first of three fish.

Cold, but not ready to give up, he built a fire and fished on. Unbeknownst to Uncle Rusty the thaw had already begun with temperatures hovering above freezing. The additional warmth inside that lean-to was all that was needed for the ice to break. They did not locate Uncle Rusty until the pond thawed and only then after they dragged it with hooks. Story goes that he still had his fishing pole held firmly in his grip and on the line was the largest catfish that had ever been caught in that pond. The fish was still alive. They set it free but not before tagging it and naming it CJ after Rusty. Seems that Uncle Rusty's real name was Carl Jacob. He came by the name Rusty when he was a little boy because he always played in the red clay all the time making him look rusty from head to toe. Mama told me that Grandmother said the bathwater looked like something rusty had been cleaned in it saying 'Rusty you are never going to come clean. This might be your color forever.' Rusty stuck just like the coating from the red clay.

"He died a true MacGyver death, didn't he?"

"Indeed, he did, David. Indeed, he did."

We decided to take a little break and partake of that homemade banana pudding. My old memory cells needed a bit of recharging, even if David's little recorder didn't. Just for a hoot I served up two bowls of pudding without spoons. I picked my bowl up to my face and toasted David. Not to be undone, he did the same, one upping me by sticking out his tongue. I then handed him a spoon and we both had a gut-wrenching laugh over our tribute to Carl Jacob 'Uncle Rusty'. It triggered another memory that I decided to save until our session resumed.

Chapter 3

Strolling down memory lane can be quite gratifying, especially when you have a captivated and interested audience. I appreciated David having the gumption to see this through. Not often do you see this generation interested in the life of old codgers, even if it is somewhat of a legacy left behind for those that have no inkling of the family tree and its origins. Some people have no interest in knowing the past. Their lives are too fast and furious in the present to care. Others pay dearly for someone to research their genealogy. But that alone does not provide the memories from those who lived the life. Connecting the dots is special unless you are Uncle Rusty on a thawing pond.

"How old are you now, David?"

"Just turned twenty-five."

"What do you remember about your grandparents, my Cicci and her hubby Ray?"

"Not much. Papa Ray was already gone by the time I was born, and Nana C died when I was two."

"That Ray up and leaving like he did, left a bad taste in my mouth. Guess I should let it be being that less than a month after he decided to call it quits, he was T-boned by a Greyhound bus. Don't much make sense a man as old as Ray deciding he no longer wanted to be married. Well, I reckon that jezebel from the Waffle House that he hooked up with convinced him otherwise. I had always thought a lot of Ray until he decided to go rogue."

"Never heard that story about him."

"You mean your folks never told you."

"No sir, they just said he had passed before I was born."

"Guess that's why it is important, us doing what we are doing, to tell it straight and set the records right. The truth needs to be told even if it is not what we would prefer to hear."

"Papa Ray had a girlfriend, imagine that."

"David, how often do you and your folks talk about the good old days?"

"Talk? We never talk about what happened today much less what happened years ago. We hardly ever share a meal together. Everybody is busy going in opposite directions. There is never the time."

"Learn from the journey that we are embarking on and make time. When we finish with our portion, sit down with them, ask them to share memories about your grandparents and other relatives."

"I will try but they are not like you. They don't get the importance of it."

"Maybe, once you share what I have shared with you, it will click with them."

"Maybe, are you ready to continue?"

"I was born ready, David."

> Some of my best days were spent there with not only Uncle Rusty but just in general, living with my grandparents. I was the youngest of my siblings, the baby boy. It was tough for me to find my place in the pecking order. I was the little bothersome kid that nobody wanted to spend time with. I gravitated to some of the adults like Uncle Rusty and crazy cousin Calvert. He wasn't really crazy, but people called him crazy because he said crazy stuff. It was almost as if he spoke a different language. People often struggled to decipher what he was saying. Cousin Calvert was a grown man that lived about a mile from my grandparents. He was a wheeler dealer. Some called him a con man but not to his face. Cousin Calvert could be quite the bruiser if you pushed him too far or double crossed him. Daddy called him a monster among men, one never to be taken lightly. Calvert was one of those third or fourth cousins twice removed or something like that. It did not really matter where he landed on the family tree, blood was thicker than water when it came to the Whitesides. Like him or not, respect him or not, agree with him or not, Cousin Calvert was Whiteside through and through.

Cousin Calvert was a full-grown man. I am guessing he was in his forties, maybe older, when we arrived at my grandparent's place. He wasn't married and had never been that I know of. Kind of like with Rusty, I found it easy to hang out with him. He didn't seem to mind and treated me fairly. From day one he called me NeddyB saying I looked like a NeddyB, not a Nelson. Go figure. Never made much sense to me but you were not supposed to question your elders no matter what you thought. I was forever his NeddyB, end of story.

I had turned seven and shadowed him when I wasn't hanging out with Uncle Rusty. Well, I reckon I shadowed him when he was around. He did not live close by for me to see just anytime I wanted. He visited us regularly though. He was fond of my grandma's cooking. He seemed to always manage to come over on Sundays. Grandma cooked enough to feed a small army. Everyone got fed under her roof. About time the dishes were being washed, Cousin Calvert would say his goodbyes and head back home. No doubting it, he just showed up for the vittles, not much else. He was not one to socialize, even with family. He was not shy, he just seemed to be a wanderer, a man in search of the next greatest deal. He could have easily played the role of Mister Haney on Green Acres. He passed on long before that television series made its debut in 1971.

Cousin Calvert taught me plenty, telling me he would take me under his wing and open my eyes to the art of making a buck. He swapped and bartered like nobody's business. He prided himself as being the one that always came out on top. Whether he did or not is not for me to say. I was a little chap. What did I really understand about his bargaining and salesmanship? What I do recall is the uniqueness of his gab, words and phrases that took on a world of their own. Cousin Calvert had this uncanny wit and perception. He seemed to be an expert on everything, and an endless supply of knowledge oozed from his pores, so he would claim. If I close my eyes, I can almost hear him spouting about this and that.

"NeddyB, don't let anybody tell you different, a possum is a flat animal that sleeps in the middle of the road. Remember, there are 5,000 kinds of slithering snakes and 4,998 of them reside in the South. And like snakes, there are 10,000 types of eight legged spiders known to mankind. All of them live around here plus several more nobody's seen before. I hate snakes and spiders. No good comes when you cross paths when them. If it slithers, flies, crawls or jumps it will bite or sting you. Don't let nobody tell you otherwise. If they do, you can bet they have never been bit or stung."

"NeddyB, I am *fixin* to go fishing. You want to drown some worms?"

Cousin Calvert took me and Uncle Rusty fishing plenty of times. He let us keep anything that we caught but if he caught a mess, he would swap them for something else. Oddly, he did not like the taste of fish. Lots of people did though. Bartering a stringer of fish for chewing tobacco or a pack of smokes was common practice. He shared the chewing tobacco with Uncle Rusty. Claimed he was the one that taught him proper spitting technique. I tried it only once. Swallowed more juice than I ever managed to spit on the ground. I don't partake in a chew to this very day, reminded by the awful burning in my throat and spewing tobacco juice from my mouth and out my nostrils. Cousin Calvert and Uncle Rusty got one heck of a belly laugh at my expense, a lesson learned, and a mistake never committed again.

Cousin Calvert owned this old jalopy of a truck. It had a flatbed with wooden siderails and no tailgate. Every Saturday he would load up an assortment of items he had collected and head over to the next county to what he called the stop and swap. It was what we call today, a flea market or a jockey lot. The farmer that owned the pasture allowed people to bring whatever they wanted to sell or swap. He charged everybody with something to sell or swap a dollar to pass through his fence gate, even the folks just coming to browse. Sometimes he would take me and Uncle Rusty along. Rusty would ride up front with him. I liked anchoring the goods in the back. I finally caught on to the rhyme and reason behind our invites. It all centered around the load being hauled. Heavy lifting and moving meant we were the lifters and movers. Cousin Calvert usually gave us two bits a piece to spend as we wished. We were cheap labor for sure. Before we left going or coming back Cousin Calbert would always ask us, 'Jaw-P?' If we hadn't, we would take time to go to the bathroom before the long ride there or back. He did not stop once we were on our way. Sometime during our long day, he would ask us, 'Jeet?' His way of asking us did we eat, short and to the point.

Seasonally, farmers brought their produce to the stop and swap. There was a little bit of everything to be had. If you did not grow it somebody else did. I remember this one time that Cousin Calbert put his hand on my shoulder, shaking his head in disbelief while we stood staring at this one feller's crop saying, 'Can you believe it. Some folks actually grow, eat and like okra. Nasty, slimy and gosh awful prickly for normal consumption.'

It used to bug him like no get out when he crossed paths with Yankees either selling or wandering the grounds. He would say there was no good Yankee. The worst were the ones that decided to stay. He called them hemorrhoids; they came here, and you could not get them to go back. Nothing ticked him off more than hearing one say it was time for lunch. He would shake his head, swearing, 'There is no such thing as lunch. After we eat breakfast, we eat dinner and then supper.' He claimed that they only came here from the North to escape the snow and to try to change the South to the North without the snow. He was not short on tradition nor opinion, and he would share either, whether you cared to hear it or not.

You would assume that a man milking the day, wheeling and dealing would own a pocket watch. Not Cousin Calvert. I asked him why he didn't have one and he placed his hands on my shoulders and said, 'You don't have to carry a watch because it doesn't matter what time it is, you do what needs to be done until it is done or until it gets too dark to get it done.'

You learn plenty hanging out with your elders, sense and nonsense alike. Cousin Calvert had both covered like a patch quilt. Here are a few his best ones. Y'all is singular and all y'all is plural. Over yonder can be in the next room, the next county or another country. You do not push buttons, you mash them. Backwards and forwards means I know everything about you. Onced and twiced are words. You call fireflies what they are, lightning bugs and if God can light up a bug's butt imagine what He can do for us. Sweet tea in the South is a house wine, a beverage fit for all meals, something babies are given to wean them off their bottles.

There is something to be said of a man who had chosen to live his life alone. I never heard him poor mouth about being lonely or hanker in having a wife or any woman to share his world. Something that concerned my folks and grandparents was Cousin Calvert carrying a heavy pocket of cash all the time. He did not believe in banks. Some said he buried his extra money in Mason jars. It was just after my tenth birthday that it happened. I remember it vividly because Cousin Calvert had given me my first bicycle that birthday. He was on his way to one of those stop and swaps, a light load apparently, because he did not ask me or Uncle Rusty to go with him. My birthday was the day before. He never made it. They found that old jalopy of his on an old pulpwood road halfway between his home and the stop and swap. To this day, his disappearance remains an unsolved mystery. Sheriff figured he was robbed and most likely murdered but cannot explain what happened to his body, even though there were no signs of fowl play at the scene. Cousin Calvert just up and vanished into thin air. My folks were thankful that neither Uncle Rusty nor I was with him on that trip. I have often wondered that if we had been would anything have happened. I thought on it a lot, the ultimate wheeler and dealer had not been able to barter his way out of whatever had ultimately happened. He had been known as the master in the art of the deal decades before Trump.

Cousin Calvert's house remained empty for years but his property over the years looked like a moon landscape, all cratered. People were always trespassing and digging holes looking for those Mason jars filled with money, No one every laid claim if any were ever found. We moved away. I never knew what finally happened to his homestead.

"Were all of our ancestors so uniquely quirky, Grandfather Nelson?"

"Quirkily unique is an underestimate, David."

"I fear a theme is emerging, that of untimely demises."

"Let's just say that FFF comes at a valuable cost."

"FFF?"

"Forced Family Fun is what my daddy called it. He said, adding that it came fast and furious from both sides of the family, his and my mama's."

"I don't get it. The fun and fellowship that you had with Uncle Rusty nor Cousin Calvert seem forced on you by anyone."

"It wasn't. It was just Daddy's perception of our dysfunctional kinfolk. He likened it to coping with untamed critters. He even went so far as to call some of our kin strays, convinced that there could be no blood ties to us. Mama would become furious with this rhetoric."

Researching the Whiteside family tree was like opening the southern version of Pandora's box, more like a storage trunk of assorted curiosities. At least in this case there was no harm allowing the family secrets to escape. The past could not up and bite you. It might distort your perception, knowing the unconditional truth, but this was not necessarily a bad thing. Even skeletons from a closet deserved to have their day in court.

Chapter 4

David asked about my parents and siblings. He already knew that I was the youngest of the brood. I had two brothers, Keith and Jeremy, and a sister, Carol. Like everyone else in my direct bloodline, I had outlived them too. Carol the oldest, was five years older than me. Keith was a year younger than her, and Jeremy followed him by another year. I was a two-year gap behind them. I was not sure why I trailed further behind them in the family bliss. Like most everything I never asked. Over inquisitive minds were never appreciated or rewarded.

Daddy's full name was William Compton Whiteside. Everybody called him Big Bill. I'm not sure why because he was not a big man, less than six feet tall and maybe weighed one eighty. Big Bill Whiteside it was though. Mama was a Barnhart before she married, same as Uncle Rusty. Everyone that knew her well called her Snookum but her real name was Eva Marie. Like Daddy, I never heard an explanation for her being called by such a silly nickname. I reckon it didn't seem all that silly to me back then because it was what I heard her being called. She was just Mama to me. Unfortunately, there is no one to ask now why the names stuck to them like glue.

Daddy was all work and no play, not uncommon for men trying to navigate through tough times and provide for their families. I suppose because of that I tended to gravitate to other adults, those that would pay me some mind and not see me as a snotty nose bothersome little chap. The children in the family were expected to pull their weight with the household and farm chores. Again, this was the norm in that era in America. We did not whine about it, we just did what we were told to do as it was expected for us to do. We didn't know anything better that the life we lived. We were not dirt poor, but times were difficult. We just did not know it. Morning came bright and early every day. Night followed and we just repeated everything again. There were few distractions in our world.

Carol and I helped Mama with the household chores. Keith and Jeremy were the outdoor hands, helping Daddy where things needed to be done. Like I have mentioned before, none of my siblings paid me much attention, mostly referring to me as an annoyance. Sadly, because of how I was shunned, I regrettably hardly have any sensational memories from my childhood spent with any of them. By the time I had gotten older, old enough to not be the bothersome little brother, Carol had gotten married, Keith had joined the Navy and Jeremy had set out on his own, joining a carnival. Poof, just like that, they all vanished from my life before I ever had a life with any of them. I had gotten used to my place in the pecking order and did not need them around to be who I had become. Thinking back on it I had never been a kid. My void had been filled by the adults I hung out with. I learned and lived in their world, not that of a child.

My parents, as most, had done the best they could. My grandparents had helped them pick up the pieces after that Killer Cow twister. Edwin and Sarah Barnhart, my mama's parents were good people, church goers and a blessing to their community. Grandpa filled in sometimes for the preacher at their church. I will say it was an odd church, a place that scared the bejeebies out of me when they made me attend. Preacher Joe McFarlan was a burley man, wild wavey black and gray hair, a thick busy mustache and anvil arms more like that of a wrestler than a preacher. Grandma said he took the devil head on, breathing in evil's fire and brimstone then spitting it back in old Satan's face just to make him pay attention to God's word. Yep, that preacher was somebody to be feared, especially when he pulled those snakes out of the box. Not just ordinary snakes, he was a rattlesnake handler. I did not get it, what did snakes have to do with church. Grandma corrected me, calling it serpent handling saying it was a religious rite.

Preacher McFarlan would quote verse, King James Bible, Mark 16:18 saying, "They shall take up serpents; and if they drink any deadly thing, it shall not hurt them." Me, I could not take my eyes off those snakes no matter what verses were quoted. I was reminded of what Cousin Calvert had said, 'There are 5,000 kinds of snakes and 4,998 can be found in the south.' He never mentioned how many of them were considered poisonous. He just hated any kind of snake and all spiders. Thank goodness the preacher did not believe in the handling of tarantulas. I never saw the preacher or any of the congregation get bitten even when some of them got touched with what Grandma called the Holy Ghost. Those snakes had folks jumping about and talking gibberish. Grandma even joined in, her eyes rolling back and her moving about like nobody's business. The gibberish was called talking in tongues. I held my tongue between my fingers to make sure it did not gibber jabber like those jumping about during the serpent handling frenzy.

My folks had never attended church much. Daddy always seemed to be working most Sundays. Mama never seemed to be inclined to go. Thinking back, I wonder if she had been traumatized as a child too, her parents exposing her to the serpent handling and talking in tongues when she was just a little girl. Come to think of it, she allowed my grandparents to take us to that church and neither she nor Daddy ever attended while we lived at their place. Were we the tokens? Her, allowing them to take us, taking them off the hook. Uncle Rusty sure liked going. It was all that grandma could do, keeping him in his seat when the snakes were out of the box. He kept saying he wanted to pet them. It explains why he was always catching snakes, any snakes and gibber jabbering at them, his version of the great outdoors prayer meeting. I don't remember one ever biting him, come to think of it. Maybe Uncle Rusty had discovered his calling as a full-fledged serpent handler. I'll just take Cousin Calvert's stance on the slithering varmints; no snake is a good snake unless it is a dead one.

At least once a week my folks invited Preacher McFarlan, his wife Missy and their two children, Casper and Reba to supper. I always knew what day they were coming because

Daddy fetched a chicken from the yard and chopped off its head on the hickory stump. He tossed the chicken into the yard where it floundered about headless like it was still alive. Oddly, I looked forward to Daddy killing the chicken. It reminded me of a carnival act when the fair came to town each fall. They had this wild man called Sabo that was fed live chickens. He would watch the chicken for a while when they tossed one into this fenced in area, they had him in. Eventually he would catch it. He would pat that chicken like it was his very own pet. It scared me the first time I saw him bite off the chicken's head and drink the blood then turn it loose and watch it flop about. Once the chicken became motionless Sabo would snatch it up and tear into it with his teeth and hands, feathers flying everywhere. It was an awesome sight and entertaining for those mesmerized by the ordeal.

Mama plucked and prepared our chicken but. not like Sabo thankfully, not that it would not have been a hoot to see her tear into it the way Sabo did. She cut it into pieces, battered it with buttermilk and flour and fried it. Yep, I always knew when we had chicken that Preacher McFarland and his family would be arriving shortly. I did not care much for Reba. She was too much of a tattletale. Casper and I had to watch our Ps and Qs when she was around. She would rat us out if we did something fun for us but not so fun for her. She was especially afraid of Uncle Rusty. To this day I am still not sure why. I never saw Uncle Rusty do anything scary around her other than talking his usual unharmful nonsense.

One time Casper, me and Uncle Rusty were able to give Reba the slip. It was not an easy feat because she shadowed us most of the time. Casper cooked up this scheme showing her one of the baby goats in the barn. While she was distracted, we snuck off to the woods behind the house. We were quite good at entertaining ourselves, playing army or cowboys and Indians, using stick guns and stick horses. That particular day we stumbled upon a huge hornet's nest in a sweetgum tree. We kept our distance and watched the hornets enter and leave the nest attached to a low hanging limb. I will blame what happened next on Casper. What started out as a dare by him ended in an all assault. He dared me to try to hit the nest with a rock. Not one to back down from a dare I took my best shot but missed. We both began tossing rocks, some coming close but none hitting our target. Out of the blue Uncle Rusty walked over to just under the nest and swatted it with a long piece of cane he had found lying on the ground. That nest came plummeting down and when it hit the ground it exploded into a black swarm of angry hornets. Uncle Rusty just stood there motionless as we began running for our lives. Those hornets chased us, landing sting after sting. We ran halfway back to the house before they stopped following us and making us pay for destroying their nest.

Casper and I had knots and red whelps forming on our heads, faces and bodies and I cannot begin to describe the pain we were in. Those dang hornets struck us like pellets from a shotgun. We were both screaming and crying. The grownups heard our whaling and came outside to investigate the ruckus. We told them hornets had attacked us for no apparent reason in the woods. We did not admit to what we had done to stir them up. Uncle Rusty messed up our little white lie when he showed up carrying the nest saying we had forgotten what had been knocked down. He did not have a single sting. They thought he was innocent, and we were the guilty ones. Just like when he caught snakes or anything else, slithering nor flying critters seemed interested in bothering him. He possessed a gift that none of us ever understood. Our folks were none too happy about our reckless behavior, but I reckon they decided that the hornets had delivered enough punishment and they did not offer any additional penalties. That little smart aleck Reba snuck in a few laughs and *told you so's* when the adults were not around. Uncle Rusty kept that nest as a trophy for a long time, a reminder I did not need for a dare gone bad.

Thinking about that fried chicken we always had when the preacher came visiting makes me associate fried chicken and the fixings with church gatherings or anytime that we had family visiting. I suppose chickens were easier to be had back then as apposed to killing a cow or pig. Plus, the only cow we ever had was a milk cow. Kill the cow and there is no more milk. Neighbors had hogs though. Unlike killing a chicken anytime you needed to, it had to be hog killing time to kill a hog. As a chap I could not wrap my head around the concept of hog killing time, but the old timers knew precisely when it was time to kill a hog. As I got older, I understood the rhyme behind the reason. Cold weather, just that simple. It all started because of the lack of refrigeration and folks waited for winter or a cold spell to do the deed. Colder weather gave way to a means to preserve the meat. Killing a hog was an intricate ritual in the south in those days. You could always count on a large gathering of folks, a feast spread out, to be had once the hog had met its end. Nothing was wasted from the harvested hog. They processed everything but the oink. Good eating was had by all.

Unlike Daddy beheading a chicken, the hog was shot and then hung from a tree or barn, dressed and cleaned. It was fascinating to watch how those doing the needful worked with the precision of a surgeon. It was an art passed down from one generation to the next. No, it was never passed on to me because we never owned any hogs. I did learn the process later from my years of hunting, especially deer. The same concept was utilized. Cousin Henry Whitefield took me under his wing and taught me all I needed to know about hunting. Now is not quite the time though to bring Cousin Henry into the picture. He would serve as a mentor a few years later when I needed someone like him in my life.

"You experienced some amazing times didn't you, Grandfather Nelson."

"Indeed, I have been blessed David with a long life and countless memories. Most have been simply wonderful, but nostalgia can pose many roadblocks, obstacles and challenges. One can pick and choose good from the bad if one chooses but to relive them properly you should include the bad, the ugly and not so happy incidences to

38

depict your past fairly and unbiased. I take it you would not wish me to sugarcoat what I often refer to as FFF, forced family fun."

"Correct Grandfather Nelson, and to use one of your favorite phrases, don't pretty it up for me," said David pressing the stop button on the recorder.

"You pay way too much attention to me son."

"A gift or maybe a curse."

"Sounds like something I might say."

"Exactly," smiled David. "Where to next Grandfather Nelson?"

"Funny thing about memories, they come in uncontrollable flashes, not necessarily in chronologic order. You might have a difficult time sorting through my little stroll down memory lane."

"I'm not worried about that. I just want to hear everything that you can remember about family and whatever impacted your life, the good, the bad and the ugly of it."

"My words again."

"Yes, they are, and I hang on every one of them. This is for me, for us, for family so that we never forget where it all began and how we got here."

"Before I am too old to remember or gone before I do."

"Your words, not mine Grandfather Nelson. I just love spending time with you, listening to anything you wish to talk about; what happened today, yesterday, or last week. Everything else is gravy on the biscuit. Yes, I learned that one from you too."

"Refresh our tea glasses while I relieve my old bladder then we will pick up where we ended or some proximity there abouts."

Chapter 5

David set the tea and plate down in front of his grandfather. "I took the liberty of sneaking some lemon meringue pie from your fridge. Looks homemade. Did you make it?"

"Will have to give credit to Edwards, store bought but closest thing to what my mama used to serve up. Thank you for catering to my sweet tooth, David, and yours I bet. Fire up your little thingamajig and I will see if I can kick start my thingamajig pea brain too."

> One's childhood is incomplete without friends and foes tossed in to help you navigate the waters or muddy up the creek. One chap I will forever remember was Pooter Price. Children are mostly colorblind or were back in my day. We befriended who we liked whether anybody else liked our picks or not. Adults often saw it differently, everything literally black and white. I reckon my folks taught me right from wrong and to respect everybody. Pooter was a Negro boy, fourteen and a year older than me when I first met him. I am not sure what his real first name was. I only knew him as Pooter. He earned that name honestly for sure. That boy was an accomplished farter. He had it covered when it came to the art of passing gas, I never experienced the likes of it back then, now or anytime in between. I have seen some people that can belch on demand, but Pooter took his gift to an uncanny level, one that was mostly unappreciated.
>
> Pooter was charcoal black. I was whiter than white. We made the perfect salt and pepper pair and that alone placed a target on our backs for many of our peers. Children can be cruel, those either brought up wrong or too jealous to admit they are envious of true friendship. Me and Pooter did our best to ignore the catcalls and threats. Sometimes we succeeded, other times we didn't. Our worst nemesis and tormentor had to be Jonesy Meany. Nope, I did not make that name up. Meany was his real last name and let me tell you, he lived up to that name, as the yard bully in school. Even worse, he lived within walking distance of us. Sometimes you only must face your worst nightmare at school and once you leave

you are safe until another day. With Jonesy, it lessened our odds. Add in the fact that Pooter and I were best friends, you had the perfect bullying storm. Toss in the fact that Jonesy was a big old boy, much larger than either of us, we had a tough row to hoe most incidences.

Pooter was the only negro in an otherwise all white school, the only school in the county. During school we did the best we could to avoid Jonesy or at least make sure we were around enough people to minimize his threatening taunts. Off the school grounds we were easy prey for the picking. We were out for the summer, just happy for an opportunity to be us. Pooter and I had just become friends midway through the school year. It had not kept Jonesy from zeroing in on us though. Pooter and I had taken the low road approach mostly when our aggressor set sights on us. The best way to defuse a bully is to just let the bully get it out of his system. Jonesy, like most, just wanted to strut his stuff in front of an audience in hopes of getting us to spar against him. Those that did ended up with a bloody nose or blackeye. He really liked using the 'N' word to get a rise out of Pooter. I hated that for him. He mostly called me a 'N' loving queer. Words can hurt. Fists can hurt worse. We took our medicine as best we could. I think this infuriated Jonesy even more.

Last bell and we exited the school grounds as quickly as we could to avoid any confrontations. We had summer vacation in our sights, one that would not be all fun. Grownups saw us as cheap labor. Doing anything we wanted to do was not exactly in the cards. Chores needed tending and those needing attending were assigned to every child old enough to pull his or her weight. Pooter's folks were no different. Playing and horsing around were in cheap supply most days. When you had a reprieve you dang well better take advantage of it. That's why we completed assigned tasks as quickly as possible. Most of the time there was no adult overseer. They told us what they expected us to do and expected it to get done. We knew the rules and held up our part of the bargain. You did not want to be on the other end of the stick if what they expected you to do didn't get done. Swift punishment was not pretty, and you still had to finish what you had left unfinished. Sassy behavior just landed you in hotter water. Most children today have it made and are spoiled rotten. We learned to be responsible and dependable whether we fully understood the concept or not. We were being programmed at an early age. Manners were not optional. They were expected.

It was not all hard labor with no opportunity for time off with good behavior. There were routine chores and then there were seasonal chores. Seasonal were probably the worst. For us living out in the country these chores mostly involved various gardening duties. Hoeing, planting, weeding, and picking to name a few. Toting wood and splitting kindling were a given before cold weather approached. We did not have the luxury of being the grasshopper. We were the ants preparing for the harshest of wintertime threats. Our folks canned what vegetables they could. Everyone had a root cellar for storing what could be saved for later. I reckon these would be considered valuable survival skills in an apocalyptic world. Common sense trumped book smart in many cases.

"David, you must excuse an old man's wandering ways. Nostalgia often stirs up plenty of memories that go well beyond the normal family ties. The old ways were hard but unforgettable. What I would not do to be able to turn back the pages of time and relive some of them. Not all of them though. If only I could choose."

"Seeing that life through your eyes Grandfather Nelson is more than I could have ever asked for. Please continue."

Pooter caught up with his chores first and was heading my way. We did not have the luxury of today's electronic communication. Spontaneity ruled. Most times I had no idea he was coming until he just showed up. If I still had chores to complete, he would pitch in and help me finish them. I did the same for him. This one occasion though he never showed up and of course I was not expecting him, so I had no reason

42

to go look for him. Jonesy had laid low seeing him coming up the road. Unlike us, he did not have much family influence to teach him right from wrong. I don't think his daddy was around and his mama did not much care what he did. Rumor had it that she feared him. Seemed a bit strange to us an adult fearing a kid. We did not realize back then just how tough Jonesy's life was. If we had, it might have explained why he took it out on us. No, we would have not felt sorry for him or had become his friend, because he was our tormentor and we disliked him for the way he treated us. Even at a young age you realize the limitations by which you are willing to go. He was a bully. We were the bullied. Once those lines had been drawn in the sand they were rarely ever erased.

Jonesy did not like any children, especially black ones. Poor Pooter was ambushed. Pooter did eventually show up that day and a blind man could tell he had been batted around and treated unfairly. After some prodding Pooter finally admitted it had been Jonesy's doing but he would not tell me the extinct of the harassment. I instantly knew it must have been awful, maybe even crueler than either of us had endured at his hands. This infuriated me. Something had to give. We had never attempted to stand up to Jonesy and we certainly had never fathomed retaliation. We knew our limitations. Neither of us wished to be beaten by the likes of him. What then? How does one defang a bully and survive doing so?

Pooter did his best to stay clear of the conversation. He was a black boy in mostly a white world. Blacks retaliating where whites were concerned was not taken lightly. Nothing made this right. It was just a different time back then. As for me, I remained colorblind. It was easy for me to take this stance. Sadly, not so easy for Pooter. This made me more determined to do whatever needed to be done to put an end to the bullying by our nemesis. Taking him head on was a 'no win' proposition. If we were going to have any chance of beating him it must somehow be an unfair fight, the edge going to us. Question remained, how could we outsmart him and beat him at his own game? Pooter refused to be involved in my scheming no matter how hard I tried to convince him that I could not do it without him. I had no idea what 'it' was.

About a week later I had completed my chores early and decided to head Pooter's way for a change. We had talked about going down to the creek and damming it off to make the water deep enough for a little swim. Swimming might be a bit exaggerated. More like soaking and splashing. Of course, Pooter did not know about my plan. If he couldn't we wouldn't. Might be that I just helped him finish his chores. It didn't much matter. I just liked hanging out with my friend. I wasn't paying much attention, throwing rocks, kicking up dust and just horsing around during the walk. A sudden shadow in my direct path alerted me, I was not alone. There stood Jonesy Meany bigger than life, fists balled by his sides and an evil grin on his face. It was too late to run. How stupid I had been not looking ahead.

"All by your lonesome I see out here in the middle of nowhere. Your little jigaboo pal made the same mistake. I reckon you know what I did to him, and I plan to do the same thing to you. I am going to take my time with you though. I am going to make you hurt really bad."

No, I did not know what he had done to Pooter. I just decided then and there that whatever he had done I was not going to let him do it to me. I balled my fists knowing darn well that I could not win a fair fight with this behemoth. If I had a rock, a stick, something, I might have a chance. Standing in the middle of that dusty dirt road offered me no options. I considered bolting but he was bigger and faster. Before I could consider any other options, he was on top of me nailing me with a fist to my right cheek ringing my bell instantly. He then spun me around and latched onto me with a chokehold from behind. Just as quickly he shoved me to the ground, his weight resting atop me. He began telling me to squeal like a pig. Pigheaded instead, I refused. No doubting it, this was not going to end well.

Suddenly Jonesy went limp, dead weight pushing against me. I pushed and somehow, he rolled off me. It was then that I spotted Pooter standing over him and pulling him as well flipping Jonesy onto his back. He had clubbed Jonesy with a baseball bat, something he would later tell me he had brought with him as he headed to my house. Jonesy was coming around shaking the stars from his head. He yanked Pooter by the leg. He lost his balance landing butt first on Jonesy's face. I pounced onto Jonesy's chest pinning his arms underneath my legs. What now I wondered. We could not hold him down forever. Panicked, Pooter cut loose a series of nasty farts. Jonesy began gagging and coughing. Pooter terrified now let them rip like nobody's business. Jonesy began bucking like a brahma bull.

Thinking quick I yelled, "Stop it or Pooter won't."

To my surprise and Pooter's, he stopped and lay still. He was still gagging though.

Improvising to save life and limp I issued him a stern warning, "Jonesy, your bullying of us stops today. If ever you lay another hand on us or even look at us the wrong way, we are going to tell everybody what just happened. You better agree. Pooter hasn't even unleashed his version of the walking farts on you yet, wet, and nasty ones. What you say? Deal?"

"Just get off me."

"Deal or no deal?"

"All right, deal."

"We still have the baseball bat if this is a trick," spoke up Pooter catching me off guard with his boldness. "You better promise as the Lord is your witness."

"Promise, just stop it and get off me, boy!"

45

"That is Mister Jamel Harrison Price to you. Say it, please get off me Mister Jamel Harrison Price and I promise to stop bullying both of you."

I was taken aback by Pooter's sudden boldness and canter. I had not known his full name until that very moment. To my shock, Jonesy did as he had been asked and said, 'Please get off me Mister Jamel Harrison Price and I will not bully you anymore.'

With that we reluctantly eased off him. Pooter was bat ready just in case. Jonesy said nothing else but gave us one parting sneer as he turned and walked away rather quickly. He never bulled us again. I figured that he was too embarrassed by the treatment he had received and was dogged by the fact that a black boy had delivered proper justice to boot. It had probably added insult to injury us being much smaller than him too. We were the cocks of the barnyard, kings of the mountain, the perfect pair to have defanged the bully. From that day forward I never took Pooter's unique gift for granted even though I began calling him Jamel. Sometimes, life tends to kick you around, but sooner or later you wake up to the fact that you are not a survivor but instead stronger than anything life throws at you.

We remained friends until the next summer when his folks moved away. His daddy had gotten a job as a repairman for an appliance store in another county. I worried that Jonesy would renege on his promise with Jamel 'Pooter' Price out of the picture. When school started back Jonesy was nowhere to be found. Plenty of rumors surfaced about what might have happened to him. None were ever confirmed. Kids were just glad he was gone; one less bully to deal with at school.

"What do you think really happened to him Grandfather Nelson?"

"My folks said something about Jonesy's ma passing. Might be that he ended up homeless or in an orphanage. Knowing his reputation, he could have landed in reform school or even jail. I sorely missed Jamel, not him."

"Did you ever see Jamel again?"

"No, I never did. We did not have social media or any other means to reconnect or follow others. I only hope that he found his way and made his mark in a world less biased and cruel to those of another color. What you say we take another little break, David. I need to recharge my old brain cells and relieve my protesting bladder yet again."

"Fine, I need to answer a few texts."

"Are you sure you are not bored? Learning about family is one thing; reliving my nostalgic nonsense moments might be a bit much."

"Loving every minute of it Grandfather Nelson walking in your shoes and viewing life through your eyes."

"All right then, the day is early, and my mind is still sharp. I like to view it this way, David. One day old folks like me will wake up and find that there is no time left to do something like this. Best path for us is to do it now while we have a willing audience and an equally cooperating mind. For as long as I have my memories, yesterday remains. For as long as I have hope, tomorrow awaits. For as long as I have love in my heart, today is always beautiful. For as long as I have the Lord in my life, most anything is possible. I cannot take credit for these words, but I can take credit for living by their meaning."

"Amen, Grandfather."

Chapter 6

Refreshed and somewhat rejuvenated it was time to commence once again in no specific order I warned David.

I was still a young teenager more influenced by adults that peers. Corrupted instead of properly influenced my mama might say. Our family tree has an endless supply of branches, some bearing inspirational fruit a plenty while others delivered kin a bit too fruity to be believed. We have no shortage of relatives in almost any version imaginable. Uncle Delmer 'Artemis' Whitefield was about as outlandish as they come. He was a man of many secrets. I cannot recall the extent of his family connections. He was an uncle and always seemed to show up when there were family gatherings. I am not sure where he and his wife Aunt Harley Ann lived. I don't think it was anywhere close by. Both were a little spooky to me. Uncle Artemis was a man of many secrets, secrets that he was not shy about sharing. It made no sense to me how they could be secrets if you told everybody what they were. Most of his secrets were lost in translation to me. He used big words and terms that I was not familiar with. Children were not his chosen audience. Most of us were bothersome. Even I could sense his dislike for us. That did not stop me from keeping close quarters when he was around, using my ears like radar to sponge in his latest tales and off the wall inventions. I think he put a capital 'C' in crazy.

Aunt Harley Ann and he must have been a match made in heaven because they were both out there when it came to crazy behavior. She was a touch healer and card reader. She was just plain scary to me. She spoke mumbo jumbo mostly and wore more makeup than all the clowns combined found in one of those clown cars. Exaggeration, yes, but I am viewing this from a teenager's eyes. By comparison she took talking in tongues and snake handling to a new level of terrifying. I was much older than those days of Preacher McFarlan, so imagine the impact. At every family event she would seek out those with afflictions, real or imagined, and

48

latch onto them like a leech. She was all about the miracle cure, one where she would weasel a monetary contribution from those she had miraculously healed. I was too taken aback by her theatrics and gimmicks to understand the con and scams being pulled. I stayed close enough to witness them but avoided making physical contact with her. Only once did I mess up, allowing her to hug me. One and done, I learned my lesson when she pulled me close and began whispering some sort of voodoo gibberish in my ear. She ended saying she had cast out a demon from my lustful loins. Looking back now I believe she was the one who possessed demonic lustful loins. I overheard mama once say that Aunt Harley Ann had a wicked straying eye for men of any age. She did not trust her as far as she could toss her.

When not attempting to cure the family of what did or didn't ail them, she whipped out a deck of tarot cards and commenced to telling fortunes and predicting futures. Predictions included wealth, fame, love and curses hellbent on ruining lives. All donations appreciated of course. For those facing a cursed future she had the ability to lift that burden for an extra fee of course. I am not sure why they invited them to family gatherings. Maybe they didn't. Could be that they just crashed them. Once there, who could make them leave? Might be that too many believed she had the power to bring havoc on those that dare tried. I never heard anyone say they were scared but what did I know back then. Aunt Paulette bucked her one time, calling her bluff saying she was a common shyster and harlot to boot after she caught her making moves on Uncle Guy. Aunt Harley Ann gave her what they call the evil eye and tossed in some of that mumbo jumbo. Three weeks later Aunt Paulette, a rather big boned woman, dropped dead at her lady's auxiliary meeting. That caught everyone's attention even though her doctor said she had died from a massive stroke brought on by high blood pressure and an irregular heartbeat. She had stopped taking her prescribed medicine according to him. Murmurs persisted from some relatives who had witnessed the exchange. Me, not sure, but I continued to give her wide berth just in case, my loins well out of her reach.

That brings me back to good ole Uncle Artemis, quite the showman as well but not nearly in the scary range as her. His alleged accomplishments were more intriguing and often unbelievable as far as Daddy was concerned. Uncle Artemis accused Daddy of being narrowminded and eat up with jealousy. Daddy did allow him to get under his skin and he was not a man that allowed that to happen very often. Uncle Artemis could push his buttons and I believe he enjoyed doing it. He claimed involvement in some of the most absurd occurrences in American history. Looking back now his fictional life resembled that of Forest Gump. Loved that movie by the way. Artemis lived those stretches of truth to the fullest. I don't recall anyone just flat out calling him a liar. The things he told were entertaining I suppose. You must remember there were not many televisions around in the 40s especially in our neck of the woods. His tales filled an empty void and took people's minds off the escalating war.

Uncle Artemis claimed he had come up with the idea for the Slinky and he enjoyed explaining his creation in detail. He said his design was developed in 1940, three years before a naval engineer demonstrated his version at Gimbels department store in Philadelphia and patented what he had meant to be a new tension spring. Of course, Uncle Artemis could not produce evidence of his design or a spring to corroborate his tall tale. It was his word against theirs and he professed that he was no match for the Navy. He said he then stumbled into a gooey glob that was ridiculously fun. Before he could introduce the world to his crazy gook it was stolen right out from under him by another fellow calling it Silly Putty. His excuse, he spent too much time perfecting his creations instead of securing patents, adding that the little man had no chance suing or fighting the huge conglomerates.

Probably one of his wildest tales had to do with a sighting of a giant lizard creature near Bishopville. He swore on a stack of bibles that he had seen this ten-foot-tall monster walking on two legs near a swamp one night while passing through the area on the way to Hartsville. Nobody believed him because they had seen him leave a local bar just prior to his encounter, saying it had been a product of his imagination and intoxicated state. Maybe it happened. Maybe it didn't. Oddly enough, in the 1980s, nearly forty years later something similar was seen in Lee County near Scrape Ore Swamp. Bishopville is in Lee County. Witnesses described it as seven feet tall, green with skin like a lizard, with red eyes. Locals dubbed it the Lizard Man. Uncle Artemis had long been dead by then, so he wasn't around to recant his story or question him about similarities. I was probably one of the few that even remembered him telling the story. Most thought it was poppycock, just another way for him to gain attention.

Almost every newfangled contraption that came along while he was around had some ties to something he had done, seen, or invented. Sometimes he would hint at his involvement in top secret government projects. He enjoyed tossing around Project Bluebook, code name for a governmental study of unidentified flying objects started by the United States Airforce in 1952. He said he moonlighted as an investigator and had seen things that would give you nightmares. It was about this time that he and Aunt Harley Ann pooled their resources. She laid claim that she could channel the thoughts of little green men through people that had been snatched by them. She also said she was an undercover consultant for the Airforce. Obviously neither one of them ever produced evidence of their involvement, claiming that it was classified and would endanger anyone privy to the existence of extraterrestrials. Project Bluebook was real and disbanded in 1969. Uncle Artemis and Aunt Harley Ann died in a fiery automobile crash in the Nevada desert in 1966. No other vehicles were reportedly involved. The accident occurred in close proximity of Area 51, a classified Airforce facility. Merely coincidental, you be the judge. They had no children, so their personal belongings were never passed on to anyone that I remember. Come to think of it I don't recall much fanfare surrounding their funeral. Had this happened to someone else, Uncle Artemis would have milked the moment for all it was worth claiming everything had been swept under the rug for good reason, government coverup.

"David, if you tire of reliving the life I share with you, perhaps you might wish to pursue the lives of Uncle Artemis and Aunt Harley Ann Whitefield and see if there is a real hidden gem inside the family closet."

"Intriguing Grandfather Nelson, but what do you really think?"

"I think I just as soon remember it the way I saw and heard it back then. I am too old to validate fact from fiction. I will leave rewriting family history to you. My job here is to just tell it like I recall it."

Chapter 7

David engaged his little recorder, and I was off and babbling once again.

World War II was raging, and my brother Keith was slap dab in the middle of it serving in the Navy. Jeremy was where abouts unknown presumably still with the traveling carney show. I wanted to enlist and serve but my folks would not sign the consent form. You had to be eighteen and I had just turned seventeen. Without their consent it was no dice for me. The United States Navy was fully engaged. Keith was stationed in Pearl Harbor when the attack happened in 1941. Over one hundred eighty US warships were destroyed, and 2,403 Americans lost their lives. Thankfully Keith was not injured but he was forever traumatized by the horrific event. He returned to us a changed man. The trauma broke him. He could barely function normally as a civilian. I looked up to him as a wartime hero. He hated that label. He would go off on me or anyone else that attempted to place him on such a pedestal. Soldiers, friends he had known died that day at Pearl. He struggled to understand why he had been spared while so many hadn't. I don't remember him being suicidal, but he pushed the envelope when it came to taking risky chances. Some refer to this behavior as having a death wish.

Keith had this dark side. It wasn't mean or malicious. Instead, it was more like he was in a funk all the time. He hardly ever smiled or laughed about anything. He no longer knew how to have fun or horse around. Daddy always encouraged us to let him be, saying he was still shell shocked from his ordeal. You must remember this was nearly forty years before PTSD would become a household name. There were no references of post-traumatic stress disorder back then. Keith refused to seek any medical help. Instead, he wallowed in his mud pit and the more he wallowed the worse he got. Seeing a shrink was taboo. Those that did were labeled crazy, nuttier than a fruit cake. People were cruel and unsympathetic to the needs of those that sought the help of a psychiatrist. Aunt Harley Ann tried touch healing him to no avail. She even attempted using tarot cards to foresee his future, but Mama nixed that idea sending her packing.

Mama's mama, Granny Sarah Barnhart wanted to take Keith to see Preacher McFarland. You remember him and that snake handling church. She had this notion that Satan had possessed poor Keith and only Preacher McFarland could cast the devil from his soul. Papa Edwin stayed out of it saying the boy needed to deal with it and figure it out for himself. So far that had not been working well for Keith. If anything, he was getting worse. A masked thug attempted to rob Creswell's Esso Station while we (Keith and I) were there for gas. Rod, the attendant had not come outside to pump the gas, so Keith took it on himself to pump it. He insisted that I clean the windshield. Remember, this was before self-service became a common practice.

We heard the commotion, more yelling than anything and then saw a masked person exit the station office. The getaway car was parked on the opposite side of the pumps where our car was parked. Keith, seeing what was going down, reacted by aiming the nozzle at the driver and dousing him in the face with gasoline. He dropped his gun and cash. Keith flicked his cigarette lighter on and warned the robber not to move or he would set him on fire. Still blinded from the gas he obliged. Rod showed up and retrieved the gun and held it on the kid no older than me until police arrived. Frank Creswell the owner was interviewed by the Daily Times and hailed Keith as a hero adding he was a war hero and now a hometown hero saying he had free gas for the next year. Keith despised the recognition and publicity he was receiving. All kinds of businesses around town were offering him jobs. Police Chief Wainwright wanted him on the force. Keith turned down all offers. Daddy was highly disappointed.

I overheard him telling Mama that he was tiring of Keith not pulling his weight, mooching off them. I had never heard Daddy say anything like that before. I didn't have the heart to tell Keith what I had overheard him say.

The grownups were convinced Keith needed to talk to a preacher to help him sort through his problems. Preacher McFarland had been ruled out, Mama lobbying the snakes might make things worse. She hated those snakes like I did. Granny took it as a sign from God when this traveling tent evangelist showed up in the area. Mama didn't buy it, but she admitted that it beat what Preacher McFarland was peddling. The advertisement said a Wednesday night revival meeting was scheduled. It was Monday and two days remained to convince Keith this was in his best interest. An adult now and veteran, she nor Daddy could make him do anything that he didn't want to do. He had a mind of his own even if he was freeloading under their roof. Daddy's words, not mine.

Keith and I were never close. I was just a snot nose little nuisance according to him. He had been a bit more tolerable of me once he had gotten out of the service. War had certainly changed him in more ways than was visible. We even talked some. Mostly I talked and he pretended to be interested in what I was saying. It was like he was there, but he wasn't. Loud noises set him off. He would clasp his hands over his ears when whatever was happening loudly about got to him. Keith despised being around large crowds too, including family gatherings. He had never been this way before joining the Navy. I missed the old Keith even if he hadn't given a hoot about me back then.

I eavesdropped as our folks did their best to convince him to attend the tent revival. I had never heard him talk back to our parents like he had during that conversation. He even used a few choice curse words. I had had never heard him curse before either. Daddy was having none of it and warned him

55

twice before hauling off and back handing him. Daddy always ruled with a stern hand, but he had never struck any of us like that, not across the face. I prepared for the worst, an all-out slug fest. Keith held his ground but did not retaliate, at least not physically. It didn't hurt Mama stepping between them saying enough. She then placed her hands on his cheeks and told him gently, 'you will attend the revival with us.' He said, 'yes ma'am.' Just like that the ruckus was over. I followed Keith, unsure what I should say or do. We ended up at the barn. Keith took a seat on a bale of hay.

"What did you think of that, Ned?"

I was taken aback. Keith had never asked me for my opinion on anything before. And of all times it would be about something like this. I squirmed and fidgeted, not wanting to take sides. He asked me again. He wasn't exactly asking me to take sides he just wanted to know what I thought about what had just happened.

Stalling I stupidly asked, "About what?"

"Me going to that revival that's what."

"I don't know. Do they have snakes in that tent?

"Snakes?"

"Preacher McFarland has snakes in his church."

"Oh that. I'm not sure what the traveling preacher uses to convince his congregation that God is the ruler of the universe. What do you think about Mama and Daddy being so pushy about me seeking help from a preacher; any preacher apparently?"

"Do you need help, Keith?"

"Do you think I need help?"

"I don't know. I reckon you have been acting differently since you returned home."

"Differently how?"

"Like you are here but you really aren't. You jump at shadows and at normal stuff that you used to not pay any attention."

"You are pretty observant, aren't you?"

"I don't know about that. What happened to make you like this?"

"Might be that I should go see that tent preacher. No time like the present."

"You mean you are not going to wait until Wednesday."

"I suspect he is a preacher today like he is any other day."

"Do you want me to come with you?"

"Nah, I think this is something best suited for me doing alone. Don't tell Mama or Daddy. Let it be our little secret."

Keith had never confided in me, nor had he ever shared a secret with me before. I promised him and I kept that promise. He did not come home that night. I didn't see him again until the next day. He did not tell me how it went, and I didn't ask him. All I know is that it was more like Keith for whatever reason. We attended the revival that Wednesday and Keith never let on that he had met the preacher prior. I don't even recall the traveling preacher's name. I am just thankful that he helped Keith be Keith again. Everything wasn't perfect but it was better than it had been. Keith got a job and Daddy mostly stayed off his back. A short time later Keith moved out. A few months later he quit his job and left after saying a brief goodbye. He didn't tell me or anyone else where he was going or what he planned to do.

Mama wasn't happy losing another son like that. There had been no word from Jeremy since he joined the carnival. Carol had moved away as well after marrying. That left me as the last child standing so to speak. With it came much responsibility. Too much for my shoulders alone. Destined now to be the chore master I had no life of my own to speak of. I was proud at first to be the perceived heir to the throne, but those expectations were threadbare quickly. I was not cut out to be the right and left hand. I was a young man with aspirations, ones that did not include following in my daddy's footsteps. I, too, ended up fleeing the nest and setting out to find my place in the world.

I didn't flee far. I had no valuable skills to support me other than taking any job to supplement my meager living. I hadn't known just how well I had it with my folks until my life virtually depended on me. I drifted about for a while, too proud to crawl back home. I ended up at my uncle's doorsteps nearly one hundred fifty miles from home. Uncle Wilson Whitefield wasn't close kin, but he was kinfolk just the same. Uncle Wilson was a pistol ball with colorful language like nobody's business. Daddy once said about him that he could put a sailor to shame with his profanity laced tongue. He and his wife, Aunty Jane, seemed a bit of a mismatch. She was timid as a mouse and mild mannered by comparison, a true testament that opposites sometimes are attracted to each other.

I was kin and welcome, but not without a hitch. Our family did not tolerate freeloaders. Room and board came with stipulations and consequences. Out of the skillet and into the fire, I became cheap labor, qualifications that I possessed but not on this level. Uncle Wilson was a pig farmer. He raised and sold the nasty critters. I found myself literally wallowing in the mud with pigs. I quickly learned the lesson behind slopping them. They had to be fed at least three times daily. The objective was to fatten them as soon as possible so they that they could be sold. The ideal target weight was two hundred fifty pounds in six months.

Pigs are supposed to be the smartest critter on the farm, but they can be scary strong too. They have the body of a bulldozer and the appetite of a hippopotamus. I spent about as much time repairing and replacing fence and posts as I did feeding them. Those snouts can dig and uproot anything. They are the perfect escape artists. Once they are on the lamb, they can unleash unimaginable destruction. Not only did I have to track them down and round them up then bring them back, I also had to do damage control. Neighbors do not appreciate wayward pigs destroying their vegetable gardens or gorging themselves on corn set out for deer hunting. Uncle Wilson's training program was hands on, more on the job and baptism by fire. He allowed me to fight my own battles whether I wanted to or not. Sometimes this required that I repair the damage on my time and out of my pocket if necessary. He had me over a barrel with no place to go unless I tucked tail and returned home. I was too stubborn for that.

Adding injury to insult I had to eat Aunty Jane's cooking. She must have been the worst cook in the Whitefield family. The menu included smoked hog snout, pickled pig's feet, barbequed chitlins and other pig parts I dared not identify. I avoided her prune preserves at all costs. Plus, I had never seen someone make and serve fruit cake year-round; her specialty as she called it. It was a compressed fruit brick if truth be told. No mistaking it, she was not in the business of fattening anyone up. That was reserved for the pigs.

Good things can result from bad situations. I transformed from a boy to a man both physically and mentally farming those pigs. I sprouted muscles where I had never had them and I matured more, learning the value of a dollar, managing my funds and somewhat being on my own, no longer depending on my parents. I was exposed to language the likes I had never heard but my upbringing fought back, and did not allow me to use any of it. I also developed a cast iron stomach and a newfound appreciation for what real homecoming was supposed to be like. I stuck it out with them for just over a year. I did write my parents to let them know where I was. They wrote back saying they missed me, but they never tried to talk me into returning home. At first, I was hurt by this. Later I realized that they were in constant contact with my uncle and aunt, keeping tabs on me. They stepped back and allowed me to learn lessons the hard way for my own good. It is called growing up. If I had stayed with them, I would have remained the baby of the family even though Daddy worked me like I was the force of three instead of one.

"Did you return home Grandfather Nelson?"

"Yes and no. I need to stretch my legs. Can that recorder thingamajig keep up with us if we take a little walk?"

"Let's give it a whirl."

Chapter 8

The great outdoors had a constant pull on Nelson Whitefield even today. Still spry and nimble he walked three miles most days. His route took him through the woods and then around the backside of a fenced pasture. David, amazed by his vitality, found it difficult to keep up with his stride and sure footedness. It was awe inspiring how a man of ninety-seven could be so fit. Not only could he do this, but he could also talk with not the slightest sign of shortness of breath. David was already winded but was determined to keep up.

"We can slow the pace if you would like David."

"That obvious, huh."

"Nothing to be ashamed of. I have the stamina because I do this regularly."

"Yeah, I could use a little breather."

"Over there, under that oak, perfect spot to take in the surroundings. You man that recorder and I will pick up where I left off."

> It had been going on two years before I stepped foot in my parent's house again. The boy had returned full grown and filled out. Not only did I no longer look the same, neither of them did it either. Mama appeared fragile, almost gaunt. She had wrinkles on her forehead where I had never noticed them before. I have heard them referred to as worry lines. How could she have gone down hill in such a short period? She greeted me with open arms embracing me with a hug. I was afraid to squeeze her hard after feeling her boney frame. Daddy looked the same yet different. Physically he was the same, but he looked like a shell of the man I remembered. His eyes were dark and emotionless. Big Bill shook my hand with a manly grip and nodded. No hug, no greeting of welcome home, just that handshake and odd look on his face. I asked about Keith, Jeremy and Carol and tears formed in Mama's eyes. Daddy answered saying I was the first one

they had laid eyes on in years. Neither Keith nor Jeremy had called or written to them. Carol and her husband had relocated to the West Coast, thousands of miles away. She had one child, but they were yet to see their grandchild. I wondered if my brothers knew they were uncles too or even cared.

I did my best to try to fit in. I helped with chores and worked a part time job at the meat market. I had learned the trade on that pig farm enough to secure a butcher's position. I could tell that Mama was glad to have me back, but I am not so sure Daddy felt the same, having me around. Might be he harbored hard feelings from me leaving. Me being there may have caused bad memories about my brothers not being there. Sad thing, once you have left the nest it is tough to return to it. Less than two months had passed, and I was getting antsy living under their roof.

I did meet a distant cousin I had never met before. He was passing through the area and my parents offered him a room. McArthur 'Gemstone' Potter was distant kin on my daddy's side. Daddy didn't warm up to him much though. The look on his face spoke volumes when Mama offered him the room. He preferred everyone calling him Gemstone, beaming with pride because of the odd namesake. I am not one best to judge a person's age, but I think he might have been north of sixty. He got around with the help of an exquisite fancy carved cane. The handle looked to be made of silver and was the head of a wolf, a very scary mean looking wolf. It reminded me of the walking stick in that 1941 classic The Wolf Man. Larry Talbot played by Lon Chaney Jr. purchased it from Gwen the girl he would later romance. She told Larry that it represented a werewolf, adding that it represents a man who changes into a wolf certain times of the year. I still remember the quote said by some of the villagers, 'Even a man who is pure of heart, and says his prayers at night may become a wolf when the wolfsbane blooms and the autumn moon is bright.' Later that night Larry attempts to save Gwen's friend Jenny from what he believes is a wolf attacking her and he kills the beast with that very cane. He is bitten during the scuffle. And the rest you know, I'm sure. Sorry, I still enjoy the classics.

No, Gemstone was not a wayward werewolf. He was an eccentric character none the less. He was a prospector and traveled the countryside forever in search of the illusive motherlode. Instead of a mule, he owned what he called a Liberty Truck. It looked like a cross between a truck and a covered wagon. It was a refurbished Class-B Standardized 1917 Military truck. It was a behemoth of a vehicle, one of a kind transportation. It was hard to visualize it being driven by a regular civilian as an everyday truck. Gemstone was not a regular guy by any stretch of the imagination.

I asked him what had brought him to the area.

"Lad, have you not heard of the lost Confederate gold? True, old Gemstone usually seeks ground gold, long lost veins or deserted claims, but I am getting no younger. Digging for gold, silver and even gemstones is better suited for those possessing nimbler bones. I am here for easy pickings, solving a mystery and walking away filthy rich. Might be that I can enlist your help. You look to be fit and muscular, just the right kind of partner that I require."

"Do you know where the gold is hidden?"

"If you are asking if I have a map the answer is no. I have a gift instead, a virtual bloodhound I am. I can sense when precious metals are nearby. My toes become all tingly and my head woozy from the sensations. I can close my eyes and visualize, honing in on what others have stumbled over and never found. Why do you think they call me Gemstone? Gold, silver, rubies, diamonds, any precious metals are for the taking. I have found them when others thought they could

63

not be found. I have been a gem gunslinger for hire much of my life but now I prefer freelancing, it cuts out the middleman."

"Do you think gold is here some place?"

"Don't tell your folks. It might damage their fragile egos, thinking ole Gemstone had other motives for graciously accepting their hospitality. It is purely coincidental that I am here among relatives. Gold fever possesses a powerful pull. The key is differentiating the real McCoy from the fool's variety. Fool's gold has ruined many."

"Fool's gold?"

"Why yes lad, fake gold, nature's way of saying 'gotcha'. The nongenuine type has driven many a feller crazy as a bat, thinking they have found the motherlode only to be fooled by mother nature instead. Gemstone cannot be deceived by nature's trickery and despicable deception. Full circle we have arrived. Let us talk recruiting you in this little venture."

"Me? I don't know anything about hunting gold, the regular kind or the fake kind."

"Not to worry, your services are not sought to be a seeker. That is my gift. You will be the excavator in this little proposition."

"Excavator?"

"You do know how to operate a shovel and a pickaxe don't you?"

"Operate s shovel and pickaxe? Never heard it said like that before."

"I presume your hands will fit the handles of either and you can excavate… dig where I instruct you to dig can't you? This is not a complicated process, lad."

"I can dig with a shovel, but I have never used a pickaxe."

"Easy peasy, not to worry, you shall have the hang of it quick enough under my tutorial guidance."

"Where are we going to dig for the gold?"

"You will be digging where I instruct you to dig. For now, that location remains a secret, my secret. Do we have an agreement then?"

"Agreement? What sort of agreement?"

"Lad you do make conversing with you quite an exasperating experience. Do you care to partner with me or not? I will make this worth your time."

"I don't know. I do have chores and a job."

"Once we locate the Confederate gold, there will be no need for you to work. You shall be a wealthy independent. Your share, ten percent of all that we recover."

"Let me get this straight, Cousin Gemstone. I do all the digging and get only ten percent while you pocket ninety percent. Seems a bit unfair to me."

"Fairness! Without me you have zero percentage."

"Without me you are the one operating a shovel and a pickaxe."

"You drive a hard bargain lad. Negotiation accepted. I will increase your share to fifteen percent."

"Make it twenty percent and you have an excavator."

"Very well, twenty percent of all that we uncover. Shall we shake on it to seal the partnership? A man's handshake makes this a contractual agreement."

"Deal. When do we start?"

"I thought you had chores and a job."

"Chores are caught up and my job is only parttime. I am off work today."

"Shrewd negotiator you are, holding back pertinent information."

"You never asked, and I was not obligated to tell you."

"This is not your first rodeo is it lad."

"Been on my own for a spell. Just came back here recently. And if we are going to be partners you can drop the 'lad' part. My name is Nelson."

"Nelson it is then. Everything we will need is in the 'Treasure-trove'."

"In the what?"

"Treasure-trove is the name of my Liberty truck. Fitting name, do you not agree?"

"Where are we headed?"

"I will know when we arrive there."

"You are quite the man of mystery aren't you Cousin Gemstone?"

"I am the master of mysteriousness and intuitiveness. Shall we venture into the world of the filthy rich?"

"You are the seeker of fame and fortune. Work your magic Cousin Gemstone. You point. I dig."

Off and on over the next week he pointed, I dug. The landscape must have resembled the craters of the moon. Our bounty included a Mason jar full of quarters tallying $27.25, a gold pocket watch gifted to someone named Harvey Bergman, one jade and silver earing, a wedding band, a tobacco bag with seven silver dollars none of which were worth more than a dollar each, a money clip with unidentifiable currency, an odd set of false teeth with inset gold fillings, miscellaneous bones and a steeple's church bell. My twenty percent amounted to $44.59. Unfortunately, Cousin McArthur 'Gemstone' Potter skipped out under the cloak of darkness one night and I nor anyone else ever laid eyes on him again. My stint as an excavator with aspirations of becoming filthy rich ended almost as quickly as it had started. All I got out of it was an 'I told you so' from Daddy. Snookered and embarrassed, I set out on my own again. It was just too tough living under my parent's roof once I had tasted the freedom to do as I pleased.

"Grandfather Nelson, it seems you and your siblings were not ones to stay rooted with family."

"And it was not from lack of having a wonderful loving family. Mama loved us dearly and Daddy, in his own way, did as well. Your observations are founded though. We were the wandering kind for sure. I had this notion I would visit my sister on the opposite side of the country. I made sure I had gotten the address from Mama before I trekked off. Grand plans are just that…plans. Sticking to and following the plan can be more difficult than expected. Life tends to throw a few curve balls when least expected. Aunt Harley Ann might call it destiny or a simple premonition from a tarot card reading of what the future held in store. Problem, I was not like my relative. I could not see into the future. I often struggled just to survive in the present. The future decided to ambush me and my plan but not before tossing some unexpected roadblocks and detours in my path."

Chapter 9

Memories can explode and nearly run you over when least expected. Mine were beginning to snowball. David sat patiently with his recorder in pause mode waiting for me to compose myself after our little stroll. I wasn't winded nor tired, but I used 'being so' as an excuse to clear my head. It wasn't that I was having any regrets or anything remotely like it. Referencing the so-called roadblock had taken me off guard. The detour had both positive and negative ramifications. I had not been prepared for what was about to come my way. I had set out on foot at first, but this was a poor choice given the thousands of miles of traveling ahead. I had my savings, more than enough to see this trip through but I did not want to waste it on a bus ticket or train fare. I had decided to take my time and embrace what this great country had to offer. Still, on foot made absolutely no sense. I was not the hitching type either. I spotted my solution on a used car lot the third day of my journey. I picked up there and informed David to begin recording or as he called it, pressing the voice activated button.

> There it stood, a red motor scooter. Not just any scooter but a used Cushman AutoGlide. I was able to negotiate a good price with the salesman who seemed eager to get rid of it. For less than a hundred dollars I was now riding instead of walking. The scooter topped out at around 40 MPH, the perfect speed to sponge in America as I traveled across country. To stretch my savings, I camped out as much as possible. There is nothing like sleeping underneath the stars in the summertime. It wasn't long into my journey when I discovered the value of my deal. The tires were worn, and I eventually had a blowout. Luckily, I was within walking and pushing distance of a small town.
>
> It was almost dark by the time I reached the town limits sign. To worsen my luck, a thunderstorm was rumbling in the distance and approaching fast. I spotted a motel just ahead and quickened my pace. About the time I arrived at the

motel's office the sky unleashed its fury. The little old man behind the desk eyed me strangely when I entered. Before I could ask for a room, he quickly advised me that motorcycle gang members were not welcome. I tried to explain that I was not a gang member, and I was riding a scooter, not a motorcycle. Two wheels and my worn-out leather jacket meant I was a gang member tried and true.

It was raining dogs and cats now, what we called back home a frog strangler. I asked him if I could wait it out. He promptly told me to get, or he was calling the police. He was not the joking type, so I did as he asked. The rain was blowing sideways as I pushed my scooter toward town. It was slow going in the blinding rain with a flat back tire. I was none too keen on being out in the open with the threatening lightning flashing. I was drenched through to my underwear as I sloshed along. I managed to see through the blinding rain what looked to be a service station just ahead. Finally arriving I parked my scooter underneath the station's awning.

A bearded man wearing tan coveralls exited the station and walked over to me. The name embroidered on his coveralls was Ned. He had a friendly smile, unlike the motel clerk. He looked at the flat and then told me to come inside. There he poured me a cup of coffee and then offered me a pair of the same type of coveralls and a towel saying I should get out of the wet clothes. He said he would push my bike in one of the car bays. I took him up on his hospitality. It did feel wonderful to be out of the rain and those wet clothes.

"Nasty storm. Where did you have the flat?"

"Blew out on me several miles back."

"My name is Bartholomew Armstrong."

I eyed the Ted patch and he eyed me eyeing it.

"Ted owns the place. Tore the seat out of mine and he let me borrow his."

"I am Nelson Whiteside. Thank you for your hospitality. I stopped at the motel down the road."

"Let me guess. Old man Carter thought you were in a motorcycle gang. He thinks anything two wheeled and motorized is associated with motorcycle gangs because he was once robbed by a motorcycle gang passing through town."

"I don't think my wounded Cushman and I are much of a threat. I didn't want any trouble. I did as he asked and vacated the premises. Can you fix my tire?"

"Not a chance. That thing is threadbare and dangerous."

"How much is a new or used one?"

"Not sure, Nelson. Ted doesn't carry scooter tires here. Might take a while to track one down. I don't think there is anywhere in town that sells them. Could be we could check Swagger's junk yard tomorrow."

"Is there another motel in town?"

"Afraid not. Where are you headed?

"My sister lives in California."

"And you were planning on getting there on that scooter."

"Beats walking."

"Have you not heard of Greyhound Bus Lines?"

"I just wanted to take my time and see the countryside."

"For sure you will have plenty of time traveling on that thing. Tell you what. You look like a decent feller and all, I got an extra room at my place if you want to stick it out through this storm."

"That would be great, Mister Armstrong. I can pay for my stay."

"Not necessary. I close shortly. Have another coffee. It's free. We have a soda and a cracker machine if it that works for you."

Mister Armstrong was a life saver for sure. After closing he drove us in his pickup to his house less than a mile away. We were greeted at the backdoor by a young lady, his daughter. Her name was Jenny Ruth. She was two years older than me. She was as hospitable as her father. She immediately took my wet clothes and said she would dry them for me in front of the kitchen stove but not before we ate. She had prepared a meal of fried baloney, scrambled eggs, and biscuits. It was the best meal I had had since leaving on my little trip.

Jenny Ruth had flowing red hair, green eyes, and a contagious smile. She was quite petite in stature and wore a snug fitting flowery dress. Like her father, she was not shy and very inquisitive. Her questions were not intrusive by nature. I found the conversation flow to be very enlightening. Mister Armstrong smoked his pipe after the meal, rocked in his chair and joined in when Jenny Ruth paused to take a breath. He finally announced that he was retiring for the night and told us not to stay up too late. They completely trusted me inside their home as if I were family or a close family friend. We chatted for hours. It was in the wee hours of the morning when we finally retired to our bedrooms. Mine was nothing fancy but it was comfortable and beat sleeping on the ground for a change.

The next morning Mister Armstrong drove us to the junk yard in search of a replacement tire. We struck out. Mister Swagger said that he would try to locate one for me.

Meanwhile Mister Armstrong dropped Jenny Ruth and me off at the town's farmer's market where she sold pies she had made. I hung out with her until she had sold all her pies, which did not take long. We then walked to the town square and sat on a bench taking in the warm sunshine while we had ice cream cones from the corner drugstore. I think by then we both knew about everything there was to know about each other. She envied me for taking out on my own, saying she could never just up and leave her father. Her mother had died a few years ago from a ruptured gallbladder. She had become the woman of the house while her father earned a modest living at the gas station.

We eventually headed back to their place, a long walk, but in her company, it didn't seem nearly long enough. She gave me the nickel tour of town. We stopped at a small park named after a previous neighbor. Jenny Ruth sat in a swing while I pushed her. As I held the chains bringing her to a stop the swing twirled slightly, she hopped out awkwardly landing in my arms. I caught her and she planted a long kiss on my lips, hinting to me that the mishap from the swing might have been no accident. I had never been kissed by a girl like that. She smiled and grabbed me by the hand. We walked hand in hand for the duration of the route back. She occasionally shouldered into me sneaking in flirtatious kisses on my cheek. To say I was smitten would be an understatement.

We arrived home long before Mister Armstrong arrived from work. I will leave the rest to your imagination. Let's just say I no longer fretted over finding a tire anytime soon. On the contrary, I hoped it would take an extended time to locate one. I helped her prepare supper trying to make myself useful. There was plenty of heat in that kitchen. We had a dandy meal once Mister Armstrong arrived home. Don't ask me what we had because my memory is a bit cloudy on that. It was a good thing I was not traveling to my sister's place on a precise schedule. Frankly, she didn't know I was coming. I

72

had planned to surprise her. I hadn't expected on being surprised myself, pleasantly so I must add.

My blown-out tire had landed me in the middle of this delay for nearly a week when Mister Swagger called to tell Mister Armstrong that he had located a tire. It was being shipped and should arrive within two or three days. I was crushed by the news. I did not let on to Mister Armstrong that I was though. I prepaid for the tire to ensure it would be sent as promised. I broke the news to Jenny Ruth. She was as saddened as was I. Not one to hold back any punches she asked me did I still plan to go to California. I wanted to say no but, in my heart, I knew I had to see this through. My parents expected me to, even if my sister was not in on it, not that I knew of. Jenny Ruth and I did not waste valuable time knowing days were limited. We enjoyed one another as much as humanly possible.

Did I love Jenny Ruth? What did I know about love? She never uttered those words to me. If she had, would I have said them back to her? No denying it, we were living in the moment. Maybe she wanted me to ask her to go with me. I kept thinking about how she thought of herself as the woman of the house taking care of her father. I could not be the one responsible for putting her on the spot, not after they had opened their home up to me. I was in the middle of the proverbial rock and hard place. My gut told me that I must leave and complete my plan while my heart said the opposite.

The tire arrived. We picked it up and Mister Armstrong changed the old for the new one. He gave my scooter the once over to ensure there were no more surprises mechanically. I was trying to read him. Did he want me to stay or leave? He had a poker face. Once the scooter was travel ready, he did not ask when I planned to leave, nor did he encourage me that I should be on the road. He wasn't blind. He had to know that there was something going on between me and his daughter. I wondered if he wanted me to ask permission for her to accompany me, but I did not have the courage to pose the question. We were all at a stalemate. Go, don't go. Ask, don't ask. I squirmed like a red wiggler on one of Uncle Rusty's fishhooks. I wished either Jenny Ruth or her father would take it out of my hands and ask me not to go. Neither did. That confused me even more. Was I reading too much into what we shared?

Moment of truth, do I leave or stay. Do I dare pop the question and ask her to go with me? Decisive had never been so confusingly indecisive.

"So, what did you do Grandfather Nelson?"

"Neither one. I decided to head back home. Traveling to California had not been what I had envisioned it to be. Besides, my gut told me that the scooter would never survive the trip. While I was taken by Jenny Ruth, I was gun shy when it came to making a commitment. When it came right down to it, I reckon I was not in love after all. I took the cowardly way out to boot and slipped away without thanking Mister Armstrong or saying goodbye to Jenny Ruth. To this day I regret my actions."

"Did you ever see her again?"

"That would have required effort on my behalf. My regret did not kick in until way too many years later. Sometimes just feeling sorry about a situation pacifies a sorrowful soul. Like my heart, my conscience managed to heal with minimal scars. Hope that this doesn't influence how you view me."

"I am not here to pass judgement or critique your decisions Grandfather. I am here to listen and learn. Please continue and tell me more."

"You are a glutton for punishment David. Pandora's box holds plenty of secrets. When we are done, you might consider editing out some of it to cut your ties with the truth."

74

"Remember, I am the one that asked. I did not ask so that I could censor any of it. Every family has their oddities and potentially embarrassing characters and situations. I never expected ours to be any different."

"Be careful about what you ask. It might be a bit skewed from what most consider the middle of the road. Then continue we will after we wet our whistles. Dry mouth tends to hinder the process of spitting out these memories."

"I will be right back with a couple glasses of tea, Grandfather."

"My thoughts will remain on pause just like your recorder until you return."

Chapter 10

I really tried my best to stay on chronological point and pick up where I had left off. It was significant to do so where this part of my little nostalgic recollection was concerned. The detour from my California dreaming plan had led me to the most unexpected discovery. I replayed the sequence of events inside my head while I waited for David to return with our ice-cold tea. I experienced a mixture of emotions, reliving what I had long ago forgotten. A chance encounter, a change in plans and a misdirection had triggered emotional results.

"Here you go Grandfather," said David, handing me the tea. "Begin whenever and wherever you feel like it."

> After my unceremonious exit I headed back in the general direction of home. I say general because I had not exactly remembered the exact path I had taken. I just rode, the wind in my face and my heart worn on my sleeve. Jenny Ruth had deserved better than how I left matters. My day had passed uneventful. New tire and my scooter mechanically sound I motored along, passing through tiny communities, none worth stopping at. The sun was on its last leg of setting when I entered the city limits of the largest town I had passed through since leaving the hospitality of the Armstrong's.
>
> I was hungry so I searched for some place to get a bite. I was in luck. There was a diner open on the outskirts of town. I entered and it was oddly almost empty. Strange for what should have been supper time. I asked the waitress about it, and she pointed to a poster in the window telling me that most folks were probably attending the carnival. It was Friday and the best show in town, so she said. She added that she would be there if not for having to work. I woofed down my cheeseburger, fries and root beer, my first and only meal since leaving that morning. I had decided I would camp under the stars. First, I must find a suitable location. I rode in no particular direction and eventually ended up at the

fairgrounds where the carnival was in full throttle. There was a grove of hardwoods adjacent to the grounds, a perfect spot to set up my little encampment. I chose a concealed spot off the beaten path, within walking distance of the carnival. I had not attended a carnival in numerous years and figured why not.

The carnival was all hustle and bustle. We always considered it a big deal when our folks took us to a carnival or the county fair. There is a difference. Carnivals cater to everyone's fancy offering rides, food and sideshow entertainment. A county fair offers all this and then some with a primary focus on agriculture. Farmers showcase their livestock at a fair and the womenfolk share their prized recipes of jams, cakes, pies and pickled concoctions, all for the hope of winning a blue ribbon and for personal pride. Carneys tend to have reputations for being con artist and shysters. Daddy always warned us when we attended a carnival not to let ourselves get snookered by the barkers on the midway. If it looks too easy and too good to be true, it was. Odd, fairs had about the same types of games and midway shows, but he didn't seem nearly as concerned when attending them. I reckon that was because a fair was sort of a sponsored event and held different standards and integrity. If they were too dishonest, they would lose their annual fall rotation.

I paid the two bits to enter. Two bits is a quarter if you were wondering. Times were different back then. A quarter went a long way. Most carney attractions including the games of chance only costs a dime for our time. I had learned from previous trips, that while spending a dime for three ring tosses or ball throws were fun, they rarely produced significant prizes for your investment. Daddy said it was money thrown away and he was right. As kids though we must learn the hard way. We blew much of our allowed money learning that valuable lesson. I walked the midway taking in the sights and sounds but I ignored the barkers vying for my money. I opted for a candy apple instead. The gent manning the booth had his back turned to me. I rapped on the counter, and he turned to attend to his customer. I was taken aback. The face staring back at me belonged to my brother Jeremy. He was as much in shock as was I. He was the first to speak.

"Where are our folks?"

"Home I reckon."

"How did you get here so far away from home?"

"On my scooter."

"Do they know you came here?"

"No. I was heading to California to see our sister."

"On a scooter, that is crazy even for you."

"I am not heading there now. I am heading home."

"Home?"

"Yeah, I decided not to go to California."

"What are you doing here?"

"I was passing through and decided to spend the night. The carnival looked like something worth doing. I haven't been to one since they took all of us to the last one while we were still living at home. I wanted one of those candy apples."

"Here. Take one and then scat."

"Why are you wanting me to scat Jeremy?"

"You don't have any business here."

"I paid my two bits already. It is my business what I do."

"Take this quarter and get."

"What if I don't want to get? And you can keep your quarter."

"Get anyway."

"What's wrong with you? Why are you trying to get rid of me?"

"Just go. Act like you don't know me or have seen me."

"That's just plain crazy, Jeremy. I know you and I surely see you."

"You don't understand."

"You got that right. I don't. Why don't you make me understand what has gotten into you?"

"I am working. I can't waste time on you right now."

"Oh, so your brother is a complete waste of your valuable time. What's gotten into you? I am used to you ignoring me but not like this. None of us have seen nor heard from you since you left. You know that is wrong."

"I didn't exactly leave."

"You certainly said you were leaving and joining a traveling carnival. Look, here you are just like you said."

"Problem Jerod," said a gruff voice from behind.

"No sir, just selling this kid a candy apple. Thank you, kid. Have fun."

"Jerod? His name is not Jerod. It's Jeremy."

"Do you know this kid, Jerod?"

"Never seen him before."

"He is yanking your chain Mister. Jeremy is my brother. I'm Nelson Whiteside."

"Jerod, I thought you said you had no family."

"That's crazy. Why did you tell him that? I am his brother. He has a sister, another brother, a mama and a daddy and plenty of other kin."

"Do you live around here sonny?"

"No sir. I was heading to California to see my sister."

"Your folks are not with you then."

"No sir, I am by myself."

"He was just leaving, weren't you?"

"Jerod or Jeremy, whoever you are, you painted a different picture, didn't you? What say we invite your brother to join us for vittles after we close tonight? Nelson, please take us up on our hospitality."

"I suppose I could. I have nothing better to do."

"He can't. He is heading out now."

"Is that true, Nelson?"

"No sir, I am staying overnight.

"And where might you be staying, Nelson?"

"Oh, I set up camp over yonder in those hardwoods."

"If that be the case, break camp and allow me to offer you accommodations with us. We can show you how we do things here at the carnival, the grand tour, the behind the scenes look that nobody else gets to experience."

"Boy that would be swell Mister…"

"Call me Roy. I oversee the carnies. Come with me and I will show you the lay of the land, all rides and entertainment on me."

"Wow, did you hear that, Jeremy? I get to do everything free of charge."

"Trust me, nothing is free here," said Jeremy as he shoved the popcorn machine over and in Roy's way. "Run Nelson," he yelled as he ran too.

I saw the terrified look on Jeremy's face and ran behind him. Roy had fallen to the ground when the popcorn machine caught him by surprise and tripped him up. We zig zagged through various midway venues until finally we were off the fairgrounds and into the woods. There we caught our breath while my brother looked about frantically, expecting Roy or somebody to be chasing us. We did hear some footfalls and voices, but they were not heading in our direction. Once Jeremy was satisfied that we had not been followed, we circled around to where my camp was located.

"We have to get out of here."

"What has you so rattled Jeremy?"

It was then that we spotted Roy and several other men heading in our direction. Jeremy pushed me toward my scooter and yelled go. He climbed on behind me and we skedaddled, kicking up dust as I sidewinded, not accustomed to riding someone on the back. I am not sure how far we rode. Jeremy was not willing to stop until we had put quite some distance between us and the carnival. When we did finally stop, it was obvious we were not heading in the direction of home. I did not recognize the area, nor the town posted ahead. Jeremy did not seem too concerned that we were probably lost.

We ended up camping in the middle of a cornfield. It was then that my brother explained the extent of the situation. He had followed his dream and had hooked up with the carnival. His dream had nightmarish results. Roy was a combination con artist and loan shark. He lured in the carneys with promises of prosperity and advancement. Neither hardly ever happened. To tighten his hold on those who worked for him he generously loaned them money with steep interest. Carneys dug themselves deeper into debt with little hope of ever paying the money owed back. To make matters worse Roy was an abusive boss. Jeremy ended up being one of those hopelessly trapped and deeply buried in a hole of debt. Loyal carneys were utilized as Roy's muscle. Cross him and he unleashed the brutes to remind those owing money that failure to so would be met with dire consequences.

When he hired on, Jeremy decided not to use his real name. Several other carneys advised him that most didn't because local law enforcement often rousted them, accusing them of various crimes when the carnival was in their town. Some were justified. Some weren't. He was also told to never admit he had family. Roy had a reputation for forcing carneys to write their family and ask for money; money they owed him, and he kept. Roy also would use family as an insurance policy, threatening to do them harm if ever the carney crossed him or fled. Jeremy saw through the scheme that Roy had in store for me, snaring me in his corrupt net as well. He would use my brother being a carney to entice me to stay. Jeremy said he would never allow that to happen to me, so he had acted spontaneously to ensure that at least I escaped. As it turned out we both were able to shake Roy and his henchmen. Harsh words, those chasing us were poor indebted carneys that had no choice but to do Roy's bidding.

Jeremy warned me that we were a long way from being out of the woods and out of Roy's reach. He now knew our real names. Roy would also be reasonably sure he knew the general area where we lived. The man would neither forgive nor forget what we had done, and that Jeremy owed him money with interest. The carnival would eventually end back up in our town. Jeremy was not convinced that Roy would wait until then. He might seek vengeance sooner instead of later. It was then that I realized what Jeremy was planning to do; what he wanted us to do. We were not heading home yet. He suggested that we lay low and distance ourselves. I had a little money as did Jeremy. It wasn't much but it would buy us a little time until we figured out what we were going to do and where we intended to go.

"With that, I need to take a short break if that is okay with you David."

"Certainly, Grandfather Nelson but I bet this is what one of those cliffhangers feels like, the ones you told me about in the cinema serials you attended as boy."

"I promise I will not leave you hanging long. Old men and their bladders cannot be placed on pause by a button like that recorder of yours. When nature knocks, best we answer quickly."

A bathroom break was the furthest notion from my needs. I needed to think before I ventured down a path that might do more harm than good. I did not share my emotions with David, but I had not thought about Jeremy and the carnival in decades. I had mixed emotions about revisiting it now. While it had been a surprise, stumbling upon my long-lost brother, fleeing Roy had been one of the scariest things I had ever done. Wondering if he would find us was even scarier. I had never understood the concept of looking over your shoulder until then. Nights were the worst of all. I worried that he would find us and sneak up on us while we slept. Jeremy had painted a picture of a ruthless feller capable of doing heinous things. Maybe he was just trying to scare me. If he was, it worked perfectly.

When this had started, I figured I would just be going through the pecking order and telling David a little of this and that about kinfolk. I had never imagined that all these memories would be conjured up and many in such detail. I reckon it is like what people say about old people; we can remember our ancient past more vividly than we can recall what just happened. I am not sure how long and how true this will hold and just what memories I will still be able to remember. At this point, I will allow it to run its course and go with the flow for better or worse. Realistically, none of it is bad as I probably envision it. Just having the ability to walk those miles again is quite miraculous. I intend to cherish every little tidbit. If I don't, it will be lost forever like we almost were.

Chapter 11

The road less traveled can be rewarding to old minds capable of remembering the long-ago times of youth and inexperience. The learning curve can be steep and cumbersome, but it is all part of the journey. Nelson cherished every incident, good and bad, and was thankful David had asked to open the can of worms known as their family history.

"Refreshed and ready, David. Is that little recording device holding up as well as me?"

"As a matter of fact, I replayed portions of the last segment and we are good to go. Begin when you are ready, Grandfather Nelson."

"I reckon it is rocker time again. The porch beckons us. While my mind is recalling it quite vividly, I think I will pick up where I left off."

> We had time to work a new plan while hiding and resting in the corn field. Jeremy still feared returning home. His gut leaned toward Roy being the vengeful type. He was convinced his carnival boss would seek us out and demand the money owed. Even worse, he figured Roy would be out to make him an example. A loan shark has a reputation to uphold. Allowing one fish to squirm off the hook emboldened others to give it a shot. Jeremy, being the older, decided we should stick to my original plan and head to California and seek temporary refuge at our sister's place. I told him that he was an uncle now. He had a nephew named Jupiter. Jeremy thought that was an odd name. I told him what Mama had said about it, 'Carol has fallen into the California craziness and has named her son after a planet.' Jeremy got a kick out of her saying that.
>
> Jeremy convinced me to pawn my scooter. It was a no brainer. The scooter would never get the two of us to the west coast. I quickly learned that a pawned scooter was not

worth nearly as much as I had forked over for it. We emptied our pockets and counted our money including the scooter contribution. We were still a few dollars shy of purchasing two Greyhound tickets to California. The furthest we could hope for was to make it to a little town in Arizona, well short of where we needed to be. Our options were slim at best. We could contact our sister and ask her to wire us the money. We were not sure how she would react being that she didn't even know we were coming. Plus, we had no idea if she had the money to lend us. Jeremy refused to opt to contact our parents saying it was best to keep them out of it in case Roy did show up looking for us. We could find work and try to earn extra money but that might take too much time given we would also have to eat and find someplace to hold up. Neither came cheap. Another option, we could get as far as Arizona and walk and hitch the rest of the way. Were we really that desperate to escape Roy? If we laid low where we were, wouldn't the carnival put distance between us and it?

Jeremy did not trust the resourcefulness of Roy. Loan sharks tend to have long tentacles that can reach farther than most people can fathom. Jeremy said criminals stick together like they have some sort of code of the west. He had witnessed it more than once when others had tried to renege on loans and attempt to outrun his potential overreach. Roy always got his man and the offender always paid dearly for his bad decision. It was that example thing going a long way in discouraging others. Most snuck away during the night. Jeremy had pulled off the perfect insult, challenging Roy in broad daylight, something utterly unheard of. Roy would be more determined than ever to make Jeremy pay for doing the unthinkable. According to my brother, he would turn over every rock and not give up until he served painful justice. I asked Jeremy how far Roy might go, and he told me it was best that I didn't know the extent. I read between those lines, figuring we were in much deeper than I had previously anticipated. That explained Jeremy's urgency to get as far a way as we possibly could.

We slept on it and the next morning Jeremy told me that we would purchase the Greyhound tickets and travel as far west as they would take us. My brother had desperation in his eyes. Seeing his desperation put the fear in me as well. We were in serious trouble. I asked him how much he owed. He would not disclose the exact amount. I then suggested we pay Roy back including the interest. He told me that would never fly. Roy would be out for more than just the money now. We had gone full circle, the guarantee that Roy would seek brutal justice in the matter. My perception of carnivals was forever changed given the ruthlessness we were experiencing. So much so that, to this day, I have never visited another one. I figured every one of them had their version of a Roy. Perhaps this is an unfair judgement on my behalf. I'm sure there is no bad carney out there looking to enslave an old coot like me and for certain, Roy has been long gone now.

This would be another first, me riding on a Greyhound bus. We barely had enough money left over to buy something to eat. This alone made for uncomfortable travel. You must also take into account that back then we were traveling the backroads of rural American at speeds nowhere close to travel today accomplished by modern vehicles on interstates. We were days away from reaching our destination when layovers were common to allow the driver to rest. More times, hungry bellies were in our future. On the positive side I had been reunited with my brother and we were bonding like we never had before. Misery embraces company and, in our case, maybe there was safety in numbers. Well as far as Roy and his henchmen were concerned, I don't think the two of us were very intimidating nor much of a challenge if things came down to it. At least we were traveling in the opposite direction of the carnival's scheduled stops in the deep south.

A couple of hundred miles into our ride and during the second stop we spent our last money on a baloney sandwich and a grape Nehi soda. We split the meal between us. It barely fended off the hunger pains. We now faced dire circumstances. Vivid imaginations can conquer up visions of starvation even if we weren't likely to die from lack of food on a bus trip. I wondered if we could play up this melodrama to our advantage. Would other passengers have pity on us and offer to help? I had never begged for anything in my life, especially not food, and I wasn't sure I had it in me to start now. I was too proud and after having worked for my keep, the thought of it seemed too unreasonable for me to ponder seriously. Jeremy had thus far offered no suggestions nor solutions to our looming dilemma other than saying we would cross that bridge when we had to. I was now second guessing, wondering why we had not swallowed our pride and gambled on phoning our sister, Carol. Too late now. That bridge was getting closer for the crossing.

One thing I learned from bus travel, there are some interesting and diverse travelers. In my time, long distance traveling was mostly done via the bus or train. Air travel was a luxury, not affordable for folks like us. Obviously, I had never flown or ridden on a train either. The Greyhound trumped vehicular travel or even my scooter. Encased inside the boxy bus, cheap entertainment includes people watching. You tend to watch fellow passengers, eavesdrop on conversations. I upped my entertainment skills by trying to guess where the various people were from and what jobs some of them might have. Most of this could have been had by merely engaging in conversation but had I, I would have had to divulge who we were, where we were from and where we were headed and maybe even why. Rather than lie through my teeth, I opted for playing my little game instead. It made time pass and distracted me from being hungry. I tried to include Jeremy in my fun, but he would have none of it. He held firm to his serious demeanor, probably still in a quandary over Roy. Guess I might have acted the same had I owed a thug money. It was bad enough being associated with someone who owed money to a ruthless individual. Brotherly love had reached new heights, one for all and all for one until death do us part.

I watched the hat guy three seats ahead and across the aisle from us. He wore a tan Fedora with a large colorful feather in the hat's band. The hat seemed out of place for his wool plaid red, black, and yellow shirt. He was constantly retrieving a briefcase and peering inside as if he expected whatever was inside might somehow disappear. After peering inside he would always wipe his brow with a handkerchief seemingly relieved that all was how he had last seen it. I had never seen someone act so nervously. I wondered if he owed a loan shark money too. I could not see the expression on his face, but I had seen him during our stops. He had a large bulbous nose and the reddish chipmunk cheeks I had ever seen on a person. Daddy said people that looked like that were heavy boozers. Possibly he had stashed a bottle inside that briefcase although he never took a swig from it while on the bus. I decided that ruled out my assumption about him. A man hooked on booze could not have lasted for as long as he did without taking a drink. Odd behavior, when we were at stops, he kept that briefcase close to his bosom as if he was trying to protect the royal jewels. I would never solve the mystery. He disembarked on the fourth stop, reaching his destination. He retrieved no additional belongings from the bus's luggage area. I watched him until he vanished around a corner regretting that I never solved the mystery of the briefcase's content.

Jeremy elbowed me and motioned for me to get off the bus at the stop. We stood outside the gas station while passengers milled about outside and inside the country store as an attendant gassed up the bus. Passengers, including us, took turns using the bathroom. I was walking around, wishing I had money for this and that to eat when, out of the blue, Jeremy shoved me into a display case holding oil cans. Unable to break my fall I grabbed the display pulling it along with me as I crashed onto the floor. A clerk was quickly standing over me offering a hand before righting the display and replacing cans. I said I was sorry until I was blue in the face.

Back onboard I was furious with my brother for pulling such an embarrassing prank. He didn't offer much of an apology which infuriated me even more. We had taken seats near the back of the bus. It was only half full prompting many passengers to move about just to break the monotony. After we were on our way Jeremy reached inside his jacket and offered me a candy bar. He then unzipped his jacket slightly to expose a bounty of treats. Putting two and two together, I realized that he had used my fall as a distraction to shoplift a few edible items. I, in no way, condoned this behavior. I had never stolen anything in my life and despised being used by him to do so. He made no apologies for his thievery and told me I didn't have to eat any of it if I didn't want to. Guilty as charged, I allowed my appetite to overrule my honesty. My life of crime began on a Greyhound bus trip. I tried to convince myself that I had not been in on it and had not actually stolen the merchandise so I must be innocent if apprehended. Then just as quickly I realized I was guilty by association and for receiving stolen merchandise. Plus, I had destroyed evidence by eating it. Revisiting this episode has shamed me once again.

Jeremy's little heist held us over for the remainder of the day and partially into the next. I cringed every time the bus made a stop and kept my distance from my brother. I refused to allow him to use me in more of his thievery. Two grown men should never have to stoop so low. Well, one grown man in this case, as I had been innocently involved. After another stop, we boarded the bus. Jeremy passed a paper sack to me and said have at it. I smelled a familiar aroma. It contained a couple of burgers. I asked him how in the world had he stolen freshly made hamburgers. He smiled and thankfully said he hadn't. He had played the poor pitiful card to a young waitress while flashing his baby blues. Taken by whatever sad sob story he had used, she offered the burgers as her treat. He had already stolen, could I believe that he was not lying to me this time? I rationalized that he could not have blatantly waltzed from the dinner with a paper sack had it not been legit. Not totally convinced though, I woofed down the burger quickly as if trying to conceal more stolen goods.

I wondered if working at the carnival had exposed my brother to unethical behavior. We had not been brought up to steal. I certainly wanted no part of being involved in a cross-country crime spree. Every stop thereafter, I kept my distance from my brother but watched for any sign of criminal activity. I wondered if other passengers were watching us like I had been watching them. I diverted my eyes when anyone looked my way. I had lost my interest in people watching, too eaten up with guilt to be preoccupied with the distraction. The bus driver announced that we would be arriving in Tucson, Arizona in two hours. Carol lived in Lancaster, California. According to the bus driver the distance from Tucson to Lancaster was about five hundred miles. Our ticket would get us close but no cigar. It might as well be five thousand miles. We were flat broke.

I could not tolerate any more of this uncertainty and was going to be no part of additional stealing to survive. I told Jeremy that enough was enough. It was time to call Carol. To my surprise he agreed. I retrieved the folded piece of paper in my billfold with her address and phone number written on it. When we arrived in Tucson, we would locate a payphone and see if Carol would accept charges for the call. She was our sister, why wouldn't she. An argument against her doing so raised its ugly head in my mind. Since moving to California with her husband, she rarely contacted our folks. It seemed as if she had disowned the family. It didn't make any sense, her acting this way. She and our folks had parted ways on good terms even if they had not fully approved of her husband choice. She had married Edwardo. His family had been Mexican immigrants. He seemed a likable guy to me, but you must remember, back in those days, certain taboo boundaries existed. People were expected to marry within their race. Edwardo was American, born and raised in the United States, but perception often trumped logic. Possibly the rift in perception had caused issues among family. If it had, neither Jeremy nor I had been part of it.

Judgement time arrived at our final stop. I dialed the number, and we received a rude awakening. The number was no longer in service. Now what? We had an address, but logic said that if the number was no longer in service, they had probably relocated as well. Here we were, stranded in Tucson, Arizona with not a cent to our names. On the bright side, we were far away from the likes of Roy. Dire straights just the same.

"What did you do Grandfather Nelson?"

"I never envisioned I would ever relive this part of my life."

"Then don't if it causes you discomfort and stress. We can skip it."

"The time comes when you must stop focusing on stress and remember how blessed you are, David. Sometimes it is easy to be hard on ourselves without remembering we each probably have chapters we would rather not read out loud. Sometimes we should just sit back, take a breath, and marvel at our life, including mistakes we have made along the way. From those mistakes we can gain wisdom and strength and continue to move forward. In the end, if we keep the faith, we will persevere no matter how dark it gets. We are not guaranteed the sun shall rise again. David, I realize that this is probably a lot of old man babble. Tell you what, I will give you the abbreviated version, something a little less painful, yet it will get us beyond this point for all practical purposes."

"This is your story, your life, Grandfather. Please tell it however it makes you feel comfortable. To be honest, you could have skipped anything you wished, and I would never have been the wiser."

"Not my style, David. I will never intentionally paint on a different canvas just for the sake of hiding any family skeletons. Let me just end this segment by saying with many challenges and much hardship we eventually returned home. We learned valuable lessons and were tested beyond what we ever thought possible. And no, for the record, we conducted ourselves honestly. There was no more thievery or dishonesty involved to assist us in our return. And, contrary to our belief, we never crossed paths with Roy after arriving back home. He never contacted our folks either. Perhaps we gave him too much credit back then. And like I said earlier, we outlived the threat and the man behind it. We feared a boogeyman that never existed beyond our vivid imagination. Good sprouted from bad though. Jeremy and I developed a close relationship, one that we had never shared growing up as kids. I dearly miss my brother and my other siblings as well. Being the sole survivor has its regrets as well as its perks."

Chapter 12

David rocked a bit before asking me about Carol, Edwardo and Jupiter's whereabouts back then. Had they known we had gone looking for them? The short answer was no. We never told our parents that we had tried either. We kept them in the dark about Roy and the bus trip. We came up with a believable shorter version of what had happened and how we had been reunited without having to conjure up a lie. Our folks were so glad to have us back home that they posed very few questions. Several years would pass before Carol resurfaced. Our folks had given up hope, thinking that maybe she and her hubby and kid had left the country and gone to Mexico. Their suspicions were closer to the truth than even they realized. I mentally revisited the remainder of our little cross county romp before dismissing it for the very last time. Brothers had survived to live another day and only I knew the rest of that story.

Out of nowhere my mind got jolted by another Uncle Rusty memory, one worth telling. Like I had mentioned to David, there was no promise that I would remember things in any logical order. Sometimes you must go with the flow, work them when they surface. There were no bad memories about Uncle Rusty, excluding the one of his ultimate demise of course.

> We were obviously still living under the same roof when this one happened. I am not sure how old I was, but I can still see what happened as if it were yesterday. It was Halloween night and living out in the sticks does not offer many opportunities for trick or treating. The closest house was not worth the walk and there was no guarantee that we would get any candy if we mustered the effort. Daddy wasn't much on what he called a senseless holiday. There was no time off for any holidays when there was work to be done. Mama was a bit more reasonable and did make some homemade cookies for our treats.
>
> Pooter was still in the picture, so we decided to celebrate it the best way we could. We wanted to do something spooky

and forbidden if there was no candy harvesting in our future. Chores had to be finished first though at his place and at mine. It worked perfectly for us because spooky didn't begin until after it got dark. We decided we would meet halfway between our houses. Mama would not let me go unless I took Uncle Rusty with me. She even bagged the cookies for us. I kept the sack though knowing how Uncle Rusty can devour anything that doesn't eat him first. It didn't stop him from whining and begging for them. I finally told him a little white lie saying we couldn't eat any until we found some spooks first, Halloween rules.

We had even constructed our outfits for the occasion. I decided I wanted to be a clown and Mama allowed me to use some of her makeup to paint a clown face. That was about the extent of my outfit. We kept Rusty's simple too. An old sheet with holes cut out for eyes transformed him into a ghost. Pooter had not shared with me what he planned to be saying it was a surprise. It was well past dark thirty as we walked that lonely dirt road. Thankfully, Uncle Rusty had a trusty flashlight. Well, it wasn't like today's flashlights. His was more of a lantern, but it worked to illuminate our way. It served as the perfect special effect for my ghostly companion constantly booing a warning for anything out and about on the darkened road.

Something directly ahead stirred in the darkness beyond the lantern's illumination. I tried to hush Uncle Rusty and his booing, but Uncle Rusty does what Uncle Rusty wants to do. He was a ghost and that's what ghost did. Cutting through the boos sounded a piercing war cry. We were about to be under attack by someone or something. Emerging from the darkness was a wild eyed Indian, war paint on his face, feathers in a head band and clutching a bow. Pooter on command cut the cheese as a warning shot to the two pale faces blocking his path.

"How, clown boy and night spirit," he greeted us.

"Nice outfit, Injun."

"Yeah, my ma painted my face. Pa made the headband from redtail hawk feathers. He even made me the bow and arrows. It shoots like a real one. Don't worry, he rounded the tips on the arrows so they can't puncture anybody. Who is your ghost friend?"

"Boooooooooooooo!"

"That can't be Rusty underneath that sheet, can it?"

Uncle Rusty just let out more boos and remained in character. Such was his way all the way all the time.

"I have some cookies for our treats."

"I got some plum jam and buttered biscuits. We didn't have any candy or cookies."

Uncle Rusty flipped back his sheet and held his hand out saying treat. We obliged, offering him a cookie and a biscuit. He scarfed both down, asking for more. I reached over and pulled the sheet back over him telling him no more for now.

"What now? We are dressed up and got no place to spook up," I told Pooter.

He rubbed his chin for a second before saying, "I got it. We could visit that old graveyard down Dry Creek Road. It is just back that way a short piece, even a shorter distance if we cut through the woods. My grandpappy says it is haunted by restless confederate soldiers, a long deserted white folk's graveyard and no place for black folks in the daytime and especially after dark."

"Then why would you want to go there if your pappy warned you not to Pooter?"

"It's Halloween and we got nothing better to do, right? Besides, ghosts aren't real."

As if on cue Rusty let out a series of boos.

"Reckon we have our very own ghost for protection, why not? Besides, he has a lantern to light our way." The ghost waved the lantern about to confirm it. "Have you ever been to that graveyard, Pooter?"

"I've never been to any graveyards except when somebody is being buried and I have only been to one funeral in my entire life. It was Uncle Samuel's, and I was just a little kid and can hardly remember much about it. What about you?"

"Never been to a funeral or graveyard. I don't know anybody that up and died I reckon. Do you believe in ghosts?"

"Never seen one except for the one standing by your side."

"Booooooooo! Cookie for Rusty!"

"Mighty hungry one we got here. The trick is to make the treats last until we get there. Okay, Pooter, you lead the way. Just one question; what are we supposed to do if we see a ghost in that cemetery?"

"Hadn't much thought on it. I reckon we will know if the time comes what is best for us to do if any of those restless solders act up while we are visiting."

"We never talk about ghosts in our house; nothing but the Holy Ghost what makes people scream and shout when Preacher McFarland breaks out his rattlesnakes in church. I don't think the Holy Ghost counts where regular ghosts are concerned but I am no expert on ghosts of any kind."

"I am glad I don't go to a church that has snakes. I don't like any kind of snakes."

"Now you sound like my Cousin Calvert. He hates snakes too. He says the south has every kind of snake."

"Don't make me think about snakes before we cut through those woods or I might decide to take the long way, Nelson."

"I like snakes," spoke up the spook underneath the sheet.

"All right, I reckon it is now or never if we are going and then make it back home before our folks wear short of patience, us milking this here Halloween night," I told them.

"Rusty hungry…more treats!" Pooter forked over a plum jam biscuit to quiet the 'haint' underneath the sheet.

It wasn't easy cutting through those dense woods. There were plenty of sounds that made us almost turn back several times. Owls probably, bullfrogs croaking and other odd whistles and what sounded like growls. The lantern didn't break through nearly enough of the darkened world we traveled. I was already regretting the decision but wasn't about to be the first to chicken out. Uncle Rusty whistled a nonsensical tune, oblivious to the perils we might be facing. I kept reminding myself that these were just woods, same woods that existed in the light of day and no scarier than that. A full moon crept from behind the clouds for the first time offering us a better and welcome look at our surroundings but also introducing some creepy shadows.

Finally, we broke through the woods and into a field. Pooter pointed to another patch of hardwoods on the opposite side of the meadow saying, "That's where we will find the confederate graveyard my pappy pointed out to me when we were cutting firewood a while back. I could barely make out the tops of some tombstones from where we stood. Pappy would not go any closer than where we were, and it was in the broad daylight then. I think he is too suspicious."

"You mean superstitious."

"Suspicious, superstitious, don't much matter one way or the other as far as my pappy is concerned. Haints are haints, spooks are spooks, ghosts are ghosts, and people are supposed to shy away from riling them."

"I am not one that likes to rile anybody, living or dead. We will pay our respects and then just get if that is okay with you, Pooter. And that means you better stifle your farts. No need to sound disrespectful. Yours could wake the dead."

"Not to worry I will let them rip while we are crossing this field and out of range,"

"Just make sure you are down wind of us."

"Pooter is a funny feller," giggled Uncle Rusty from underneath his sheet, "Toot, toot…toot, toot. Booooooooooooo."

We finished the short trek across the field and, sure enough, nestled among the sparse grove of hardwoods was a scattering of tombstones, all shapes and sizes. I gulped loudly as I swallowed, breaking the deathly silence. Pooter responded, hopefully with one last series of puttering poots. Rusty laughed while fanning his sheet to acknowledge the uncanny accomplishment. We were the Three Musketeers, heading into the jaws of uncertainty. Simple, we had agreed, no lollygagging, no stopping and gawking, just walk through it and be on our way, simple bragging rights that we had finished what we had set out to do. The quicker the better as far as I was concerned now being within a rock's throw of the sacred ground. Had I slowed my pace or was it just my imagination?

"Cookies, Rusty wants more cookies." Without thinking I stuffed one into the sheet where his mouth was supposed to be. A hand emerged from underneath and snatched it from me. I shushed him, knowing before I had that there was no such thing as shushing Uncle Rusty. He was the most unshush-able person I had ever known. He didn't even know how to whisper either. Talking about waking the dead, if anyone could, Uncle Rusty certainly could. I almost cringed at that thought.

We were standing at the edge of the graveyard. An eerie awareness overcame me. It was deathly quiet for the first time tonight. None of the nightly sounds we had been hearing were happening here. "Shouldn't we go around it?"

"Shortest way is through the middle," said Pooter, sounding way to brave for my liking. "Try not to step directly on top of any of the graves."

"How am I supposed to know if I am or aren't? And why are you actin g so calm?"

"My pappy says you always act respectfully when around dead folks. I reckon these are about as dead as it gets. He says to always say a little prayer for those who are no longer with us."

"What kind of prayer? Like lay me down to sleep or something like that? They are already dead asleep and hopefully restful to boot."

"Hush, don't say nothing if what you got to say don't make much sense, Nelson."

"Boooooooo!"

My heart skipped a beat or two when I turned and spotted Uncle Rusty standing on top of a gravesite, both his hands on the tombstone, shaking it back and forth. It was moving way too much and quite disrespectful at that. Before I could yell at him to stop, he stopped but not before it crashed to the ground in front of him. I rushed to his side and stared at the dislodged chunk of granite wondering how we could upright it, and undo what he had just done. I could not make out the name, but the born date and death date told me that a baby had been buried there. I thought this was for confederate soldiers. What struck me next was what I could read underneath the dates, *Rock A Bye Baby*. Uncle Rusty had rocked the baby, like it said to do. Had he been able to read it or had something reached out from the grave and made him do it? All I knew was that I was ready to get out of there. I didn't much care if Pooter thought I was a cowardly chicken. Before I could, we heard another ghostly voice. It was not a boo. Uncle Rusty was still beside me. Pooter's eyes were larger and whiter than I had ever seen them. Without so much as a warning, he let out of there like his clothes were on fire. I willed my legs to follow him, yanking Uncle Rusty by his sheet. The sheet came off in my hand as I ran like the wind. Thankfully the moon lit our way because Uncle Rusty had the lantern somewhere behind us.

Our feet reached the old dirt road and we never looked back until we came to the end where it intersected with the road that connected our homes. It was then that I realized that Uncle Rusty was not with us. I still clutched his ghostly sheet though. Pooter looked at me and I shrugged. Neither of us made a move to head back to look for him. I shamelessly justified my actions saying he was a grown man. Pooter didn't question my actions. What were we supposed to do now?

It was then that we heard shuffling footfalls, almost as if something or someone was being dragged against its will. That did not set well with either of us. Then we saw a glowing light and oddly shaped shadows. Whatever we thought we had outrun, we hadn't. We were conflicted with running or standing our ground. I am not sure why we were so conflicted. We never said it but maybe we thought whatever was coming had Uncle Rusty and it was our duty to rescue him. The glowing grew brighter but partially blinded us. We remained frozen in our tracks. We prepared to face our worse fears. Then we heard the familiar 'booooo.'

101

Uncle Rusty approached with the lantern in his left hand and something else tucked under his right arm. When he got closer, he turned loose of what he had. Jonesy Meany crashed to the ground after being released from a headlock.

"Look who I found making funny noises," announced Uncle Rusty.

Jonesy stood and said, "Keep your crazy uncle away from me before I smash both of you to smithereens."

Uncle Rusty patted him on the head again saying he was such a funny feller. Jonesy knew better than to challenge Uncle Rusty. Not that he couldn't lick him, but he knew that taking on a halfwit adult would bring the wrong people knocking at his door. He dusted himself off, warning us that we had not seen the last of him. We learned later that he had followed Uncle Rusty and me and heard what we planned to do. He got there before us to scare us. Uncle Rusty had intervened as only he could. The man child did not understand the concept of bravery, but he was fearless of any living creature, man or beast. That ended up being the most memorable Halloween I have ever experienced. We rewarded Uncle Rusty with the remaining plum jam biscuits and cookies, our treat for his trick on Jonesy Meany.

"Grandfather Nelson, did that incident hold some significance for why Jonesy had it out for you and Pooter?"

"I'm sure it did. He did not take kindly to being bested by us, especially where Uncle Rusty was concerned. Even he knew Uncle Rusty was off limits though. If Uncle Rusty would have been our age, he would have been fair game."

"Well, where do you wish to go next?"

"Mighty fine question, let me think on it. Sorry for getting sidetracked on this one but when they pop into my head it is best that I tell them before they disappear again."

Chapter 13

Nostalgia can be an awakening experience for those fortunate to either remember or have photographs and other family artifacts that trigger them. For Nelson Whitefield they seemed to just materialize out of thin air. He was almost gifted in a sense. A man going on ninety-eight could still capture the vividness of ancient times, incidences and the people that contributed to making them unforgettable. David hung on his every word, sponging it in and recording it for others to enjoy.

"David, you are too young to remember the twins Vern and Bern Whiteside. They were my daddy's brothers. They were identical twins and were nearly ten years older than my daddy. Vern and Bern acted nothing alike though. Vern was outgoing and a people person. Bern was almost the exact opposite, introverted and quite bashful around people, even his own kin. He was a bookworm while Vern was a jokester and a cut up. Funny thing about Bern was that he was wonderful with young'uns, had this uncanny ability to relate to them. Vern was okay with kids too but not the same way as Bern. I wasn't around them much, especially, like Carol, they moved to California. I don't know why California had such a magnetic pull to some of our kinfolks. What I about to share is mostly secondhand as told by Daddy and my grandparents."

"Recorder is on and will begin when you speak."

"I am not sure of the exact year, but it would have been in the fifties after Disneyland had opened."

"Hold on a second, Grandfather Nelson. Let me google it. Okay, Disneyland officially opened July 17, 1955. Interesting sidenote, it says that tickets were a dollar for adults and fifty cents for children. The Park had thirty-five rides with the price to ride them ranging from twenty-five to thirty-five cents. My how times have inflated those costs. Sorry for the trivia, please continue when ready."

I mention Disneyland because it seems Vern and Bern both landed jobs there. California was the land of opportunity and Walt Disney was hiring plenty of folks to operate his dream venture. How the twins got wind of this is anyone's guess. Story goes that Vern became a ticket taker and sometimes worked the information booth. He was like a pig wallowing in mud when it came to interacting with the tourists, razzle dazzling them with his vast knowledge of the theme park. Bern landed quite a unique position. He became the resident Goofy. Bern was supposedly a natural when he slipped into that Goofy character costume. Shy as the day is long, the job fit him like a glove. None of the characters were allowed to speak to the visitors. It was the perfect job for an introvert. His identify was concealed and he didn't have to talk to anyone. The big kid had found his dream job entertaining the children and adults alike.

From Goofy, Bern morphed into another Disney character, Pluto. I have never understood the reasoning behind both characters. Goofy is a dog and so is Pluto. One wears clothes and the other a collar.

"Just googled it, Grandfather. According to Disney, the character of Goofy was created to be a human and Pluto is supposed to be a pet. Goofy can talk, except when in costume at a Disney theme park. Pluto is just supposed to bark and make other canine noises. He is owned by Mickey Mouse. I can see how the contrast can be confusing especially since in the costumed theme park, Pluto walks on two legs instead of four."

"I reckon that made it a lot easier for Bern to dress up and portray both. Getting about on all fours wouldn't have been an easy feat inside one of those suits."

"Are there any funny stories about him acting in either role?

"Matter of a fact, I was getting to that, David."

Neither Vern nor Bern were married, and they shared an apartment. It was cheaper for the brothers to pool their resources. It seems Bern came down with a bug like the flu. It couldn't have happened at a worse time. It was during Christmas. The Park, like today, goes all out for holidays. Bern was slated to pull double duty and swap in and out of character, performing as Pluto and Goofy throughout the day. He was in no shape to report to work and was fearful of losing his job. Bern had the day off. What sounded like a good idea might not have been. Bern convinced Vern to do what he was supposed to do saying who would be able to decipher the difference. After all, they were identical twins. Reluctantly Vern agreed for the worst of reasons, worrying that if Bern lost his job the burden of the household would be on his salary alone.

Nothing to it, right? A costume is a costume and all one must do is act a little 'goofy' and silly for the patrons in the park, pose for a few pictures and go where they direct you to go. Christmas introduced a twist. Goofy and Pluto were in high demand. Various families were in the park celebrating the holiday and with it came some special perks when preplanned. Goofy and Pluto would alternate appearances at special family meet and greet gatherings. Nothing had prepared Vern for these up too close and personal situations. Another added handicap, with so many costume changes, once inside the costume it was easy to forget which character you were portraying.

Strolling through the park was one thing; being in confined spaces in close proximity of a family unit introduces more perplexing challenges. Vern did not possess the training nor discipline of his brother. Children, especially a herd of siblings or cousins can be a recipe for disaster. Dares, taunts and unruly behavior can be the norm. One must remember that Bern was the children person, not Vern. Vern interacted better with adults seeking information. He could only be tolerable of little chaps for short spurts. Walt Disney expected his characters to be the perfect Fantasyland ambassadors.

I am not sure if Vern was in his Goofy or Pluto garb, but things were about to take an ugly turn. A gaggle of young'uns were up to no good. A mixture of older ones with all believing little bitty ones became the perfect storm to test Vern's fortitude. You know how the routine goes. The older ones have reached that ripe old age where they no longer believe in Santa Clause, the Eastern Bunny or the Tooth Fairy and they are hellbent on convincing the little ones that none of them are real. A Disney character is no different. Cartoons are not real and none of the characters in the park are either. Let the games begin. Poor Vern had not signed up for this thinking all would be easy peasy. It had been a long day to boot for someone not accustomed to wearing those suits and remaining in character for better or worse.

Dares or just plain meanness ensued, Vern never the wiser that a plan had been put in motion, one to discredit whatever critter he now portrayed. It began as an innocent taunt, one of the older chaps yelling at him saying he wasn't real, just a person dressed up. Vern stood his ground and remained in character, whichever one he was at the time. He wiggled his oversized hands, danced about and just ignored the rants. Then one tugged at his costume telling the younger kids that it was just some sort of fabric, not fur. One must ask, where are the parents when something like this is transpiring? Tugs and pokes from various sides made it difficult for Vern to ignore and remain calm.

Unlike Bern, Vern had a narrower threshold when it came to testing his tolerance. The character on the outside was smiling and oblivious to the assault. The man behind the mask was steaming mad, growing a bit weary of where this was heading. One is supposed to grin and bear it but grinning and bearing it was reaching the end of the rope. The final nail in the coffin occurred when the prank went just a tad too far. Old school, one kid got down on all fours behind the mythical Disney character while the largest of the tormentors gave him a blindsided shove. Poor Vern fell backwards feet in the air crashing to the concrete in a thunderous thud. Once grounded, it is not easy to right oneself in such an awkward costume. He rolled about this way and then that struggling to get to his feet all the while laughter and crying reaching epic levels.

The foolproof plan worked much better than expected. Vern ripped off the head of his costume and eyed those responsible for doing it while ignoring the younger ones and the parents now eyeing the shenanigans. He let some choice words fly while pointing his huge, gloved hands at the perpetrators. Cat out of the bag, there stood a Disney cartoon character with a man's head cussing like a sailor at children of all ages. The parents were appalled and demanded that something be done to rectify this awful behavior. Their vacations had been ruined and their children's bubble had burst when it came to the perfect experience in the wonderful world of Disney.

Vern did his best to take the brunt of the rath from their superiors saying Bern shouldn't be blamed for his bad behavior. The deception by the twins could not be overlooked nor ignored. Both were fired. Their dream jobs had gone up in smoke just like that. Harsh lesson, never cross the Big Disney Cheese. Their stint in the wonderful world of California had come to an abrupt and untimely ending. Tinsel Town had shunned the twins, the episode landing front and center in the newspaper and local television segments. Disney did not take kindly to bad publicity.

"Gosh, how terrible. What did they do then?"

"It's a Small World and a terrible analogy on my part. They were devastated and returned home, tails tucked between their legs and an embarrassment to the family. Once acclaimed and placed on a pedestal for working at Disneyland, they were now at the lowest point of their lives. This next part came second maybe even third hand so keep that in mind when I share it."

The twins were engulfed in guilt for the ruse they had attempted to pull at the Magic Kingdom. Bern sorely regretted having asked his brother to do something he had not been trained to do. Vern was infuriated that he had allowed the kids to get under his skin and had broken a cardinal rule while wearing a Disney character costume, breaking character. Not merely breaking character but exposing the person inside the suit. He had disgraced both the family name and that of the old man's, Walt Disney. The brothers struggled to find themselves and restore what dignity remained.

Vern fared a tad better than Bern. He tried his hand as a used car salesman. The gift of gab offered a ray of sunshine in his newly chosen profession. His pearly whites and twinkling blue eyes soothed those in search of the perfect vehicle. He could connect with men and women alike, an honest approach to helping them figure what type of transportation best suited them and at an affordable price. He took pride in what he was doing. That took an ugly turn when his boss encouraged him to con a young couple to stretch their financial limits and purchase a real lemon and take out a loan at the car lot, an affordable monthly payment with an outrageous interest rate. Vern confronted his boss telling him that the newlyweds deserved better. The owner would have none of it and poked Vern in the chest one time too many. He coldcocked his boss ending that career move.

Meanwhile, Bern did his best to stay the course and follow his dream. With no Disney nor theme parks in his future he settled for small time gigs. Grand openings for various venues often included character mascots representing the store's brand. His first starring role placed him inside a pig costume for the grand opening of a grocery store. As he had been trained at Disneyland, it required that he be animated and interact with customers, having no speaking parts. He gave out balloons to the children and acted whimsical around the adults. The pay wasn't great, but Vern followed his dream as best he could.

Vern had stints at peddling life insurance and Fuller brushes. He realized quickly that he was not cut out for the rigors of cold calls. His charm was no deterrent for doors being slammed shut in his face. Nope, those that knew him could never envision him as a salesman of any kind. He pumped gas far a while, anything to make ends meet. Sadly, the owner of the gas station expected him to do more. Poor Vern was not a grease monkey. He did not have a mechanical bone in his body. He quit before he could be fired. Options were not exactly falling from the sky.

Bern remained true to his aspirations and continued to seek any opportunities that showcased his ability to be the man behind the mask. An introvert by nature shined like the brightest star when he could be anything but himself. He eventually perfected a lovable clown personality. Disguised by the whimsical makeup, he hired himself out for children's birthday parties. He learned to make balloon characters and even mastered a few corny magic tricks to entertain the children and adults. He utilized hand gestures to communicate with his audience preferring to remain in character and not speak. Speaking more times than not turned into a stuttering mess. The money wasn't great, but it didn't really matter to him. His lifestyle required few perks. The joy of the job was what was most important to him. Making children happy, who cold ask for anything better than that.

Vern and Bern rarely crossed paths, each doing his own thing. Some said they never reconciled the debacle that had ruined their careers at Disneyland. While neither seemed to hold any animosity for the other, unspoken words seemed to be a powerful sign that things were not right between them. A couple of years after their Disneyland departure, Vern was found dead at his flat. The cause of his death remained hush hush, but rumors circulated that he had taken his own life. One year to the day after his death, Bern died at his apartment while in full clown garb. Red tears were painted on his cheeks. Family said he died of a broken heart having never gotten beyond losing his twin brother.

Vern and Bern had shown such great promise, each securing their dream jobs in California. Poor judgment had been their undoing. Neither could outrun the shame and disappointment. It haunted them until their dying days. Ironically, last wishes from each, they were buried with no fanfare and in unmarked graves. Family made sure that they were reunited in their final resting place, the clown prince and the pauper.

"Wow, what a sad ending to such a spectacular beginning, Grandfather Nelson. From promising careers at Disneyland to tragically struggling to find themselves. How old were the twins?"

"Not sure, maybe in their early thirties, if I had to wage a guess."

"Our family sure seemed to have some dysfunctional tendencies, didn't they?"

"The Whiteside clan have always had their moments for sure. The Barnhart side of the family, while not quite as quirky, have a few interesting skeletons in their closet as well."

"Like Uncle Rusty?"

"Well, Uncle Rusty was more of a gift than an embarrassment. He could not help being born the way he was. Others had choices though. My, my, where do we dare go now?"

"Tell it your way and about whatever you feel comfortable sharing, Grandfather Nelson."

"As it has been and should be, David. I reckon there is no value in holding back punches at this juncture."

Chapter 14

The day was growing short. Nelson was still spry and sharp. David's recording device had plenty of battery and storage remaining and he could think of no better place that he would rather be. Nelson pondered where he should go next. There was no need to fill in every nook and cranny of the past. He should focus on those that held some family significance for better or worse. Picking and choosing was better said than done though. Dysfunctional to the core but family bonds were sealed in fate. What might seem normal to him might be a bit skewed off the charts to others. He had been exposed to the haves and have nots when it had come to common sense and practicality. He walked a fine line of being neither proud nor ashamed of the branches that solidified the family tree. No need pausing at this juncture; might as well go full throttle and let it fly.

"David, we're going to fast forward a bit. Just leapfrog over what doesn't amount to a hill of beans in the big picture of things."

"Proceed at your own speed and spot, Grandfather Nelson."

"I will do just that then. Next stop, the 50's. Mama was in poor health. Daddy was doing his best to get by and age not exactly his friend either. Big Bill Whiteside was a fighter, a tough old bird from the old school. Juniper and Clarice Barnhart, my mama's parents, were doing poorly as well. Roles had been reversed and my folks had taken in her folks to care for. What goes around comes around and family always came first. Some of my memories might be a bit a fuzzy but there is nothing fuzzy about family loving family."

> I was thirty-two and married to my first wife Bessy. It was our second year of forty-three blessed years. Bessy had been raised by her grandparents; an only child orphaned when she was six. Both her parents had met their tragic and untimely deaths when their house had caught fire in the middle of the night. Sparks from an open fireplace had set the place ablaze. Smoke killed them while they slept. By the grace of the Lord, young Bessy had been spared when a next door neighbor,

heading to work early that morning, had smelled the smoke and then spotted the flames. He had rescued the little girl but by the time he got to their bedroom they were both dead from inhalation.

Bessy was my heart, a gift sent me from the heavens for sure. I was working in construction then, operating heavy machinery mostly doing what was asked of me to guarantee a paycheck. I helped when I could to support Mama and Daddy and my grandparents who lived about fifty miles from where Bessy and I resided. Bessy worked in what most called a shirt plant. She sewed up men's shirts and trousers for catalog sales distribution. The Sears catalog was our version of ordering online of today. Almost anything imaginable could be had for a price from the pages of the Sears catalog. It was known as the wish book. Folks could hardly wait for it to arrive in the mail so they could thumb through it and wish they had this and that. Young'uns used it to choose what they wanted from Santa. The latest toys could be found in it.

Jeremy and Keith had become drifters again. No grass grew underneath their feet. Guess I could say the same for Carol. She had three children by then, Jupiter, Rachel and little Petey. Her second husband had hauled her off to Missouri. Jeremy had tried marriage, but it hadn't worked out for him either. She up and left him, ran off with a carney, of all things. That was the ultimate insult to injury for my brother. The last we had heard from Jeremy he was up north somewhere and doing who knows what. He would call my folks once in a blue moon but would never say much about exactly where he was or what sort of job he had. Keith had joined the French Foreign Legion. Go figure. We all thought he had seen enough of the war and fighting. I reckon he had overcome the trauma he had encountered at Pearl Harbor. I wondered if that death wish thing of his had resurfaced.

Helping with family landed square on my shoulders. Daddy was quite blunt with his read on calling my siblings a bunch of ungrateful deserters. Daddy was speaking his mind a plenty, more so than usual. Mama just made excuses for them and for Daddy acting like an ass. Sometimes I felt like an only child. And an only can be quite a lonely place in the Whiteside household. Family is family, even when you have already started your own family. You must do what is expected of you, no grumbling and no questions asked.

It was about then that I met a Homer Godsell. Mama introduced him saying he was a fourth cousin twice removed from her side of the family. I wasn't sure how a person could be a fourth cousin then could be removed two times and still be a cousin. Nobody back then explained it to me in terms that made any sense. I still am not sure what to make of it.

"Grandfather Nelson, all due respect and I apologize for interrupting you but, why not allow me to Google it for your sake and mine."

"Google, the know and tell all of everything you wanted to know but might have been fearful of asking. I reckon this is as good a time as any to solve this unsolved mystery for us both. Work your Google magic, David."

"It states that when two cousins share the same common ancestor but do not share the same number of generations in decent from said ancestor, we use the term 'removed.' It further explains that if the cousin in question is a great-great-great-great grandchild of the common ancestors, then they are a fourth cousin twice removed."

"Google needs to learn to talk in terms that we average folks can comprehend. Thanks for asking, David. Reckon I will continue with how Homer Godsell entered and exited my life."

It seemed we were a family of drifters. Nobody wanted to stay anywhere long. We were a bunch of roamers, refusing to be rooted. Homer Godsell was close to my age, but he sure looked a lot older; what we called rode hard and put up wet.

At least he didn't show up making claims of digging for gold. Still, that didn't make him a square shooter by any measuring stick. I am not sure straight shooting is a predominate gene in the DNA on either side of our family. Homer was a curiosity by any standard. Daddy referred to him as a genuine snake oil peddler even though I never witnessed him peddling a magical elixir. I must be a magnet for attracting the craziest of the crazies. Not to be sounding rude and crude about Cousin Homer but he was a rare bird indeed.

Paranoia dominated his life. Everybody was out to get him for one reason or another. He was convinced that the federal government was a conspirator to almost anything imaginable. He didn't hold local government in high regard either. The difference, he didn't stay in one place long enough for local government to sink their claws into him. He swore that the feds had planted secret devices inside of his body so they could track his whereabouts. Might not be so far fetched in today's times but back then it was a bit too much like science fiction. Homer was the only kin or kin twice removed to ever call me by my middle name, Rutherford.

"Come over here Rutherford and sit a spell. Big things are happening today, things that you need to know. Mighty important it is."

In the early going I had no cause to question his integrity or his knowledge about anything. I always did my best to respect kin or anybody as far as that goes, whether they be older, equal or younger than me. My folks had offered him a room to stay a spell, so I had no reason to be suspicious of his antics. Well, except for Daddy saying he was a snake oil peddler. Daddy said a lot of nonsensical stuff back then. Mama thought he was coming down with the beginning of 'old timer's' disease even though I didn't see him as that old. He had become quite opinionated, that was for sure, and sometimes forgetful about the simplest of things. Anyway, I did as Homer had requested.

"Can you feel it, Rutherford?"

Doing my best not to insult him I just asked, "Feel what?"

"Its presence. My skin is all tingly. Is yours not all tingly?"

I must admit a chill did run the length of my spine, but I could not contribute it to a strange tingly experience, so I just shrugged rather than go down the rabbit hole with him.

"Not to worry, I can feel it for both of us. Stick close by, safety in numbers works sometimes but not always. The signs are weak right now but when they strengthen it can test the strongest. Not my first rodeo though. I have the tenacity, fortitude and experience on my side to handle most anything tossed my way, long as I see it coming. Being blindsided poses a different set of circumstances though. You don't want to be on the wrong side of that fence, let me be the first to confess."

Don't know what made me do it but, I glanced over my shoulder like I was expecting somebody to sneak up on me. My concerns did not go unnoticed.

"You do feel it, don't you, Rutherford. I can see it in your eyes. The gift has been passed to your genes like it always has been from one generation to the next. Your mama is from the good stock. Sometimes it skips a generation or two and when it does that person what gets it can be counted on to fight the good fight. It's the power of clairsentience. There are thirteen signs of clairsentience and only the most special are gifted with all thirteen."

"Clairsentience? I have never heard that term before Cousin Homer."

"Not to worry, the term is not what's important. It's the signs what are. Have you ever entered the room and felt an energy in the room?"

"Maybe, I'm not sure."

"I will take maybe as a yes. What about crowds, do you ever have difficulty being around crowds?"

"I reckon I have sometimes suffered anxiety when there are a lot of people gathered in one room. I just thought it was a bout of claustrophobia."

"No sir. It was a sign as sure as I am standing here. Do you completely trust your feelings all the time?"

"I reckon I do trust my gut mostly."

"Check off another one then. What about the news, do you avoid the news?"

"News?"

"The news what is reported every day, do you find yourself avoiding it?"

"I can't say that I listen to or watch the news on a regular basis."

"Check. Do you have strong initial feelings about people?"

"I reckon that I am pretty good at reading people, if that's what you mean, probably better than some."

"Ah yes, another checked box. What about feeling comfortable in what you wear and how you feel inside your home?"

"What I got on feels just fine. Bessy and I love our home."

"You are proving your worth Rutherford. How would you rate your sensitivity?"

"Not sure what you mean."

"Are you a sensitive person toward others or one that doesn't wear your emotions on your sleeve?"

"I pride myself as treating people like I would expect to be treated."

"Yes, yes, indeed you do. What about folks that ooze negative vibes? Do you stay clear of them?"

"I suppose I don't like being around people who are always down on everything, looking for the worst in people and feeling the gloom and doom."

"Fine answer, Rutherford. Do you ever sense bad events before they happen?"

"Maybe. If you look at a situation long enough you can see there is a right way or wrong way to approach it."

"Splendid, four more to go. What about mood swings?"

"Everybody suffers from mood swings, even if they refuse to admit it."

"Number eleven, do you have a special connection to animals?"

"I never mistreat animals if that is what you are asking."

"Bingo! Have you ever experienced the presence of spirits?"

"This one time in a cemetery when me and my old friend Pooter visited it on a Halloween night, we thought we heard ghosts, but it turned out to be Jonesy Meany."

"Graveyards and ghosts qualify. Lastly, do you ever feel the pain of others?"

"I felt for what my brother Jeremy went through when he worked a carney and what my brother Keith suffered because of the war."

"Say no more, you have checked all thirteen boxes of clairsentience. You are spiritually sensitive and a chip off the old family block."

"I am? What does that really make me?"

"You have psychic abilities. You are special. You can acquire knowledge by means of feeling. That sets you apart from most and will be most effective when sensing that the feds are out to get you or those you love."

"I cannot read cards nor tell fortunes like Aunt Harley Ann."

"I knew Harley Ann. She did not have the gift as we do. She did what she did for profit. It was all about making a buck, putting the fear into people. She was a charlatan of cheap fortune telling tactics. What you and I have is the real deal, Rutherford. It comes in mighty handy when fending off the corrupt federal government, out to steal our souls and make us pay for what belongs to us, not them. That's why I stay on the move, a vagabond always one step ahead of them. If they cannot find me, they cannot latch on to me to take my money for their illegal tax purposes. Greed has no boundaries nor scruples."

"Did you do something to make them want to hunt you down?

"They require no reason to take what is mine or yours. Overreach is their mantra. Pure treachery it is, unlawful and only lawful because they make the laws to will their power over us."

"It is illegal if you don't pay taxes on what you earn isn't it?"

"It is only illegal if they know what you have earned fair and square. It pushes an honest man into a corner where dishonesty is the best policy. Their techniques are forever improving. I hear they can plant devices inside people to enable them to locate you wherever you go. Doctors are in cahoots with them. That's why I never visit a doctor. They always want to poke and prod you and eventually they will come up with an excuse to stick a syringe into our veins. Don't think for a moment that what is inside that syringe is some miracle cure for what they say ails you. It's a tracking serum. Once it is inside of you and takes root you can't undo it."

"Doctors are sworn to an oath to help us. I don't think they would do anything like that Homer.

"That's what they want you to believe. It's smoke and mirrors, the ultimate deception and a total conspiracy. Why do you think free clinics pop up all over the place? The lure of free entices folks into their web. Trust me when I say it, there is no such animal as free. You lose your freedom if you believe everything government promises they will do for you to make your life perfect. It is all about control. They are out to control everything we do or want to do. They are worse than blood sucking leeches, bloated ticks, vampire bats all rolled into one. You have the gift, the power to see through their wicked ways to protect you and your family, Rutherford. Do not squander it."

I didn't know what to think about what he had unloaded on me. Was he crazy or did he really know something most people didn't? Did certain family members have this so-called gift? He said I had checked all thirteen boxes for this thing he called clairsentience, a term I had never heard until that very day. It was scary, a bit too spooky, like how Aunt Harley Ann acted. He said she was a fake but maybe she

121

wasn't. She was probably more blood kin that he was with all this twice removed stuff.

"Grandfather Nelson, perhaps this is another Google opportunity."

"Cousin Homer would have accused Google of being a governmental operative and he might not have been that far off base, given the suspicions some of us have about it."

"No denying it sir, even I understand manipulation when I see it. Still, it is much quicker than flipping through a dictionary."

"Handheld devices were old school before technology caught up David. Smart gadgets are wonderful but there is nothing more satisfying than holding a binder clad book. Please Google and let's see what the wise one has to say."

"Just like Cousin Homer described it, clairsentience is the psychic ability for a person to acquire knowledge by means of feelings. Are you a clairvoyant, Grandfather Nelson? Do you possess the ability of perception of what is not normally perceptible?"

"Having gut feelings don't make a person special by my book. I have never felt like I was something special, not even after passing Cousin Homer's taste test. As those info commercials go, 'but wait there is more'. I have always wanted to say that."

> Cousin Homer was determined to convince me that I had been gifted with unique powers. The proof is in the pudding and there was no evidence to back up what he was saying. I could not recall ever having any definable premonitions. I certainly wasn't fearful or suspicious of the government, federal or local versions. I can't say inconclusively that I trusted the government but there was little I could do one way or the other. If Cousin Homer would have been around today, his banter would have been perfectly acceptable, at least his feelings about government overreach.

> "Politicians are the devil's disciples no matter which side of the fence they claim they are on. Promises broken is their

motto. They will use slight of hand to get what they want. While you are watching their little juggling act, they will have one hand in our pocket. You have the power to see through their deception, Rutherford. You can protect your family from their ruthlessness. You are the 'all and powerful Wizard of Oz', the man behind the curtain pulling strings that they have no idea you are pulling. You can beat them at their own game Rutherford."

"Homer, I am a mere simple man, not one to stir up or look for trouble. Gifted or not, I am not about to go toe to toe with the government."

"It is your rite of passage son. You cannot ignore your responsibilities. It is the core value of our family."

"Then explain to me how you are abiding by these responsibilities by moving about so. To protect family, shouldn't you be with family?"

"Ah, excellent question, Rutherford. I am what they call a covert operative. I must remain undercover to thwart their evilness. To ensure my success, family members invest in my abilities. Mere contributions are good as any insurance policy. Fox and the hound, I lure them, bait and switch, they forever hunt me and leave the family alone. The investment produces sound dividends. A tiny sacrifice I assure you."

"Let me get this straight Homer; you take money from family members to supposedly entice the government into a game of hide and seek. They chase you and will leave us alone."

"Exactly, and you are one of the privileged as well. Together success is on our side Rutherford. Ask and receive. Your parents will gladly contribute to the cause if you ask them."

"Excuse my bluntness, but you are a Flim-Flam Man, a snake oil peddler just like Daddy said you were. You are selling nothing for something and once you have it you will vanish like a puff of smoke until you find another next of kin and lobby your 'fourth cousin twice removed' nonsense to pull the wool over their eyes. You are much worse than Aunt Harley Ann."

"Harsh words Rutherford, my feelings are beyond repair. Your ma will be devastated by your accusations. Kinfolk should not treat kinfolk with such disgraceful manners."

"Hold on a minute Homer, I am experiencing a psychic episode. Clarity has never been clearer."

"See, work it, Rutherford. Let it take you to the truth and they say, the truth will set you free."

"What I envision with clarity, as you put it, is you skedaddling the heck out of here. Get before I forget my manners, fourth cousin twice removed. Don't bother gathering your things back at my folk's house, just leave and be thankful I don't turn you over to the sheriff. If you are what you really profess to be, I imagine they would gladly welcome you, the government grateful to reconcile the wrongs you have done all in the name of protecting family. Don't say a word. Scat and get those feet moving now."

That was the last time I laid eyes on good ole Cousin Homer, fourth and twice removed. In never told Mama what had really happened nor why he up and left so abruptly. I almost told Daddy. He would probably have understood and appreciated what I had done. I figured it was best to protect family, a lesson learned. My fees were simple, love thy family and expect nothing in return.

No sooner had Homer exited the premises, Cousin Danny Whitefield showed up out of the blue. It seemed we had cousins falling from the sky, this one on Daddy's side. I had never met him either. At least he didn't claim to be kin removed by some crazy number. Daddy welcomed him with open arms. That alone spoke volumes for the mystery man now at our doorsteps. I had barely caught my breath when arrived. Mama had invited me and Bessy to Sunday dinner. Not one to pass up her fixings, I accepted.

Cousin Danny was a lot more tolerable than the con cousin that had exited the premises. He was a world traveler, another Whitefield that never let the dust settle underneath his feet. I figured this cousin must be legit because Daddy was the one that offered him lodging for as long as he wished to stay. Around the kitchen table for any meal is the ultimate Whitefield social activity. Plenty can be learned, and gossip is never in short supply. Daddy was in his element, chewing the fat. He certainly had that old sparkle in his eyes chatting with Cousin Danny. He appeared revitalized, a previously broken man on the mend once again.

Cousin Danny was indeed the real deal. A world traveler with purpose. He was what was referred to as a great white hunter. He was a professional big game hunter. We were captivated by his tales of safaris and close encounters with the mighty beasts of lore. Well, maybe Mama and Bessy were not as thrilled with his stories as Daddy and I were, especially the bloody parts. Still, the women folk were taken in by the travels to countries that tested the imagination. He even had photographs to share of some of his greatest adventures and trophies. I guess he was proof that every Whitefield does not have a dark and tainted past. Cousin Danny was my elder, gauging he was probably in his sixties, but I never asked his age.

Unlike with Homer, I learned valuable lessons and skills hanging out with Cousin Danny while he was around. He stayed with my parents for almost a month, something unheard of by all accounts. When I wasn't working, I spent what time I could with him and Daddy. He taught me the craft of hunting, not just for sport but for food. We managed to fill my folks and our freezer with meat a plenty. No, we had no big game to offer but Cousin Danny embraced any opportunity to test his skills. He did score a trophy buck, teaching me how to look for signs and track what ones are worthy of the hunt. I learned to be patient and remain motionless while inside a constructed blind. Daddy and I scored some shots as well. Nothing worthy of bragging about but it put venison in the freezers. Any game was fair game, rabbits, squirrels, quail, ducks and doves. I would never measure up to his marksmanship, but I wasn't half bad, making mostly clean shots.

I was heartbroken when he decided to leave. I am guessing Bessy wasn't though as I spent more time with him than I did with her while he was around. I hadn't thought about it that way until after he was gone. She made it a point to put it in perspective for me. I spent a while making it up to her. I'm sure Daddy hated to see him leave too. He had been as happy as I had seen him in a long time, caught up in the male camaraderie. Mama took it better than Bessy, glad to see him revigorated and happy. Cousin Danny gifted me one of his guns, a thirty-five-caliber rifle equipped with a scope. All these years later I still have that gun.

About five years after his visit, we received news that he had died. Information was sketchy at first. I envisioned he had met his end while encountering a fierce lion or being run through by rhinoceros. He had already shared close calls with us and had shown us the scars from the mishaps. A few months passed before we learned what had really happened. His boat had sunk during a violent storm while in the Congo. Flood waters had been responsible for his untimely death. His body was never recovered, lost along with six others of his party. He had been in search of a killer crocodile that had been responsible for the deaths of hundreds. A better ending would have been he died in the jaws of the massive reptile doing what he always loved doing. Or maybe the behemoth upended his boat during the encounter. Not to be, a mere accident had been responsible, an act of nature just the same.

"I would love to see the rifle he gave you, Grandfather Nelson."

"And it would be my honor to show it to you, David. Wait here and I will fetch it."

Chapter 15

I wasn't sure just how long David wanted to take this today. We had covered plenty family memories and dark secrets so far. I can't deny that my juices were flowing freely reliving them and thinking on others I had not shared yet. My old brain was working in overtime cherishing the nostalgia waiting at every turn. All of those who shared these memories were long gone. It would have been a hoot to be sitting around a fire with those that could add to the stories and rekindle others. David was my captive audience and just having him interested in hearing them was beyond satisfaction for an old coot hankering to tell them. We had gone longer than I would have ever imagined, and I had conjured more than I could have ever expected. So many of them I had relived as if they had only happened yesterday. I wondered if others would appreciate the thought that he and I had put into this.

"Are we good to go or would you prefer pausing this until another time, David?"

"Are you tired. I can understand if you are, Grandfather Nelson. If you would rather, we could pick this up another time."

"Me, tired. I am as rejuvenated as my daddy was when we were living the adventures of Cousin Danny. I am good to go, if you are while my old brain is fully engaged and cooperative. This has been Godsent for me, cherished blessings worth revisiting, reliving and sharing. When I am gone so will they be if we don't capture them on your little contraption. Hope I haven't worn you out or worse, bored you half to death."

"Not in the least, you have so vividly painted the canvas that I feel I have walked in your shoes in many incidences. I am game if you are to continue."

"Then continue we shall. What say you plan on spending the night here."

"I would like that."

"Then I reckon we might be pulling one of those all-nighters if everything goes as it has been going. We can keep on until I run out of things to remember or until that recorder runs out of memory or battery life."

"Deal, pick up wherever it suits you, Grandfather Nelson."

"Well, in no particular order, here goes."

Some years later after the death of Cousin Danny, my daddy had what the doctor called a massive stroke, lucky to have survived it and be alive. Surviving is one thing. Being alive is a whole different ballgame under certain circumstances. Daddy was partially paralyzed from his close call. He was unable to speak or do much of any kind of communicating. He was no longer my daddy, not by a long shot. Mama was not in the best of health either, the burden of taking care of him pulling her down even further. Bessy and I did what we could to check in on them. We were furthered tested by family consequences. My grandfather had passed, and my grandmother was now in one of those nursing homes, having gone downhill fast after his passing. Some days she knew who we were but most days she didn't. My mama's folks were not faring much better. Old age was taking its toll in that generation. Jeremy had shown up but wasn't much help. He was quite sickly looking, not willing to share where he had been nor what he had been doing. I loved my brother, but he was more of an added burden than a blessing. It was about that time that we received word that brother Keith had gone missing on some Foreign Legion engagement, sketchy at best. I was able to contact Carol. She and her third husband were living in Chicago. She passed along her condolences in a tearful conversation but never offered to return home. She had three children and all of them were in the custody of the welfare department. She nonchalantly mentioned it as fact during our conversation, seemingly sharing no remorse for what had happened. She simply added that they were better off not being with her and left it at that. I had not laid eyes on her since she left for California with husband number one. I had a one niece and two nephews I had never met and now it seemed I never would. Shameful legacy for our family it was.

Bessy and I kept doing the best we could to hold everything else together. It was far from being a perfect life but what did I know about perfection. My life had been chaotic at best, the comings and goings that could be the makings of one heck of a soap opera, The Whiteside Wild World of Wandering Ways. I had lost my previous job and turned back to something I could do to get by, butchering in a local grocery store, a Piggly Wiggly. The pay was not what I had been accustomed to, but long hours and overtime offset some of my bring home wages. Bessy hung in there, working at the shirt plant. She had been promoted to a planner position. No longer on production scale she was now salaried which meant she was making less than what she was used to making. We were never promised an easy go of it. Hard times made us hunker down and persevere as best we could. We didn't whine nor complain. We simply did what we needed to do. There were a few perks in working in the meat department. I got some discounts here and there, mostly outdated and unsellable goods. I hunted when I could to supplement the rest. Bessy had a small vegetable garden. We got by.

I tried to encourage Jeremy to find a job but was only met with belligerence. My brother had a huge chip on his shoulder for reasons unexplained. He despised the world in general and family didn't rate high in the pecking order either. I struggled to understand where all his hate and resentment had originated. He became just one more mouth to feed, an ungrateful one at that. I began to resent him as well. Soul searching and prayers often prevented me from going all-out assault on him. He was flesh and blood after all, not removed kin like Cousin Homer. He was my only brother unless Keith was somehow found from where he had been lost in that secretive mission. I was back to feeling like an only child, no pity party, just a factual assessment on my part.

Bessy delivered some wonderful news. She was with child. I was going to be a daddy. I was excited with a mixture of dread. How could we bring a child into a world so topsy turvy and filled with such uncertainty? I thought about what a terrible parent Carol had apparently turned out to be and couldn't help but question if it might be in our family genes. Keith, Jeremy, Carol had not exactly turned out to be the cream of the crop. Not bragging, but I had fared better than them, at least so far. Mama was jubilant over the premise of being a grandmother. When Daddy was told his facial expression never changed, as blank as ever. I had hoped it would free him from the cage that held him captive, but it hadn't. Mama sat on her mother's bedside and shared the news but like Daddy, she had no reaction. Jeremy shook my hand and congratulated me on my news before sulking away like he always did. I cringed thinking of him as my child's only uncle. I held onto hope that Keith would somehow be found alive.

We were certainly living up to our dysfunctional family reputation no matter how hard I tried to alter the perception. I was not a model Whiteside, but I was better than most. Bessy and I did our best to break the mold, to be the do-gooders, the trail blazers, the ones making a difference, always placing family first and foremost. We were not ready to climb on a pedestal. We were simply doing what was right. Just three days before Christmas, Daddy died in his sleep. He would not live to see his grandchild, my child. A week later, after burying him and still mourning the loss, Bessy had a miscarriage. I had lost my daddy and my child in that short span. Bessy, Mama and I grieved together. Keith attended neither funeral and the morning after we buried our baby, he up and left again, without so much as a goodbye. We took in Mama at our place and sold theirs.

We were just getting our life back in order when this young man that I had never laid eyes on before showed up at the Piggly Wiggly. Call it clairsentience but there was something familiar about the stranger, I just couldn't quite put my finger on it.

"The woman at the checkout told me Nelson Whiteside worked in the meat department."

"That would be me. What I can I do you for?"

"My name is Jupiter. I believe you are my uncle."

"You are Carol's boy?"

"Yes sir, pleased to finally meet you."

"Same here, is Carol here too?"

"No sir and she doesn't know I am here either."

"How did you know where to find me?"

"Like I said, the lady at the checkout pointed you out to me."

"No, I mean how did you know we live here?"

"I went to the address on some letters my mother kept. A man there told me that the Whiteside family no longer lived there. I think it was where my grandparents were supposed to live. That gentleman told me to come to this town and try the grocery store where he thought you worked. It took me a couple of days to get here. I walked and hitched when I could catch a ride. Did the same all the way from Chicago too. I lost track of time, but I finally got here."

"How is Carol...your mama?"

"I wouldn't know. I haven't seen here since she gave us up. I was the only one old enough to walk away from the orphanage. The rest are in foster care or other orphanages somewhere. They wouldn't tell me where they were."

"And you came all the way here by yourself."

"Yes sir. I didn't know where else to go. I sure didn't want to go back with her. She didn't want me in the first place. All she ever cared about was hitching up with the next man, somebody to take care of her while not caring to take care of any of us. I can't say I ever really had a mother. She is messed up, always has been or has been since I have been old enough to know better."

"I was not much older than you when I set out to visit Carol in California. I hooked up with my bother. Me and Jeremy, your uncle, got as far as New Mexico when we ran out of money. We tried phoning her for bus fare, but the number was no longer in service. Dead end, so we eventually made our way back home. I have not seen her since she left us for her first husband."

"That would be my father. I never really knew him. He ended back up in Mexico. Mother said he died there but who really knows what is true and what is not. She lied so much to us and probably to all of you."

"I bet your grandmother will be tickled pink to meet you. She lives with us...my wife Bessy and me. My daddy, your grandfather died not too long ago. Your great grandmother is still alive, but she is in a nursing home. She is in a bad way, unfortunately, but I will take you to see her once you get settled in. Our home is your home, Jupiter, and what last name to you go by."

"Just Jupiter is fine."

"When is the last time you had a decent meal, Jupiter?"

133

"Not had a decent or indecent one in a while."

"I'll have Cornelia in the deli shop make you a sandwich and give you a soda. Hang around there until I get off work at seven then we'll head home."

"Thank you, sir. I look forward to that."

Amazing, I had lost my daddy, my child and now had gained a nephew. I could see Carol in him, more in the eyes than anything else. Regardless of his circumstances and upbringing he had turned out to be a pleasant young lad, oozing with manners. A chip off the old Whiteside block, he had traveled such a great distance, determined to meet his relatives. He had completed the journey Jeremy and I had started to find his mama. Somehow everything felt like it was supposed to feel, him being here. The planet Jupiter had returned to mother earth. I ached for him. He either did not know his last name or did not want to use it because of the ordeal he had endured.

I finished my shift and we headed home. My mama beamed with such delight, meeting her grandson. Bessy, even with our recent loss, embraced him with open arms. The poor lad was taken aback with all the gushing love smothering him like a wet blanket. I had not witnessed so much slobbering since it had last been hog killing time. Our home suddenly felt alive again, something we all needed.

"David, what you say we take a little supper break. There are plenty of leftovers. When our bellies are full, we shall dive back into the nostalgic pool for more Whiteside spills and thrills."

Chapter 16

Thinking back on the arrival of my nephew, Jupiter, had brought on a flood of memories. Most of them were wonderful thoughts. Sometimes we must trade something bad for something good; even steven my old pal Pooter might say. As we feasted on the leftovers my mind wandered from this to that as I tried to corral the frenzy of emotions surrounding that time long forgotten. At my age it was a wonder I could recall with such vividness those accounts long forgotten. I reckon the old brain is smarter than we give it credit. It possesses this unique filing system for storing what we might some day need to research. Scary thought: by experiencing this sudden rush of nostalgic moments, does this somehow mean I am approaching my end? I am not even sure why I am interpreting it in this manner. The brain has the wheel. I reckon it is driving me where it wants to take me. I would rather just enjoy the ride and worry less about journey's end. Bless David for kick starting the process.

"I don't know about you David, but I am about to pop like a tick that has found its way inside a blood bank. Dishes washed and put away I reckon we can see where this old brain of mine is willing to take us next."

"I'm gorged and ready, Grandfather Nelson."

> Jupiter had fit right in as if he had always been with us. That boy needed some loving and family fellowship for sure. He was not quick to open up about the life he had lived. Understandably, Carol married all those times and then him being handed off to strangers and separated from his siblings. It was no telling where his sister Rachel and brother Petey had landed, and if they were together or had been separated. Jupiter, for reasons only he understood, did not want to latch onto his daddy's last name. Edwardo Valdez had seemed to be a likable feller what little time he was around us. As mentioned, mixed marriages of any kind were not accepted by everyone back in those days. Maybe them moving to California where there was a more robust Mexican

population made it easier on them as a family than around our parts. That's pure speculation on my part though.

Mama and Bessy had just about ruined that young man. He filled a huge void left by Carol, Jeremy and Keith still AWOL. That boy was spoiled and near rotten to the core, but it was a blessing having him around. One thing for sure, we couldn't just keep introducing him to everybody as Jupiter, Carol's boy. Everybody deserves a last name even if it isn't one that fits your fancy. I decided to do a little poking and prodding. Jupiter had been around us long enough to know that anything we said or did was not meant to be harmful to him.

"Jupiter, what say we take a little walk and do us some man to man talking?"

"Whatever you want, Uncle Nelson, it is a fine day for a walk."

"Fine day it is. Late spring is my favorite time. It is that in between season, not too cold and not too hot. I expect here is a lot different than California or Chicago."

"More ways than you could ever know."

"How old were you when Carol and Edwardo left California?"

"I don't rightly remember. Maybe four or five. Mother said that he wanted to visit his family across the border. Scary places down there, especially in Tijuana where we stayed for a while. I wish I would have known you and Uncle Jeremy were hunting us. I guess it really doesn't matter since we were already gone then."

"How did you like your daddy's kinfolk?'

"They were okay, but I couldn't understand a thing they said. Guess they could say the same thing about me. Mother was

136

not happy about us going there though, when she found out he had another wife."

"You don't say. Edwardo was married to another woman before he married Carol, never heard that before."

"He was still married to his first wife. They never got divorced. Seems I had three half brothers and one half-sister, all a lot older than me. Mother was fit to be tied, saying she would not share her husband with another woman. One afternoon while he was at his cantina job Mother packed up what she could, and we crossed on foot back across the border. She didn't leave a note or anything. I found out later that it was Mother that wasn't really married to Edwardo. They faked their marriage just for the sake of making her parents happy. I was a mistake, and they just did what they did to make it look right."

"I didn't think much on it back then, being young and all, but I reckon it is a might peculiar that they supposedly got hitched but never invited any kin to the wedding. I do remember Mama being quite hurt because of it. Is that why you refuse to use his last name?"

"He is my father, but he was never married to my mother. I suppose that ate away at me once I found out. I understood the meaning of being one of those bastard children. He treated me like a son, and I guess if I step back and look at it now, she left him. He didn't dessert us."

"Would you consider using his last name? It doesn't seem right you not having a last name to go with your first."

"I would rather not after all these years of not admitting to it. Having his last name without him around doesn't fit who I am and what I look like."

"You mean because you do not look Hispanic."

"It makes it tougher to explain and I really don't want to have to justify who I am to anybody. I fought my share of fights in the orphanage fending off the ones that looked down their nose to me just because of my last name."

"I might have a solution for you then. Why not take up your mama's maiden name and be a Whiteside?"

"Can I do that?'

"You are half Whiteside, why not?"

"Jupiter Whiteside does have a nice sound to it."

"Fits right in with my mama's daddy being named Juniper Barnhart. Jupiter could pass for a spinoff of Juniper. From here on out you will be Jupiter Whiteside."

"William Jupiter Whiteside, mother named me after hers and your father."

"That's right, Daddy's full name was William Compton Whiteside. A lot of people called him Big Bill."

"Big Bill?"

"Funny when I take a better look at you, you and he were about the same size, had a similar build, but I think having one Big Bill in the family is a plenty."

"That's okay. I will settle for Whiteside. Thank you, Uncle Nelson for making this happen for me."

"It is what it is, and you are a Whiteside, blood kin and I am proud to have you here with us. What about your brother and sister, do they share the same daddy?'

Jupiter hung his head shamefully before answering. "It isn't an easy thing to admit, especially now that I understand it more so than back then, but I believe Mother got pregnant just to hold onto the men in her life. Rachel's father was a man named Russel Cabot. She didn't marry him either, his choice not hers. We were living in Texas then. He worked the oil rigs. Rachel wasn't quite a year old when he left one day and never came back. We eventually ended up in Oklahoma where she hitched up with another man, Joel Peterson. There are two years difference in Rachel and Petey. He walked out before Petey was born. It was about a year later when we moved to Chicago then our mother left us on the doorsteps of a church and told us to wait there while she ran some errands. She never came back. We landed in one orphanage after another and in many foster homes. When we got older, they split us up. I never saw either of them again."

Carol had three children by three different men and had never been married to any of them. That explained why she never wanted to return home. I have a niece and a nephew out there somewhere. My attempt to locate Carol had failed royally years ago. I doubted that another attempt would amount to much then. I felt for Jupiter, now understanding the plight he had been exposed to all these years. He didn't push the issue of seeking his siblings, so I left well enough alone. If ever he decided that he wanted to find them I would be all in to help him. My task for now was to welcome the lad with open arms, restore his faith in family and provide him an environment that put him at ease. It would be on him if he decided to stick it out with us. We would not desert him. My gut told me that he had found his rightful place among the Whiteside's. After all, he had traveled a for piece to find us. As for Carol, that would be a different chapter yet to come.

Jupiter Whiteside was not a freeloader. He wanted to earn his keep and contribute to his new family household. I wondered where he had learned these principles. I could not imagine that he had received such scruples from my sister or any of the men that she had bedded. One way to find out, I asked. Jupiter was not shy on answers either. All his experiences had not been terrible, so it seemed. He had landed with one foster couple for a spell, the McMurtry's. He had spent almost two years with them and from his description they were a loving family. He was removed from their care only after Mrs. McMurtry became ill and passed. Older by then, it had been tougher to relocate him to foster care and the orphanage did not provide the warmth and love he had been accustomed to having with his foster parents. That placed him on the road for leaving when he was old enough to opt out.

I had returned to construction work. I secured Jupiter a position working at McDougal's Pharmacy. He helped stock shelves and delivered orders on a motor scooter I got for him. He made payments to me until he paid it off. That was his idea, not mine. Bessy continued to spoil him, providing the motherly love missing from his life. The sparkle that boy put in her eyes was worth every second of having him around, a blessing indeed. About six months later she shared another blessing with me. She was with child again. We were both excited and walking on eggshells. I was worse than a mother hen making sure she did not overdo nor take any unnecessary risks.

Mama's health deteriorated and she came down with double pneumonia. She suffered something terrible before she finally drew her last raspy breath. She was reunited with Big Bill and left a huge void in our lives. Jupiter took it hard, having finally found his grandmother only to lose her in just a short time. There was no way for us to contact Carol, Keith or Jeremy. We had no phone numbers or addresses. My recollecting, I didn't think they deserved to know, given how they all but abandoned the family. Bessy didn't see it the same way as I did. She was too warm hearted for her own good. I was the blessed one, having her as my wife.

Seems there are always wandering kinfolk out there, mostly ones I have never heard of until they show up at our doorsteps. What made meeting them tougher now was the fact that my grandparents and parents were gone. I had no way to vet them, to validate if they were real kin or not. Sometimes that made it difficult to meet and greet them with open arms. It wasn't like they could present papers certifying that they were true blooded and not somebody of flim-flam origin out to take us for a ride. Sounds harsh, me putting it like this, but we had been burned by those that my folks stood up for, and now I had to rely on my gut. I had to keep reminding myself that if I had been a hard ass, I might have turned away young Jupiter. It wasn't like he arrived with any identification to prove who he was either.

One such scoundrel darkened our doorway one Sunday afternoon just as we arrived home from church. He was on foot, claiming he had arrived earlier on the Greyhound. I was suspicious from the get-go because the bus doesn't usually run the route at the time, he said he got there. I held my tongue only after Bessy delivered a swift elbow to my ribs. She had anticipated where I was going with my questioning and promptly reminded me of my manners.

He introduced himself as Randolph Boone and that alone made it a tough row to hoe because there was no sign of a Whiteside or Barnhart attached to the feller whatsoever. He claimed he had roots to Mama's side but never explained fully to my satisfaction just how connected we were supposed to be. I wanted no part of this little reunion, gut mostly telling me to be very wary. Bessy would have none of it and invited him to Sunday vittles. I was being double teamed. Jupiter warmed up to him instantly. That boy just hankered to get close to anybody that laid claim they were kin.

This Boone feller could tell some good'uns, entertaining the lot with his worldly escapades. I immediately thought back to the last time I got snookered by Cousin Homer Godsell the conning prospector. He hadn't shown up with any papers either but, no doubting it, he was certifiably crooked as the day is long. I considered myself older and wiser and not one willing to get burned twice. P.T Barnum said, 'there's a sucker born every minute.' I just hoped in that very minute I wasn't the sucker in question.

Dang that Bessy, she went right from offering him something to eat to offering him a place to stay. I drew the line though and quickly told him that there was a small bunk house attached to the barn. No way was this complete stranger going to sleep under **my** roof. Boone didn't even flinch at the offer and just said he was much obliged by our hospitality. Jupiter showed him to his accommodations. Seems I was still being double teamed. One thing about Boone is he had a nasty tobacco chewing habit. He spat places I didn't appreciate him spitting. My bruised ribs prevented me from giving him a little lesson on manners. Reckon I was learning lessons on manners from my lovely wife.

One night stay quickly surpassed a week. Randolph Boone had settled himself in to that bunkhouse and it didn't seem he was moving on anytime soon. I guess I shouldn't piss and moan too much, he was lending his help around the place doing just enough to keep me off his back. We had a sizable garden, and the corn was coming in. That Boone rolled up his sleeves and went to pulling it. He taught me something by shucking it as he pulled it, leaving the shucks in the garden to be plowed under later. The crop hadn't yielded what I had expected it to yield though. It was far short of my expectations.

Might near a month later we were still blessed with his presence, but it seemed he was backing off the chores. This didn't set well with me, and I was just shy of having a little talk with him when my dear wife intervened again. I had learned by then to protect my ribcage. I came home from work one afternoon and spotted Herschel Hoge chatting with Boone. When they spotted me, they ceased their conversation and Herschel gave me a little wave before hoping in his truck and driving off. My gut was churning something awful and without Bessy anywhere around I decided I would go with my hunch.

"What did Herschel want?"

"Nice feller, good to meet your neighbors from time to time."

"Herschel isn't exactly a neighbor, Randolph. He lives on the far side of town. I know him by sight only. Me and him have hardly ever exchanged words. What brought him all the way out here?"

"He was asking if we had seen his lost coon hound."

"Why would he think his hound had wandered this far?"

"He said somebody had stolen it and was wondering if anybody had come around here trying to sell one."

"Seems a might peculiar just the same."

"That man is fond of his hounds. I told him we would be on the lookout."

"What have you been doing all day?" I chanced the question without Bessy being around to jolt my manners.

"Rheumatism has been acting up and has me feeling poorly. I'm not worth a plug nickel if I push myself when it gets a foothold. A little rest and I should be good as new."

I eyed him suspiciously but held my tongue. The man was up in age and might have a spell of rheumatism. Then again, no doctor had confirmed he was stricken by it. No papers and no medical records, this just got better and better.

143

"You can tell Bessy not to fret over me like she did this morning. It was nice of her bringing me breakfast, but I think I can manage to make it for supper."

It was one thing feeding him but catering to him like a hotel guest just about sent me places Boone didn't want to witness me going. Before I said something I probably wouldn't regret until Bessy caught wind of it, I turned and headed to the house. Jupiter was in the kitchen helping her prepare the meal. He had gotten off early. Mr. McDougal had closed the pharmacy to attend a funeral. I asked Bessy if she had seen Herschel Hoge arrive. She hadn't. Jupiter said that he had seen him and another man leaving about the time he got home. Another man? Jupiter said he didn't recognize the other man either. I almost asked Jupiter what kind of dog the feller had lost.

Too many red flags were waving inside my head. Something smelled mighty fishy, but I couldn't quite figure out why. Two men show up out of the blue and end up having conversations with Boone. This place wasn't exactly on the main road, a regular well-traveled route from here to yonder. Over supper I planned to ask Boone about this other feller that just so happened to drop by. It was about then that I heard a vehicle coming down the drive. I peeked out the kitchen window and saw another truck I didn't recognize. This time Boone met him and handed him something through the window. One thing I noticed; Boone was not moving like someone stricken by rheumatism. He instead had too much pep in his steps, and he was looking about as if expecting somebody else to show up.

Enough of this horse manure, it was time to get to the bottom of it. I exited the house and headed in their direction. Boone saw me coming and said something to the driver. He whirled around and kicked up dust like a scalded dog as he left the premises. Boone ducked inside the barn.

"Randolph, get your Rheumatoid ass out her now." All sense of compassion was lost in that demanding yell.

As if on que, he slowly limped from the barn; noticeably more crippled looking than when he had entered it. He was wiping sweat from his forehead with a handkerchief. He smiled too much like the Cheshire Cat for my liking.

"Who was that and you best not say he lost some kind of critter too."

"Never seen him before, he was asking for directions to town."

"Plenty of signs on the main road, why did he come down here?"

Boone shrugged, "Don't ask me. You should have asked him."

"What did you hand him?"

"Oh, that, I wrote down instructions on that paper sack for him. He didn't seem to be the type to latch onto word directions, so I wrote it down for him. That boy was dumb as a rock."

"And you were able to figure that out and write it down for him just that quick."

"I am a good read on folks and have been gifted with mighty fast penmanship. Did you come to fetch me for supper?"

"You were moving pretty good, weren't you?"

"Yeah, about got it worked out. Funny how it can come and go like it does. Tell Miss Bessy I will wash up and be there in a jiffy."

Nope, I wasn't buying it but conversing about it was getting us nowhere. Randolph Boone was hiding something, and he was doing it on my watch. That didn't set well, by a long shot. You're supposed to be innocent unless proven guilty. By my recollection, he was guilty as sin for something. I just had to prove just what he was guilty of to knock that innocent look off his face.

A day or two more passed. I was no closer to solving what was eating at me. Boone had been overly helpful since our little conversation. He was volunteering to this and that and doing so with vigor; no sign of his rheumatism at all. Apparently, it had come and gone. We finished up early on the site where we had been excavating and I headed home. I pulled into the drive and got out to check the mailbox figuring I would save Bessy a walk. A Caddy pulled up beside me and man smoking a cigar asked me if this was the place where he could find a feller named Boone. I nodded saying he lived here on my place, and I asked if I could help. I received my answer loud and clear and informed him to follow me.

We parked at the barn and called out to Boone. He strolled out of the barn like he owned it.

"Hey Randolph, this gentleman is looking for you."

"So, you say; never laid eyes on him before."

"He's here to buy some shine. Said he heard you were selling it."

"Now where would he get a notion like that?"

"He said Herschel Hoge told him; reckon he found his hound didn't he. Mister, you can leave now; seems Boone is closed for any future business."

When the Caddy departed, I asked, no, I demanded that Randolph take me to where he had his still hidden. After a brief debate and after he got up and dusted the dirt off his britches, he led me down into the holler where it was located.

146

Corn liquor, my corn at that, had been used for his little
enterprise. I did some quick mathematical figuring and then
held my hand out for him to fork over what I considered to
be reasonable compensation for my crop, his room and
board, and a fee to disinherit him from the family. Basically,
I made sure he emptied all his pockets. I then escorted him to
bunkhouse where a search of his belongings uncovered the
rest of his booty. I left him with bus fare and one last kick to
his duff as I sent him packing. I warned him if he did not
catch the bus the sheriff would be his newest family member
and the jail would be his new address,

I agonized over what I would tell Bessy and Jupiter.
Randolph Boone certainly didn't deserve their admiration nor
respect. Honesty is the best policy, so I told it like it was, and
to lighten the agony, I gave Bessy the contribution he had
made for the hospitality that had been provided. She said
little, understanding where I stood on the subject. I then
asked Jupiter to accompany me to the still. We dismantled
and destroyed the Boone farm operation. Not a drop would
ever be served to more wanderers seeking lost coon dogs.

"Grandfather Nelson, do you think Randolph Boone was a relative?

"David, I can't prove that any more than I can disprove it. What I did
prove was that he was guilty as sin, dishonest from the first step he
set forth on our property. He did say he hailed from somewhere in
Tennessee, but he was never specific about any town. Making and
running moonshine in that state was right popular. I don't recall us
ever having kin in the Volunteer State but who am I to say we didn't.
And I can't throw too many rocks at the man because our family has
had its fair share of swindlers, con artist and mumbo jumbo
soothsayers. It seems we are a tarnished and corrupted lot as well. I
wish I could pretty it up but if it quacks and walks like a duck it is
probably a fox dressed in a feathered outfit. Don't look at me
sideways, David. I am your elder and my words might not matter or
make sense sometimes, but you're supposed to nod your head like

you think they do. Might I remind you; you asked for this. Wishing what you want and getting what you get might not always turn out the way you thought it would."

"I couldn't have said it better, Grandfather Nelson,"

"Boy, you are hankering to move to the front of the line in my will, aren't you?'

"I have all I need right here, spending time with you while you are on this side of that will."

"I am rubbing off on you, that's for sure."

"I'm on pins and needles. I can hardly wait to hear where you take us next."

"Reckon there is no better time than now to get on with it."

Chapter 17

David was sponging in everything. Not many these days are interested in what any of us have to say. I credit him with the enthusiasm, heart and patience to listen and record everything on that little thingamajig. I'm still not sure what he plans to do with all that I have shared with him. I reckon that is more his business than mine. He asked. I have been delivering on his request as best I can recollect. I have certainly surprised myself, remembering so much and in vivid detail. They say you can't go back, can't turn the pages of those forgotten times but I beg to differ. I am reliving mine and enjoying most of it. Unfortunately, my old brain doesn't work like a colander. I can't sift the bad from the good, not that I would wish to if I could. I figure it is best to just tell it like it was and let David censor or erase what he wants. It is my story to tell as I see fit, letting the chips fall where they may. You cannot pretty it up by putting lipstick of the pig. So, ready or not, let me shove the old shovel into the dirt and see what I can dig up next.

> Bessy had her second miscarriage. It seemed we weren't destined to be parents. The doctor could not find a source for her woes. He said sometimes these things just happen for no rhyme or reason. I can't say that talk reassured either one of us. He added that we were still young, and he was right. Folks got hitched early in those days. Most parents didn't stand in their children's way. I reckon us flying from the nest meant less mouths to feed. We both took the loss hard. I think that Jupiter was affected the hardest. It reminded him of losing his two siblings all over again except they didn't die. Well, we didn't know for sure if they were alive or dead. One thing for sure, it weighed heavy on our hearts and minds for quite a spell. We needed a distraction. Watch for what you think you need.
>
> Keith showed back up out of the blue. I was at work as was Jupiter. Bessy found him there on the front porch sitting in one of the rocking chairs. She didn't know how long he had

been there, and he offered no explanation for how long or where he had come from. Fact is he had little to say about anything. She invited him inside and offered him something to eat. She told me later how he devoured it as if it was his first meal in quite a long spell. When I arrived home, I spotted a bearded, stringy haired, scroungy man sitting in one of our rockers smoking what didn't smell like a cigarette.

My first thought was what kind of stray had wandered here this time. As I got closer, I asked, "Keith, is that you? You have been missing in action!"

"In the flesh, Bro and missing is just the way they like to frame it."

Bro? He had never called me Bro. "You look like…"

"Your long, lost brother, right," he interrupted me. "Would you like a toke?"

"A toke?"

"Marijuana…helps sooth the soul if you still have one."

"Grandfather Nelson, y'all smoked reefer back in those days."

"I didn't David; never have. Some people think that marijuana arrived on the scene in the hippie days, but it was around a long time before then. There was a movie made about it in 1936 called Reefer Madness, before my time. It was made illegal around that same time too. I read it somewhere. Like I said, it became more prominent around the time of the Vietnam War and the hippy movement. My brother got hooked on it, but he stayed mum on the particulars."

"Sorry I interrupted. Please continue."

I didn't take too kindly to how my brother looked and how he was acting. His eyes didn't seem quite right and when I got closer, I got a good whiff of the stench oozing from him. He smelled as if he had not bathed in days, maybe weeks. He had this gnarly unkept beard. I had never seen him with a beard and that's why I almost didn't recognize him. He held out his hand and offered me a pull from that wrinkly cigarette. I had never taken up smoking and wasn't about to do it then.

"Keith, that thing stinks. Where did you find it, in the garbage?"

"Trust me, this is genuine, the good stuff. Takes away all the pain and makes you see things clearer, Bro."

"First of all, I am not in pain, and I can see as plain as day that you must be a hobo or something. You stink to high heavens. When's the last time you had a bath or a haircut?"

"Don't knock it if you've never tried it. Hygiene is wildly overrated."

"Have you eaten anything lately?"

"Sister-in-law fed me. You did good by her, Bro."

"When did you get here?"

"I don't know. Time is not important. I'm here in the moment."

"Where have you been all this time and what really happened to you?"

"Here, there, everywhere and nowhere. It's all beautiful if you take the time to breathe it in. What happened is just a happening, nothing more. Can I crash here for a spell?"

"You can stay as long as you want but first, you're going to have to clean up. Are those the only clothes you got?"

"What you see it what I got and all I need."

"Get rid of that stinking cigarette, Keith, and come inside. You can take a bath; use my razor and I'll bring you some clean clothes."

"You look good Nelson, fit as a fiddle. Fine place you have."

"How did you find us?"

"Where there is a will there is always a way, our old man used to say. Where are the old man and old lady?"

"Dead and buried, but you wouldn't know that, would you Keith? We had no way to contact you."

About that time Jupiter rode up on his motor scooter.

"Riding a bike, must be your kid. I remember how you and Jeremy tried to ride one all the way to California."

"Jupiter, meet your Uncle Keith, mine and your mom's brother. Don't mind his appearance. He'll smell better once we get him cleaned up."

"Jupiter? Wait a minute, you're Carol's kid, aren't you? Where's that sister? I would like to see her too."

"Me too. If you find her Uncle Keith, you can tell her that for me as well."

"She's not here with you?"

"Long story, Keith. Plenty of time to talk later after you bath that filth from your body."

"You never were one much for talking, were you?"

"Seems to me that you had the market cornered on that and still do."

"All grown up now, talking like a man. All right, Bro, point me to your sanitation room and I will do my best to put a smile on your face."

152

After I escorted him inside, I returned to the porch where Jupiter now occupied one of the rockers. "What's wrong with Uncle Keith? He doesn't look so good, and I have seen plenty of kids that were in bad shape. He might be the worst I have ever seen though."

I had no explanation for my nephew. I had way more questions than I was getting g answers from my vagabond brother. I switched the conversation to small talk, how his day had gone and summed my up as well. Bessy joined us on the porch saying she had run a hot bath for Keith, remarking she would do her best to clean his clothes but had her doubts they could be salvaged. To say we were all awe struck would be an understatement. Temporarily we had a reprieve from agonizing over the loss of our child. Jury was still out if we would like the alternative any better than the grieving that had been consuming us.

Keith finally made his way back to where we were all gathered. He smelled better and looked considerably better wearing my shirt and pants, but he had not shaved his beard. When I asked why he hadn't he said it identified the person he was, whatever that was supposed to mean. Bessy excused herself and stepped back inside, giving the menfolk some space to talk as she put it. I asked again where he had been, and he just waved off the question and began jabbering more nonsense that neither I nor Jupiter understood. I worried that he was still being haunted by his war time experiences and as much asked him about it. Keith just laughed it off then rolled and lit another one of his skinny little marijuana cigarettes. He inhaled that thing, like there would be no tomorrow.

Jupiter sat there speechless, not knowing what to make of his new uncle. I was a bit perplexed as well. This was far from the Keith I had known, and I had already seen him in a depressed state after the war. He looked so much older and haggard. My clothes hung from his torso. The man underneath must be skin and bones as best I could tell. His bearded face was so gaunt, cheeks sunken in and there were those awful dark circles under his eyes, much worse than mere crow's feet.

"Keith, are you ill or something?"

He sucked in another deep pull from the marijuana, blew out a cloud of smoke and then said, "I got nothing against dying. I just don't want to be anywhere close by when it happens if I can help it." He laughed and coughed more; deep coughs, those that sound like your lungs are rotten.

"Are you in some kind of trouble; is that why you're here?"

"Trouble, trouble, toil and trouble, right side up is the wrong side down. You can't change what can't be changed even if you thought you could. Trouble is just a word. You can't start trouble nor seek it, for it is always there before you arrive."

"Does that mean he is or isn't in trouble, Uncle Nelson."

"Beats me, Jupiter. Do you need some money, Keith?"

"Got no money, got no evil; you earn it when you learn it."

"I have no idea what you are jabbering about. It's like you learned a new language since last time I laid eyes on you."

Jupiter nudged me and said, "Is all our family nutty as a fruitcake? You seemed normal compared to mother and now this."

"I can't deny that we don't have our share of quirkiness in in the family genes, but I am just as puzzled as you. Keith was never the same when he came back from the war, but his behavior now is not like the Keith I used to know. Matter of fact, I have never been around anybody that acted like this, including the snake handlers at Preacher Joe McFadden's church."

"What?"

"Another time, another story, Jupiter."

"Y'all talking in front of me like you think I am crazy and can't hear you. Guess what? I am not deaf. I can hear every word and y'all have never seen crazy like I have. It's out there everywhere just waiting to expose itself to nonbelievers and believers alike. Crazy is what crazy does and when it decides to latch onto you, you can't shake it free. It sinks it claws and teeth in and hangs on like nothing that has every got hold of you before."

"Keith, you are my brother and I want something fierce to help you whatever way I can, but you got to talk sensible and in words I can understand. All this babbling you are doing is muddying up the water. And put out that dang marijuana cigarette before it fries your brain worse than it already has."

Keith took one last long pull before he snuffed it out between his fingers. He then placed what was remained behind his right ear. "Okay, Bro, are you ready to hear real or do you want me to tell you what you would rather hear?"

"Just be honest with me Keith so I can help you and please stop calling me Bro."

Keith rubbed his bloodshot eyes with both hands before rubbing them through his long stringy hair, finishing off by stroking his beard. "I am homeless. Been homeless a longer time than I can remember. Life in the streets is another world, one you never want to live in, I promise you. There's terrible carnage out there, things I won't talk about. I have done stuff I will never share with you, bad, an awful gut-wrenching hell. I am not here to complain nor beg forgiveness. It is what it is and what I have done is done. You

155

asked if I am sick. Probably. You asked if I was broke. Most definitely. You asked if you could help. Not hardly. You fed me, cleaned me, clothed me and welcomed me unconditionally. That's more than any man, any brother deserves. I am not sure why I am here. Maybe I just wanted to see my family one last time. Maybe I had no other place to go. Maybe I don't know why I came here. I'm here though, but I am not here to stay. I never stay anywhere. I'm long past growing roots. You know me as well as anybody does. I have never been rooted if the truth be known.

I love you, my brother. I cannot change what cannot be changed. I do dearly regret I was not here more for mama and that I didn't even know she had died. And you nephew, I am sorry what your mama must have done to you that left you here with my brother. Carol has trouble growing roots too, always did. As for Jeremy, I haven't seen him either. I hope he is okay. It seems you are the only rooted one of the bunch, Nelson, the youngest and the smartest, the one with a heart that has always loved family. You are and have always been the real McCoy. I am proud of you and of who you have become. You welcomed me without hesitation into your home. I guess I should thank that sister-in-law. She welcomed me with open arms even before she realized who I really was.

If it is all right with you, brother; I need to walk this off and think a bit. Seeing you has brought much clarity to my sorry soul. Meeting you, nephew, has brought me happiness. I hope Carol and Jeremy find their way back and experience what I have firsthand. Now, please excuse me while I gather my thoughts."

I watched as Keith strolled across the yard and eventually entered the barn. I was relieved, hearing him as he soul searched, seeing how badly he wished to be back home among those who dearly loved him. I gave him the space he requested and looked forward to him establishing roots for a change, if indeed that was possible for him. I went inside and recapped for Bessy what had happened. After a while, I sent Jupiter to hail Keith for supper. A few minutes later he returned all wild eyed and stuttering up a storm. He found my brother, his uncle, hanging by a rope. Keith left no note, no explanation for doing what he had done. We buried him alongside our parents. Yep, we had needed a distraction and by golly we had gotten a humdinger.

This prompted Jupiter to thinking. He wanted to find Rachel and Petey and his mother. I did, as well, and I added Jeremy to that list of lost souls even if I had no idea how to kickstart the process. All I knew was that I had to do everything humanly possible to prevent anything like what had happened to Keith to happen to any of them, if it wasn't already too late. Our family was a messed-up bunch if ever there was one. Keith credited me with being the best of the lot, so it was on my shoulders to do what I could to salvage the others. I wasn't sure if my shoulders were broad enough to support the load of that burden and responsibility, but what I did know, I had to try.

It seemed like Chicago might be the best place to find a trail for Rachel, Petey and Carol. I was blood kin, and I was a grownup. People in those orphanages should have no cause to keep information about them from me. I had a right to know where they had landed. As for Jeremy, I was clueless as where to start. I thought about the carnival but could not imagine him ever going back there, not after all this time. One thing at a time, help Jupiter find out what happened to Rachel and Petey. With any luck, maybe we could cross paths with my wayward sister.

Chapter 18

Who knows what triggers a memory? One thing for sure, I had hardly thought about this one since it happened. Why would I? I had tried to block it totally from my head but poof, here it was. I almost skipped sharing it with David, but I had made a commitment to tell what I remembered about our kin. Well, Livonia Barnhart was kin whether I wanted to claim her or not.

"Grandfather Nelson, are you all right? You have a peculiar look on your face."

"I bet it looks like I have been sucking on a lemon. Feels like it to. I had one of those out of the blue recollection, not one I am too fond of I must admit. One must be a might careful when shaking the family tree; you never know what rotten fruit might fall to the ground. God has blessed us with some wonderful kinfolk; a strange and odd bunch in some cases but you must play the hand you are dealt. Satan can be a hell of a dealer as well and there is no doubt in my mind that he had something to do with spawning Livonia Barnhart. She was my mama's aunt, and the old witch was still kicking after mama died. She and mama were close to the same age. It was one of those situations that happens among kinfolk where an elder isn't necessarily an elder. I can't remember the particulars in the family pecking order and for this account, I don't reckon it really matters. She was blood kin on mama's side so I will just leave it at that."

"Don't share it if it stresses you Grandfather Nelson."

"Well, it's on my mind now and not something that I can shake. Might as well get it out in the open and be done with it. It takes forced family fun to a new level."

> It had always been a tradition on both sides of my family to have family reunions every year. As a little chap I loved going and playing with cousins and eating home cooked vittles until I popped. As I got older, I wasn't as drawn to

them, but I went just to appease mama mostly. After she passed, I didn't feel the need or pressure to go and usually found every excuse in the book not to attend. The Whiteside reunions fell by the wayside and never were a sure yearly event. The Barnhart clan were sticklers though. Come hell or high water there would be a reunion and if you didn't attend it was about the same as being blackballed. I would almost take being blackballed as a blessing to the alternative. Invites were usually done word of mouth, some phone calls and few letters if necessary. There was no RSVP. If you were notified you were expected to be there.

I tried every trick in the book to avoid going but in the end my dear Bessy convinced me otherwise, saying it would be wonderful for Jupiter to meet his relatives and for them to meet him. Guilt ridden and backed into a corner I had no choice but go. We were still reeling from my brother's suicide. It seemed the lesser of two evils. The place and location had already been decided. There was no family vote. For us it would mean almost an eleven-hour drive. No getting out of it, this would not be a simple one afternoon event. We would have to stay at least one night, probably more. Bessy could not be happier. We had never had a vacation since marrying. I couldn't disappoint her. Jupiter was excited as well once the cat got out of the bag.

I dreaded going because I would have to face the usual questions like where was Carol and Jeremy, and there would be those wishing to pry into Keith's death seeking any little dirty detail they could uncover. While Jupiter would indeed be introduced to his kin, he would also be poked and prodded about his past. The Barnhart side of the family was a nosey bunch. Livonia was hosting it at her house. I dreaded seeing her most of all. Evil incarnate, the devil's disciple if ever there was one. I never knew a single person that was filled with so much hate and jealousy as that woman. Family tolerated her because that's what family does. I wasn't like

159

most family though. If she pushed me too hard, I tended to push back. When you pushed her, you placed yourself in her crosshairs. It was better to not start a fight you had no chance of winning. And when I say fight, I mean it. There was no such thing as a civil discussion or a mere exchange of opinions. It was always her way or the highway. I was tempted to preview Jupiter for what most certainly was ahead but explaining her would not do it justice. Seeing it firsthand would leave a lasting impression and then he could decide for himself how he felt about her.

The reunion was still a month away. Anything could happen in a month. We might have one of those cow killing tornados or a locus plague or something to prevent us from attending. I hadn't heard of a horde of grasshoppers organizing a takeover nor was the weather this time of year prone to spawn a tornado. I certainly was not going to pray for a disaster but that didn't mean one couldn't happen. I was all gloom and doom while Bessy and Jupiter were anything but. It was wrong of me thinking this way when they were so excited about going. Well, I would not be the cause for us not attending, but if a natural disaster happened it would be taken out of my hands.

The weeks passed and there was no reprieve, not for me anyway. It was time to bite the bullet and pack up the car for an uninspiring road trip to kinfolk hell. Harsh thoughts. All my relatives were not intolerable; forced family fun just the same. Mama couldn't help it. She was born into it just like the rest of us were under her watch. With Keith now gone and Carol and Jeremy's whereabouts unknown, I would be left to face them alone. Bessy wasn't full-fledged bloodline. Married into it wasn't the same. Jupiter was blood kin, but I didn't wish on him what I expected him to be exposed to. No doubt in my mind, I would take the brunt of it. Sounded like I was preparing to walk to the gallows and then it hit me, Keith swinging from that rope in our barn, and I quickly dismissed that analogy.

It was an hour before dawn, we were loaded up, bags packed for a brief stay, and I meant the briefer the better. Bessy had made us some country ham and cheese biscuits since we had skipped breakfast. We had a thermos of brewed coffee and a gallon jug of sweet tea. She had made several pies and one cake for the reunion. Because of the 'all day' drive it would be impossible to cook up any other vittles for travel. She had agreed to bring desert. The smell of freshly cooked pies set my belly to growling.

"Uncle Nelson, how many kinfolks usually attend these reunions?"

"Varies from year to year as does where they settle on having it. This one is probably a far piece for some to drive. It is being hosted by Livonia Barnhart, your grandmother's aunt. Don't go thinking she is old and decrepit though. She and your grandmother are about the same age. I haven't seen Livonia in a couple of years (Not enough years I thought but didn't say). I think this is the first time she has ever had the reunion at her house."

"Did my mother ever take me to one when I was little? I can't remember ever going."

"Nah, Carol had moved away from here before you were born. She never came back to any," I thought thinking how smart she had been,

"I have butterflies thinking about meeting kin that I have never met before."

"I have butterflies and I know them."

My comment prompted a swift elbow to the ribs from Bessy. I flinched and glanced at her, only to receive 'The Look' that

161

look that only women can deliver effectively. It meant watch your tone around Jupiter.

The sun made its presence known about an hour into our trip. Hindsight, we should have left much earlier to have avoided the heat of the day. Late summer would deliver brutally hot temperatures. The windows down would make for windy conditions inside the car. It was going to be a long, brutally sizzling day. Barring any unforeseen issues, we should make it to our destination before dark. Against my better judgment I had agreed to stay at Livonia's home. I had exactly agreed. Bessy had said yes to the invite. We hadn't received any other offers. Hers was the only option unless we located a motel. Sadly, there was no motels within fifty miles of the town where she lived. Driving fifty miles didn't sound so bad. I was apprehensive to say the least. Livonia had never been one to invite any relative to stay at her house. I certainly wasn't her favorite, given our track record. Might be that curiosity had gotten the best of her with Jupiter in the picture. Speculation was getting me nowhere except reaching new levels of dread. Dread led to anger, and anger would only cause conflict from the get-go.

I tried to keep Jupiter entertained with one of my favorite childhood games, counting cows. He wasn't a child. The premise was lost quickly when he asked why he would lose any cows he had counted when we passed a cemetery on his side of the car. Cows were not buried in people cemeteries. It made absolutely no sense to him. Thinking on it, he did have a valid point. I don't know why I hadn't questioned it when I was a little chap. I dismissed sharing with him one of my other favorite road games, that of picking a make of car and tallying the number of them spotted. At least it made sense losing your car count when you passed a junk yard. Instead, I just let him enjoy the ride as best he could and chit chat when chit chatting was required. I played the radio when any good stations came in. I especially enjoyed listening to Paul

Harvey and managed to locate his radio show. He always started with 'Hello, Americans, I'm Paul Harvey' then after he had begun a story he would eventually say, "In a moment, the rest of the story.' And later he would say, 'And now you know the rest of the story,' always ending his broadcast with, 'Paul Harvey…good day.'

We had eaten the ham biscuits earlier. That had been hours ago. Bessy broke out bologna and cheese sandwiches. There was not the abundance of fast food franchises back then. You prepare picnic fashion if you wanted to eat without searching for a nice restaurant or diner. Our pockets weren't deep. Preparing ahead worked better for both thrift wise and saving on stops. Lemonade would wash down the sandwiches. When we saw a service station with a restroom we stopped. If you didn't have to go you still went anyway. We had burned eight hours of our eleven and to say it was hot as blue blazes inside the car was an understatement. Air blew in through the windows, but the breeze was far from cool. Bessy didn't complain nor did Jupiter. I constantly wiped the sweat from my face and dobbed the handkerchief on the back of my neck. We had topped off the gas once when had stopped for a potty break.

We motored along, inching closer to Livonia. Darkened thoughts had engulfed my head. I envisioned anything but a stay oozing of hospitality. Hostile yes, but hospitable, I doubted it. She had not invited us to stay out of the goodness of her heart. There must be other motives in play. The old gal wasn't one to appreciate family, not unless there was something to be gained for her. She was a taker, not a giver. She used people, any people, family or not. It almost bothered me thinking of her like that, almost. We might stay at her house, but no way would I allow her to use us for any notion she had in mind. Livonia had been married four, maybe five times, maybe even more. Mama called her the black widow. She bled her husbands dry and then buried

163

them while making sure that everything of worth came to her. She was a wealthy independent woman, not one to break a nail doing any kind of work. Again, those were mama's words, not mine. Gloom and doom filled my head as we crept closer to the gates of hell.

"You've been mighty quiet, Nelson. Penny for our thoughts. You are thinking about her, aren't you?"

"Penny bought you first prize Bessy. Why are we putting ourselves through this? You know how she operates. Bad things, very bad things are going to come of this, us staying at her house."

"You know why. You said it yourself. Jupiter will have an opportunity to meet some of his relatives. The boy has only known us." She said this openly because Jupiter was sprawled on the backseat sleeping.

"Reckon so, but why in the world did I give in to staying with her?"

"I seem to remember you saying it was cheaper than a motel."

"Cheaper but at what cost? Why didn't you talk me out of it?"

"Two days and it will be behind us."

"Two minutes alone with Livonia is two minutes too long. She's a parasite. She bleeds anything she touches. A bloodsucker if ever there was one."

"You are overexaggerating Sweetie."

"Just wait and see. If I'm lying, I'm dying. I am not going to put up with her hogwash. I will not hesitate to put her in her place if she pushes me too far."

"Hush now. Two days and it will be over. We will enjoy your family and you will look back and think how blessed we were to have attended."

"Blessed when we are heading home you mean."

Bessy squeezed my arm reassuring me that everything would be all right. That same squeeze was used when she tried to calm me down. Her touch was always the miracle cure. She said she was the ying to my yang, whatever the heck that meant. She was the calm preventing my storm for sure. The next four hours passed quickly, too quickly. We had arrived. There she stood on the front porch, arms crossed and that little leaning hitch to one side. She was dressed to the nines. She was all show, the stage hers to shine and put on the big put on. She was as old as my mama, but makeup and surgery had hidden the years, at least until you got close enough to see through the smoke and mirrors. Not so much as a smile or wave, she just stood there like a cold and unfeeling stone statue. So much for the welcome mat. We exited the car. She waited us out, never taking a step in our direction. Come to me said the spider to the unsuspecting flies. Well, in this case one fly suspected the worst. We breached the steps and now stood on the porch mere feet from where she stood.

"Nelson, Bessy, you look weary from your trip and in need of a hot bath."

Who greets someone telling them they need a bath? I just mustered a smile and a nod.

"And this must be Carol's boy. I am your great aunt, Livonia Barnhart Compton. I believe I recall your mother named you after one of the planets, didn't she? Pluto, Mars, Saturn?"

"Jupiter, ma'am, my name is Jupiter Whiteside."

"Whiteside? I recall Carol marrying a Mexican, Warez or Diaz or Perez."

165

Without so much as a flinch Jupiter replied, "Edwardo Valdez but they were never married."

"Oh lordy, where is your mother and this man now?"

"I don't know. Last time I saw him I was little, and he was in Mexico. Mother left me and my brother and sister in Chicago some years later."

"Three children and she never married this Valdez?"

"He isn't Rachel or Petey's father. Rachel's father was a man named Russel Cabot and Petey's was Joel Peterson. He left before Petey was born."

"Tell me that at least one of these gentlemen was the standup kind and married your mother."

"Nope, afraid not. Mother often said she wasn't the marrying kind. Apparently, she wasn't the motherly kind either because she left us at a church in Chicago and we never saw her again."

"Nelson, did you know about this?"

"I know about it now."

"You can't condone what your sister has done."

I clinched my jaw but before I could speak Bessy squeezed my arm.

"Leaving him, them was a travesty but I didn't know where Carol was or anything about her business until Jupiter showed up at our place. What's done is done and there isn't much anyone can do about it." Bessy could feel my tension and squeezed my arm again.

"These poor bastard children have been brought into this world by your sister. She has forever tarnished our family name with her promiscuous whorish behavior."

166

Bessy squeezed my arm and stepped around me delivering a thunderous slap to the right side of Livonia's face and then saying, "Come on Nelson. We're going home."

Without another word being spoken, we loaded back in the car and wheeled out of the driveway, literally leaving Livonia Barnhart Compton to eat our dust. I gave Bessy a little affectionate squeeze on the arm. It put a smile on my face and still ranks as one of the best things my dear Bessy has ever done. On the return trip I treated us to an overnight stay at a motel and a fine spread at a little diner. The three of us celebrated a little Whiteside reunion. I have but one regret, that Jupiter did not have an opportunity to meet the kinder and saner side of the Barnhart family. He took it like a champ though, not a negative word spoken of the ordeal.

Chapter 19

Nelson basked in the memory while David took an incoming phone call. Bessy could be a little pistol ball when riled or pushed as far as she was willing to be pushed. Pound for pound she could hold her own given her small stature, five feet, seven and weighing about one hundred ten. Livonia Barnhart Compton would not forget the encounter anytime soon. That would be the last time any of them would lay eyes on the uppity busybody. None of them would lose sleep nor fret over her absence in our life.

David returned.

"Is everything all right?"

"Yes sir. That was Dad. He was wondering where I was. I told him what we were doing and that I was staying over tonight. There was a long pause. I thought the call had been dropped. He finally said he would see me tomorrow. He didn't say have fun, enjoy or anything that would make me think he approved of what I...we are doing."

"Don't hold it against him, David. Edwin has never been one interested in the past."

"Why is that Grandfather Nelson? Is he ashamed of his past or something?"

"Something maybe. Since we are on the subject, might as well jump to the most blessed day of my life, our lives, mine and Bessy's, the birth of your father, James Edwin Whiteside."

> Nearly three years had passed since Bessy's miscarriage. We had all but given up hope of ever having children. We had also given up hope of finding Rachel and Petey, one dead end after the next. Carol had not surfaced either. While Jupiter had adjusted to life with us, it was obvious that he suffered from underlying depression. It was tough on him not knowing the whereabouts of his brother and sister or mother. Were they doing well or not? Were they dead or alive? Not

knowing can often be far worse than knowing. I had failed on my promise to find them. I don't think he held my failure against me, but it dogged me just the same. Neither Rachel nor Petey even knew that they had ties to the Whitesides, so I did not expect them to come looking for us. As for Carol, she had completely vanished too, no calls, no letters.

I had gotten Jupiter a job with the construction company where I worked. He picked up on things quickly and had climbed the ladder. He operated one of the dozers for larger jobs or could just as willingly take on the grunt jobs when grunt work was required. He became the son it appeared I would never have. He had graduated from that old scooter to a Chevy pickup. Being single, he did not require the luxury offered from a sedan or a family wagon. He had not had a serious relationship either. Given his upbringing or lack thereof, I think he feared getting too involved and God forbid, being married. A capital 'D' defined our dysfunctional family.

It was might near hog killing time when Bessy began feeling poorly. She lacked energy and appetite. I ended up calling Doc Ferrell. Back then the medical doctors made house calls. I waited in the parlor while he practiced his bedside manner in our bedroom. I about wore a hole in the rug pacing the floor. He and Bessy were behind closed doors much too long to suit me. When a doctor visit takes that long it usually leads to news you are not expecting nor willing to listen to without feeling a bit squeamish. Finally, the door opened and out stepped Doc Ferrell without my Bessy. I wanted to ask how she was, but the words were cut off in my windpipe.

"Nelson. Bessy needs to take it easy. When I say easy, I mean no tough chores, heavy lifting, anything that requires straining and considerable effort."

I could not muster the spit to ask why. I reckon he saw it in my face and then to my surprise he offered the slightest of smiles.

"Nelson, Bessy is with child. But before you cut cartwheels, I must warn you that her pregnancy will be difficult and risky for her and the child."

I stood there dumbfounded and speechless. He placed his hand on my shoulder and did his best to explain the circumstances so that even I could understand them. Giving Bessy's history, the miscarriage and the condition of her female parts, it was going to be a dice roll if she managed to make it full term. It would be up to both of us to take the necessary precautions to give the baby a chance to be born. The fact that she was with child gave me all the incentive I needed to protect her with every fiber of my being. Doc Ferrell said if God be willing this baby would be born. I shook his hand like I was pumping water from a well until he finally pried his hand from my grip. I eased into the bedroom after I walked the doc to the door.

Bessy smiled as I entered the room and motioned me to have a seat beside her on the bed. Tears flowing freely from both of us. Happy tears. Joyous tears. We were going to have a baby. I laid down the law saying how she was not going to do this and that. She patted my hand, reassuring me that she would do nothing that would compromise her pregnancy. She added though, that she was worried about the burden it would put on me. It was then that it hit me like a bolt of lightning. How could I take care of her when I was at work all day? Sometimes it even required that I was away from home days, even weeks, contingent on the location of the site we were working. Same went for Jupiter. I faced a quandary, but I did not let on to her just how concerned I was. I could ask Jupiter to quit and stay home but that was not fair, me asking that of him. Whatever I did it needed to be done now, not later, not tomorrow.

Jupiter arrived home about an hour later. He saw the frustration on my face and asked me what was wrong.

"Nothing is wrong, should be wrong that is. I am going to be a daddy. Well, to make sure of it we must keep close watch over Bessy. Doc Ferrell said things are complicated and Bessy need not exsert herself. Her having this baby is going to be tricky. I, we must do everything around here to keep her from overdoing. That means we will be doing most of the chores that she usually does."

"Congratulations Uncle Nelson. Not to worry, you can count on me to do whatever you need me to do."

"I appreciate that, Jupiter. I never doubted that I could. Got another problem though. Both of us work. Nobody is here to see to her needs and do what has to be done when we aren't here."

"What are we going to do then?"

"I haven't quite gotten that far yet. Doc just left about an hour ago after he laid it on me. I am going to ask the foreman for a day off tomorrow and see what I can work out."

"Is there anything I can do?"

"Try to cover me, pick up the slack as best you can if you don't mind."

"I will. Anything else?"

"Pray." I said that and immediately thought about Preacher Joe McFarlan. Not sure why, he had been long dead and buried.

"I can do that too."

Our foreman Travis Kennedy was a compassionate and understanding man. He understood how badly Bessy and I had wanted children and gave me his blessing, adding we would be in his prayers as well. He even said if I needed to, take an extra day. I wasn't sure what I was going to do the first day, much less a second one. My mind was drawing blanks. I knew that I better clear those cobwebs and get to figuring this thing out. This was no time for dillydallying. A smile eased across my face when I remembered what the most important part of the equation was; we had a chance to be parents if we did what was needed to ensure everything went right. It was too late today to reach a resolution. I would sleep on it and attack it on all fronts tomorrow.

With Jupiter's help we managed to rustle a supper of pork and beans, fried fatback and cornbread. It wasn't much to brag on considering what we might have had if Bessy had prepared the meal. She didn't complain and we woofed it down as well. I saw to her every possible need until bedtime. I did everything but pee for her and I would have done that if I could have. I didn't sleep nary a wink that night. My little ole pea brain did its best to formulate a plan to address our needs, her needs but solutions were in short supply. Every time Bessy moved, grunted or snored I almost peeled out of my skin, fearing the worst.

I clambered from bed long before daylight and well ahead of my normal get up time. After changing and washing up I headed to the kitchen to muster some breakfast. I am not a biscuit maker but luckily there were some leftover biscuits. We had eggs. I scrambled eggs and sliced open the biscuits and added cheese then toasted them open face in the oven. I might have charred the biscuits a bit, but Bessy never complained. I made Jupiter cheese and egg biscuits and bagged them for him. He left for work while I worked on what I was going to do.

172

Bessy could read me like a book and suggested that I should see if any of the ladies from church could help while we were at work. Good idea but I wasn't on a first name basis with any of them. A life in construction did not offer many opportunities to attend church regularly. She tossed out a few names. I asked her to write them down and how I could reach them. Dead end, she didn't know any of their phone numbers and few addresses. I did not cherish the notion of knocking on doors and parlaying with strangers.

Midday arrived and I was no closer to solving this problem than I was yesterday. Travis said I could have an extra day if I needed it. If I couldn't figure this out today what made me think tomorrow would be any better. Dillydallying soon turned to extreme procrastination. Neither were particularly becoming saddled on the shoulders of someone deeply in trouble. After seeing to Bessy's needs, I went outside for some fresh air, hoping the freshness of the great outdoors would do wonders to clear my foggy head. I sat on the steps and ran my fingers through my hair resisting the urge to pluck some of it out by its roots.

It was then that I spotted dust being kicked up by an approaching vehicle. I shaded my eyes with my hand attempting to get a better look from the blinding sun. I didn't recognize the owner of what looked to be a blue Plymouth station wagon. It rolled to a stop and a rather large black woman emerged from the backseat. The driver was an equally large behemoth, both black as spades. I did not recognize either of them. I stood and asked if I could help them.

"Are you Mister Whiteside," asked the woman.

"Yes ma'am."

"My name is May Young. This here is my brother Marlon. Doc Ferrell sent me. Said you was looking for some help."

"Yes ma'am. I reckon I am."

"Doc said your missus is feeling poorly and needs to be tended to while you are at work."

"Yes ma'am. She is with child and the doctor said she can't be doing any heavy lifting or normal chores."

"He told me as much. I sit with the elderly some and sickly folks too. Doc Ferrell refers me to people that might need some sitting and tending to. Your missus would be in good hands with May."

"If Doc Ferrell recommends you, then I am sure you are trustworthy and dependable."

"As the day is long I am."

"When could you start?"

"I got no folks what needs sitting right now. I can start now, tomorrow, whatever suits you and our missus."

"What do you charge Mrs. Young?"

"Call me May. Got no husband. He run off long time ago. My children are grown and gone too. Let's see to what needs to be done first and then we can settle on what we both can live with."

"I work long hours May. Sometimes I can be gone days or even weeks on a job."

"I got no reason to stay home when somebody needs me. Long hours, days nor weeks scare me much. Don't fret Mister Whiteside. I am not out to steal you blind."

"I would never infer anything like that May."

"I live with my brother. Marlon would jump at the chance to have me out of his home for a spell. Room and board, a share of the meals and I think we can make it work."

"I don't reckon I will receive another offer so generous. Let's give it a try. Can you start tomorrow?"

"I can start today. I'll have Marlon bring my belongings from his car."

Nelson smiled, "You were that sure of yourself, were you?"

"You got the need. I got the solution. Now take me to your missus so we can get acquainted."

"We have a little room off the kitchen. Not much to it but I can round up a cot or something for you."

"That will be fine. I don't take up much space. I'll make do and if I can't, I let you know."

Doubtful I thought. She was about as round and wide as she was tall, and she wasn't that tall. She moved with the grace of someone much smaller. She was pitch black and wore a colorful yellow scarf on her head. Her dress matched the color of the scarf. She hardly had a distinguishable waistline.

'You are a straight shooter, May. I like that about you."

"Beating around the bush just makes it awkward for all concerned. May thinks it and mostly it escapes my mouth. If ever I say or do something that doesn't set right with you then you set old May straight and we will fix what needs fixing."

"Marlon, take my things to where Mister Whiteside says they should be. Point me to your missus and give us some time."

"Yes ma'am."

"Y'all will get use to her bossiness after a spell," said Marlon. "One warning, stay out of her way while she is in your kitchen. Let me know when you are tired of having her around and I will come fetch her. Keep her for as long as want though."

I couldn't tell if that was meant to be a joke or not. Marlon sure didn't smile when he said it. And her belongings were just one bag, more like a satchel, and a croaker sack tossed over her brother's shoulder. I fretted over if I should take Travis up on that extra day, just to see how things were going to go. I finally figured if we were going to give a shot, tomorrow was as good as any day to try. Bite the bullet, my daddy would say.

May wasted no time getting at it. She was a whirlwind, not a lazy bone in her body. She fixed us some fine vittles that night for supper and had tended to Bessy's every need without missing a beat. Jupiter and I watched in amazement as she accomplished more than the two of us could ever have accomplished and in half the time. Me going to work tomorrow posed no problems nor offered any concerns. Bessy would be in good hands. Heck, all of us would. May Young was a Godsend indeed and we were certainly in need of someone with her character and tenacity.

Seven and a half months later Bessy birthed a fine eight-pound three-ounce boy, James Edwin Whiteside. May performed the role of a midwife and brought him into the world. She stayed on. May Young was part of the family. With Jupiter's help, we added onto the house giving her larger living quarters. Five months later Bessy was again with child. This time she was not having as much difficultly as with James. May still hovered over her like a mother hen. We eventually brought Clara Faye into our little growing family. She was named after my grandmother, Clarice Barnhart. By then Jupiter had moved on still intent on finding his brother, sister and even his mama. I couldn't fault him for that. I still regretted that I had let him down. I wondered though if he had really moved out to give up his room for the young'uns. The house was busting at the seams with us, the chaps and May under one roof. I hated to see the lad leave. My nephew felt more like a son to me.

Then came that terrifying accident not more than a year later. Carelessness while operating big equipment is taboo on a construction site. Something had happened about a week prior that I let dog me something fierce. A letter had come in the mail. It was from Carol, but it had no return address. It was postmarked as being sent from Reno, Nevada. Carol wrote that she was in a bad way and needed to come home; home being where we lived. I'm still not sure how she got hold of our address. She asked if I could wire her bus fare to the Western Union in Reno. Without hesitation I did. Jupiter always kept in touch, and he was living in Saint Louis and planned to be there for a while. I phoned him to tell him the news. He was so excited that he said he would head back as well.

Within a couple of days Jupiter had arrived anticipating the long-awaited reunion with his mother, filled with questions as to why she had abandoned them like she had. Days passed and Jupiter faithfully waited at the Greyhound station when buses were scheduled to arrive from out west. The buses kept coming but Carol was never on any of them. It hurt me to the core seeing that lad disappointed time after time. I was guilt ridden being the one that had broken the news to him, building his expectations so. Nothing to do now but wait it out.

Another letter came. It was from Carol. This one was postmarked from Las Vegas. She was asking for more money saying she had to flee Nevada for reasons she did not explain. She offered no explanation for not fleeing here. The jig was up in my mind. She had no intention of returning to family. We had been who-doed. Jupiter decided to catch a Greyhound to Las Vegas. There was no talking him out of it. I drove him to the bus station on my way to work.

The construction site was within drivable distance of home. No overstay required, not that it mattered with May living with us. Still, it allowed me to spend time with Bessy and the children. I was operating a front-end loader the first part of the morning and allowed my mind to do too much wandering. I drove too close to a steep grade and before I could correct my ill-fated mistake the loader tipped then overturned, flipping more times than I dare count and tossing me like a ragdoll from my perch. By the grace of God, I was not rolled over. I was alive but the extent of my injuries was anything but minor.

I woke up in a hospital bed with little recollection of what had happened, thanks to a concussion. I had a broken left arm, dislocated left shoulder and several busted ribs. My left foot was fractured as well. Bessy was sitting in a chair pulled next to the bed and had my right hand in hers. She touched my cheek and kissed me. Thankfully my lips were still intact and had survived that terrible accident. She then offered me a sip of water and praised the Lord for my awakening. Travis Kennedy was in the hallway. He stepped inside and then explained as best as he could what had happened, once he realized that I did not remember. He said not to worry, he would see to it that everything was taken care of for me and my family. He was more than just my foreman. He was a friend.

The doctor said I was lucky, but mending would take some time, patience and rehabilitation. Time was my enemy. I needed to work. Patience and rehabilitation would just get in my way. First things first, I had to get out of this hospital. Anyone trying to hinder my progress would have their hands full. I sounded bitter and maybe I was, but I was only angry at myself for allowing it to happen. Sure, I cursed Carol for setting it in motion with her selfishness and destructive paths. Poor Jupiter was out there searching for my sister, his mother, as sorry as she was, and it was doubtful that he would find her. If he lucked up and did it was doubly doubtful, he would pry any answers from her. why she had done the things she had shamefully done without remorse. Without remorse, my words, not hers. Who knew what she was thinking when she did what she did?

Carol was in a bad way all right. To what extent was anyone's guess. Any circumstance has issues and can be resolved. It takes the person being impacted by them to be willing to accept help and do what is needed to overcome them. Carol was not at that place yet. If Jupiter, by some chance found her, maybe he would be the match to light the fuse for her recovery. I doubted that even she could offer any information about where Rachel and Petey might be. If I were a betting man, I would not bet on a successful outcome no matter if he did or did not find her.

Three weeks later I was back on the job. Was I mended? Nope. Was I mending? Slowly. Travis would not allow me to operate anything larger than a bobcat and that was only after two weeks of gopher work from the construction trailer. Humbled yes but working was working. I was not one for handouts. I was getting around with one crutch mostly, a cane sometime. My arm and foot were in hard casts. My ribs were sore as was my shoulder, but I ground my way through the pain.

Happy Cameron, one of the fellers working the site, claimed to have done some cowboying in a previous life. He said he hailed from Oklahoma. We were having our lunch one day sitting outside on a stack of lumber when he offered me some advice.

"You are one tough'un, aren't you, son. Broken up like you was and here you are, manned up and spitting in fate's face."

"I don't know about all that."

"I know a man when I see a man and you got what it takes to be somebody to be reckoned with, Nelson. I like that about you."

179

"I just try to give anything my all and treat folks decent if they will let me."

"Cowboy Code."

"Cowboy Code?"

"Yep, you would have done it right, Cowboy Code. Live each day with courage. Have respect for everyone you meet. Be confident in your dreams. Always do what's right. Take pride in your work. Talk less and say more. Know where to draw the line. Always finish what you start. Be tough but always fair. Cowboy Code!"

I nodded. Cowboy Code was a sure-fire way to live your life by. Thinking about what Happy had said made sense. I reckon I abided by most of what the code meant to a cowboy. Happy gave me a painful slap on the back as he headed back to his grader. My thoughts reverted to Jupiter and his search for Carol, the very thing that had landed me in this predicament. We had only heard from him twice since he had arrived in Las Vegas. He had not located her to no one's surprise, but he had not given up yet. Cowboy Code! Jupiter fit the mold too.

Some time passed and I was about as mended as I was going to be. A few aches and pains persisted. Seemed I got stoved up more than I used to, and it took me longer to limber back up. Doctor told me I was doing fine even if my body argued against his medical opinion. Jupiter had returned to Saint Louis, no closer to finding Carol or any answers. I was in the back chopping some wood, my version of extended rehabilitation, just keeping the old limbs flexible, when a shadow appeared from behind. There was no mystery as to the owner.

"May, what brings you out here to my world of manly chores?"

"We sure don't need any more wood, so my guess is you do this when you got some thinking to do."

"My brain works better when my body tosses in its two cents worth. You didn't answer me. To what do I owe the honor?"

"You and Miss Bessy have opened your hearts to me and made me feel like one of your own. Sometimes colorblindness is not curable in these parts and these times. In this house and this family everybody is equal and for that I am forever grateful."

"May, why do I feel a 'but' coming?"

"I reckon it is time for May to move on. Y'all are doing fine and will be just fine without me here bossing yawls business."

"May, the children don't want you to go and neither do we? Why now?"

"It's just something that needs to be done."

"Where are you going to go?"

"That brother of mine said I could stay with him a spell."

"So, you have really made up your mind."

"The time comes when you need to wean the pups off the tit. That time is now."

We hugged and I had a hard time turning her loose. She was family, more family than most blood kin I had. She didn't give us much notice. Her brother picked her up the next morning and just like that, May Young was gone. Barely two months later we were attending her funeral. She had been sick but had not let on to us that she was. She had weaned us off her before the worst of the sickness took hold of her. She had not wanted the children or any of us to see her die at our home. She had spared us, always putting us ahead of herself.

We loved May Young and her passing left an empty spot in our hearts, weaned or not.

Low and behold, some surprise, I received a collect phone call, this time from my wayward sister, the day after we buried May. Carol was in Bakersfield, California and crying to beat the band as she told me how she missed me and was ready to come home. Burned too many times, I called her bluff telling her I would come get her and bring her back. The line went dead. I thought she had hung up figuring she realized she could not get money from me this time. She said fine through her sniffles and sobs then gave me an address. She then begged me to hurry. I caught Bessy up to speed and caught the next Greyhound.

"I reckon that's enough for right now, David. Couldn't hurt to stretch our legs. My old butt has nodded off and requires some circulation."

"This is one of those cliffhangers again, isn't it?"

"More like jumping off a cliff, David. Memories got a way of turning ugly even when you thought you had seen and already experienced the ugliest. We're not done, not by a long shot. Just a bit of a break, no more. Just humor an old cuss."

"I had no idea that our family had so many skeletons, Grandfather Nelson."

"Nothing swept underneath the rug, just not something we talk about and like I said, I am the last one standing to set the record straight. Blood letting ain't pretty, no matter where you fall in the pecking order."

Chapter 20

Funeral directors say bad things always come in threes. Good for their business. Bad for the rest of us. Well, I had finished one and was working on number two. Reliving this portion of my life was like bottoming out on bad shocks in a worn-out rutted road. No matter which way you steered, another pothole was there to rattle your teeth and jar your tailbone. What I would give for a smooth stretch of freshly laid asphalt about now. One thing about the past, you can't undo it and make it something else, something you would have rather it been. And trying to outrun it is a wasted effort.

"Well, David, some say that old age comes at a bad time in your life. Seems when you finally know everything, you start to forget everything you know. I reckon I have not quite reached that age yet."

"I can see that this is difficult for you, and it need not be. We can skip it if you wish Grandfather Nelson."

"Skipping is for throwing rocks across a pond or preventing from being entangled in a jump rope. Words are powerful and if used wisely can change your life. People, including kinfolk, come and go, only the right ones stay. Sometimes you are doing or saying enough, even if it doesn't feel like it. Failure is when you don't try and just flat give up or lose the notion. People offering random acts of kindness can make everybody feel better, but kindness of any sort is worth practicing. There are those that believe living for today and not tomorrow makes them stronger and refusing to look back is better practiced because there is nothing there for you. I say, hogwash. Too much overthinking only promises unhappiness. What I got to share is worrisome, but it happened. As you know by now our family is a festering sore, oozing pain and hurt like having a case of the shingles. Mostly incurable, you got to let it run its course."

"I'm not sure that I followed all that. Might take me replaying it a few times."

"Life is filled with lessons if you can just look pass the regrets. The youth of today, present company excluded, don't grasp the concept of communication. They don't listen to understand. Instead, they focus on their reply. Stressed and blessed might sound similar from a wordy perspective but that's where the similarity stops. Speaking of, I am getting a might too wordy and a bit too preachy. Time to cut to the chase. Mash the button on that little recorder, David."

There is no quick way to travel coast to coast unless you are willing to fly in an airplane. I wasn't. It better suited my billfold to buy a bus ticket. Driving was out of the question. I hated leaving Bessy to tend to the children alone now that we no longer had May. Travis gave me what time I needed to do what needed to be done for my sister. We were kind of between jobs which made my asking a little better timed.

Riding that Greyhound to California brought back a flood of recollections, ones of me and Jeremy heading there to find Carol and coming up empty handed. I could only wonder if the same outcome awaited me this time. She had sounded so desperate and fearful of whatever was going on in her life without stating any specifics. Either she was ashamed or scared or both. Not knowing what scenario I would be walking into was concerning to say the least. She was my sister. I would muster what was necessary to face it head on. The important thing was to bring her home while she was willing to return.

Greyhounds hadn't improved much from my last ride on one. People watching was still a way to pass the time. Other than that, you could gawk at the passing countryside or think yourself half to death. At least I had cash in my pocket and there would be no shoplifting required. It was an agonizingly long ride anyway you measured it, three days there and three days back, not counting time spent there. I had not purchased return tickets yet figuring I needed to assess her situation first. In the back of my mind, I wondered if she would still be there when I arrived. Carol was not dependable, not by a long stretch. Ask poor Jupiter. If all went well and I managed to bring her back with me then I would call Jupiter. The boy didn't deserve anymore false hopes.

With no craziness like my last trip, we finally arrived in Bakersfield in three days as scheduled. I showed the taxi driver the address scribbled on a piece of paper. He nodded and we were off. I became a bit concerned as we traveled deeper into a seedy part of town. What did I know about Bakersfield? Maybe all of it looked like what I was seeing. He finally pulled the taxi to a stop and announced we were here. I watched his eyes in the rearview mirror. He was looking about nervously as he held his hand out for the fare. I only had a small bag so there was no need for him to help me with it, not that he ever offered. I stepped out, closed the door and was about to ask if he would wait for me. He sped away before I could utter my request. Probably just as well. I had to locate Carol and had no idea how long it would take.

The streets were filthy and almost deserted. Many buildings had their windows boarded up or were missing glass all together. I instinctively removed the cash from my wallet and slipped it in my sock along with my driver's license. The area reminded me of a ghost town, if tall buildings would have existed in the wild west. I looked at the address on the paper and began perusing the doorways on my side of the street. The taxi driver said we had arrived so I must be close.

Rustling from behind alerted me I was not alone. I snuck a peek over my shoulder. A ragged old man flopped down on the sidewalk with a defining thump. He never looked in my direction. I quickened my pace looking for the address I had scribbled on the paper. The building numbers were ascending so that meant I was walking in the wrong direction. I must backtrack. If I did, I might have to pass the old feller now sprawled belly up on the sidewalk. Thankfully I spotted the building number. The nine in 106 almost threw me off until I realized it wasn't nine but a six, the number loose and upside down.

I pushed the door, and it made an awful screeching noise, one of accumulated rust and no oil. The stench of rotted food and feces almost took my breath. I quickly placed my handkerchief over my nose and mouth then stepped over and through the mounds of garbage and who knows what else. I made haste and quickly found the apartment number Carol had provided. Luckily it was on the first floor if there was any such thing as luck in this hell hole. I knocked on the door. No response. I reluctantly rapped louder hoping not to bring any attention to myself. Still, there was no answer. I mustered up a 'Carol' just above a whisper. Nothing! I knocked and said her name louder. A door opened down the hallway and a head, mostly eyes peering from it before the door slammed shut. Sweat was running down the back of my neck and dripping from my nose. I tried the doorknob and found it wasn't locked. I eased it slightly open and called out to Carol. No answer. The stench from inside took my breath. I stepped back sucking in some fresh air, at least fresher than I had just inhaled.

I closed my eyes and whispered a quick prayer before trying a second time. With the handkerchief still in place I stepped inside. Rats scurried away as did the largest cockroaches I had ever seen. Flies were buzzing about; those large green blowflies that were usually drawn to animal carcasses. The room was one huge garbage pile. I stepped over and around as much as I could until pushing some aside with my feet.

Oh Lord, I saw a tiny foot protruding from the boxes. It wasn't moving and it was shoeless. It left no doubt that it belonged to a child and the child must be dead. I emptied the contents of my stomach adding to the stench that could not be escaped. I stumbled backward over a stool and fell on my backside my fall broken by a mattress on the floor. Anchoring the other end of that nasty mattress was my sister Carol in a sitting position, eyes and mouth open. She was dead too. By the condition of her body, she hadn't been dead long. Dead was still dead no matter how you figured it.

She had said for me to hurry. Three days had been three days too long. I was too shocked to shed a tear. Instead, I exited the building in search of a phone. I had to walk nearly ten blocks before I located one that worked and had more close calls with those that lived in the area than I could ever count. An ambulance eventually arrived and took hers and the child's body to the nearest morgue. Against policy they gave me a ride. I identified her body but could not identify that of the fragile little boy. The coroner thought the child was probably hers. Both suffered from malnutrition. Carol had signs of drug abuse and she had been physically abused as well, according to the coroner.

I arranged for both bodies to be returned and that had to be done by train. I traveled back on the train as well, wondering what the boy's name might have been. Carol had left no notes or information. It would remain a mystery as to where she had been all these years and I could only imagine what life she had lived. I wondered how many other children she had birthed whose lives had ended tragically. I did contact Jupiter before leaving and brought him up to speed. He would be there and waiting before we arrived home. Bad things do indeed happen in threes…May, Carol and most likely my nephew and half brother to Jupiter.

Bessy thought we should at least give the child a name. I left that up to Jupiter. Without hesitation he named him Michael Whiteside. When I asked why Michael he said, "Michael is the archangel who led the other angels in a war against Satan. I read this in the Bible. I believe my little brother was a warrior and he fought a good fight against the devil and everything that was thrown at him, good versus evil, until he could fight no more. He had to depend on himself and not our mother."

"Michael it is then and a fine name and wonderful reason for the namesake, Jupiter."

"You gave me the Whiteside name, Uncle Nelson. I felt he deserved it as well."

That was that. Carol and Michael Whiteside were laid to rest. Carol did not receive the fanfare that Michael did. I still could not fathom what her life must have been like, but I was making no excuses for my sister's behavior. Unlike Michael, Jupiter had been lucky to have survived what must have been an awful ordeal. With any luck and God's grace, Rachel and Petey had as well wherever they might be. As for me, I had lost a brother and sister to tragic circumstances and like Rachel and Petey, Jeremy was still out there somewhere. The difference, Jeremy had made his choices. Rachel nor Petey had any say in theirs.

Not surprising but disappointingly so, Jupiter didn't hang around very long and returned to his life in Saint Louis. Bessy, me and the children did our best to return to ours. Through the tragic circumstances we found ourselves blessed yet again, Bessy now with our third child. We would be without May Young this time. Thankfully, according to the doctor, she was not in a fragile state this time. Third time was the charm. Her body had gotten used to spitting out these little pups. We were blessed with another son. We named him Michael Nelson Whiteside. He would be our last, three being indeed the charm.

Mostly, life for the Whiteside, was normal, almost boring for years to come. This was a pleasant change given our family's ugly history. Jupiter had gotten hitched and started a family. He made a fine daddy. Bessy and I had fared well too. Our young'uns sprouted like beanstalks, none of them showing any of the crazier Whiteside traits. James Edwin, (Jimmy), had shown an interest in becoming a schoolteacher. Clara Faye was musically inclined. Michael marched to his own drum beat but leaned toward wanting to be a policeman. We never tried to influence any of them, preferring to let them decide what they wanted to be.

It had been almost twenty years since we buried Carol and Michael when, yet another surprise graced our doorsteps. Jeremy returned out of the blue. We had not heard from him at all during this time, expecting the worse given my sibling's history. More surprising, he was married to boot. Had been for almost ten years. He had two children in tow, seven-year-old twins, a boy and a girl. At first glance, seemed he was a little late in life starting a family. His wife was much younger than him. Jeremy looked as if he had been rode hard and put up wet. The years had not been kind to him by the looks of him. Still, he seemed content and happy with his marriage and children. Her name was Meagan, and the children were Alvin Stewart and Alvina August. The boy went by Al and the girl August.

Given the family history I was waiting for the next shoe to drop, something dark and dirty from the past to tarnish what on the surface looked to be a normal family. Bessy kept hushing me up saying just let it be and accept them for better or worse. I wasn't marrying them so this better or worse didn't hold water. So far, no 'worse' had raised its ugly head. It didn't mean that I wasn't expecting it though. I just kept it to myself, avoiding more elbows from my wife and less bruised ribs.

Jeremy was hush mouthed about sharing where he had been all these years. Given what had happened to our sister I was just glad to see him above dirt. He had not known of Carol's death. I caught him up to speed. Not much really to tell. We did talk about old times, those days escaping from the carnival's clutches and our adventures out west. We laughed about them now but there was nothing funny about them back then. He was thinking about settling down in the area. I was shocked, hearing him utter the words 'settle down' but was glad to hear him say it. Seeing was believing though. Had he really changed? None of my siblings had ever been the homey settling type. I was the one that had broken the mold or curse depending on how you wanted to spin it.

Bessy and I took a liking to Meagan. She was courteous and down to earth. Al and August were well mannered too. Maybe it had taken someone like her to turn Jeremy's life around. I asked him what he wanted to do as far as work was concerned. He wasn't sure. I told him I could put in a good word with Travis. He and his son now ran the construction business. Travis had made me a crew leader, so I was an overseer now and rarely ever operated any equipment. Other than that stupid accident, I had been blessed with a healthy body and soul, even though I missed operating the heavy machinery.

It was Fall and the County Fair was in progress. I watched Jeremy closely for any signs that he might be hankering for that life again. So far so good. He never mentioned it. I refrained from monitoring it also. Jeremy seemed committed to being a family man, but I found it odd he was not quick to commit to finding a job. I stopped bringing it up. He had taken up board at the trailer park near town. They always had vacant trailers for rent at Happy Valley Trailer Court. Most were not in the greatest shape. I thought back to how I had found Carol and Michael and the conditions didn't seem so bad by comparison.

It was going on two weeks that they had been back and then something changed. I couldn't put my finger on it though. It was more of a feeling than anything. Bessy noticed it first, saying Meagan was acting a bit peculiar. She had asked her if she could keep the children a few times. She never mentioned why, and Bessy didn't feel it was her place to ask. I was off on a worksite for about a week and when I returned, I found Bessy tending to them again. She missed having ours around. Jimmy had gotten hitched. Clara was away in college. Mike had joined the National Guard and was off on an assignment overseas. He was studying to be a lawman.

We were about to break bread and have supper when a knock on the door stopped us dead in our tracks. It was a lady for the social services accompanied by a deputy sheriff. She asked if Al and August were with us and then said she was there to pick them up.

"Hold your horses little lady. These chaps belong to my brother. They are fine. We are taking care of them for a spell."

"I hate to be the one to tell you, but these children are not your nephew and niece. They belong to Meagan McGrath."

"Aka, Wanda Horton," added the deputy. "We picked her up for prostitution."

"Now, please Mr. and Mrs. Whiteside, I must remove these children from your custody," said Mrs. Cranston the social worker.

"What about my brother, doesn't he have a say in this, even if they aren't his biological children? They're married. These are his stepchildren."

"Sir, your brother is in custody to for solicitation of prostitution. He was Wanda Horton's accomplice, drumming up business for her. And no, they aren't married. Like Mrs. Cranston said, these are not his children," said Deputy Wainwright. "We're both just here to do our jobs and I respect you for doing what you thought was right."

Bessy and I watched, jaws unhinged, as these two precious children were placed with Mrs. Cranston in the backseat of the patrol car. My brother and his alleged wife were common criminals. My family had reached new lows, lower than I thought possible given how my sister had deserted her children and my other brother had taken his own life. It was hard to figure how I had turned out like I had having lived under the same roof and under the same conditions. I was now wondering if I had a dark side that hadn't emerged yet, something that hadn't been triggered. One by one they had each done the despicable, the unthinkable, and mostly without any remorse. I could nor would ever defend any of them and their actions, blood kin or not.

Bessy and I were awe struck and dumbfounded by what had just happened. I believed that my brother had returned with honest intentions, homesick, ready to plant roots and reunite with family. How had I, we been so easily deceived? After the carnival close call, I would have thought he had learned his lesson. What had he gotten into the last years while he was missing in action as far as family was concerned? I reckon it was obvious given the path he had chosen. Brothels had always existed but now men had taken the reins, seeking those who would pay for whatever fantasy they craved. My bother was now one of those filthy scoundrels.

Not a surprise, Jeremy exercised his right to a phone call and called me. He begged me to pay whatever money they wanted to spring him from the poky. I had been burned by Carol, not knowing she was conning me; may she rest in peace. There was no doubt that Jeremy was conning me. He just wanted out at any cost, and that cost would come at my expense. I almost agreed with stipulations for him to walk the straight and narrow but then I came to my senses. He would say and do anything to obtain a get of jail free card and then would most likely hightail it out of here. He never mentioned

193

me helping his professed wife Meagan McGrath, aka, Wanda Horton. It being all about him spoke volumes.

Bessy was more forgiving than me. She leaned toward us helping. I couldn't do it. To me it would be no better than aiding and abetting my brother. He would promise anything to get what he wanted. He had already proved my point through his deceitful lies. Bessy was worried about Al and August even if they weren't kin. I sympathized with her feelings but told her it was not our business. The deeper we allowed ourselves to get involved the tougher it would be for us to get out of it. You can't save the world. You must pick your battles. We certainly owed this Meagan or Wanda anything. My gut told me this was probably not her first run-in with the law. My gut was telling me the same thing about my brother. Might be that they came here to escape where they had come from, the heat having gotten too hot for the kitchen or worse.

Jeremy had made his bed and it was now time for him to face the consequences. This didn't make my decision any easier to swallow. He was my brother and I loved him. This wasn't like marriage though. For better or worse did not apply as far as I was concerned. I had already ventured down the 'until death do us part' road with Keith and Carol. I did my best to convince myself that jail time might be what he needed. Perhaps it would help him turn things around. Then again, maybe he had already served time and if he had it, had not rehabilitated him. There were not enough prayers to help our dysfunctional family.

As it turned out, and as my gut had directed me, this was not his first offense. He had many incarcerations including shoplifting, embezzlement, skipping bail and now this. He had indeed been moving about to stay ahead of the law. There were warrants for him in five states. At least he had not committed murder nor robbed any banks or at least he

194

had not been caught and convicted for any. There was no bailing him out of this one, even if I wanted to, given what else they had on him. When the dust had settled, he would be doing some serious jail time but not here. Other warrants required him to be extradited to another state.

I did visit him once before they extradited him. He remained smug, unremorseful and extremely angry at me for not trying to help him. You cannot help someone who is not willing to help themselves. Jeremy cared for only Jeremy. He cursed me for all it was worth saying I would get mine one day and hoped he would be around to see it. His words unsettled me thinking that a family curse did indeed loom over our heads. I was the last one unaffected for now.

"David, knowing what you know now, do you regret opening Pandora's 'Whiteside' Box?"

"I said from the beginning Grandfather Nelson that I wanted to hear it all no matter what. You are no more responsible than my dad or me for what happened all those years ago."

"Your dad was married and far away when the Jeremy family blemish occurred. I didn't try to hide it from him. It has always been his choice not to ever share it with you. Maybe he is ashamed or has just swept it under the rug. I reckon there is not much to be gained airing such dirty laundry. Some things are best left buried but burying it does mean it didn't happen. Ugly is ugly."

"I am not holding it against him for not sharing it with any of us. I suppose he has his reasons."

"Well, David, some live by simple rules, not always easy to follow but rules just the same. A feller once told me that he abided by eight pieces of wisdom and took the time to share them with me. I will repeat them as best as I can remember. He said that words were powerful, adding that it was important to use them wisely. He always said that people come and go in your life, but the right ones usually stay. Failure is nothing more than not trying in the first place.

195

He professed that practicing random acts of kindness will make all who are involved feel better. He believed that you must always live for today and not for tomorrow. He said that it was best to not look behind you because there was usually not much there in the first place. Lastly, he would grin like a possum when he said people overthink too much and it is bound to ruin happiness if you do. Feller's name was Gabriel Fowler, the best crane operator I have ever been privileged to work with. Died in an explosion on an oil rig in the Gulf of Mexico some years later. He had tried to get me to go with him. I could not wrap my head around living on one of those platforms in the ocean with no land in sight."

"Did Uncle Jeremy ever get out of prison?"

"He did."

"Did you and he bury the hatchet?"

"That is a bit more complicated than saying yes or no. There is more to share before we arrive at that juncture."

"You have the keys, drive where you wish, Grandfather Nelson."

"You would think I should be running out of members from our family tree by now. My generation was surely falling by the wayside. We'll leapfrog a bit further, more into your daddy's stretch and my young'uns making their mark."

"Am I really prepared for this revelation?"

"It is part of the journey. Without it, you wouldn't be here, David."

"Fire away then Grandfather Nelson."

Chapter 21

"I'll pick up with your daddy, James Edwin Whiteside and your mama Angela Kay. They were blissfully happy and had known each other since the first grade. As you know, your daddy followed his dream and became a schoolteacher. He was a natural at it and his students loved him. Well, most did. There are always bad apples in the bunch."

"Yes sir, I know he was a teacher, but he never said why he stopped teaching."

"Well, you were young, David, the youngest. I suspect your daddy didn't know how to explain it to you at the time. He had his reasons. I am probably talking out of school so to speak if I take it on myself to tell you. I should leave that to Jimmy. We could skip this part and you could ask him."

"I have asked him before and he just said it was his time to give it up. His time? That doesn't make sense. He did not retire. He just quit. He's not going to tell me so you may as well do it."

"I don't want him to be mad at you nor me, David."

"It's part of the family story, right? It is more personal to me than most of what you have shared so far."

"All right then, we will take our lumps like Whiteside men if we must. Once I tell you, you might decide that just knowing is enough without letting him know that you know."

"I can't make any promises Grandfather Nelson."

"Best not to make what you are not sure you can keep. Mash the button and here we go."

> Jimmy was an honor student in school. He had indeed followed his dream in college to be a teacher. We were proud of all our children. Clara Faye had stuck with her music and even went into teaching too, becoming a music teacher.

197

Michael navigated a life in the armed forces with the Guard while pursing a life in law enforcement. His would eventually take a different path but that is another story as well. Jimmy and Angela Kay got hitched shortly after high school which slapped them with an extra burden, Jimmy working his way through college while doing his best to raise a family. Oswald was born their first year. A wife, a child and school were a handful for him. He worked a fulltime job at nights while pursuing his college degree. Bless Angela Kay for holding the family together like glue with all this going on. Jimmy schooled, worked and slept, leaving him little wiggle room to be the husband and daddy I know he wanted to be. As parents and spouses, they made many ultimate sacrifices to secure their future.

His second year in college Anna was born. Two children now in the mix and two more years of schooling left. Angela Kay would not hear of him giving up on his dream. They made do and dealt with everything like true champs. Bessy and I helped where we could but them not living close by prevented us from doing more. He was starting his third year while raising a two and three year old. I'm not sure I could have toughed that out. I worked to make ends meet when Jimmy, Clara and Michael were young, but I had help for a spell with May. I was not burdened with college. That boy had gumption and determination. It helped to have the support of Angela Kay. And we had hit a stretch where we didn't have family craziness disrupting the apple cart. That alone was a mighty huge blessing. That didn't mean there were no distractions.

His final year was his toughest. The Viet Nam War was in full swing, and colleges were often in the middle of it, protesting the war. Jimmy did his best to stay out of the fray but sometimes the fray had a different notion. Peer pressure can be mighty persistent and impatient. Picking sides was expected and those in college were expected to side with what they called 'the movement.'

Anti-war protesters were the 'in thing'. Jimmy did his best to avoid the controversy but ignoring it just drew more unwanted attention. To pacify his classmates, he participated in one of the sit-ins just to get them off his back. What harm could it do? Lesson was learned the hard way when his photograph with the rowdy bunch was plastered on the front page of the newspaper and then picked up by one of the television networks. He was the one standing closest to the photographer holding a sign 'End the War in Viet Nam', making him the protester poster boy. He became the campus hero. This did not set well with us, and especially with his brother Michael serving in the Guard, when we saw him on the news. It made it tough on all of us, living in a community where everybody supported the soldiers and the United States of America. How dare our son be one of those violent America hating traders. Jimmy swore to us that he wasn't one of them and even though we believed him, a picture is worth a thousand words. The jury had convicted him guilty as charged.

He did his best to stay out of the limelight and on the sidelines, but the activists would not allow it. He had to play the part, but he wanted none of it. Keeping the peace at college required that he support peace and the end of the war. He did manage to not get caught on camera again, but the damage was done. He was a marked man, one of them, like it or not. His saving grace if there was one, he had a job that left him very little time to march and spew the mantra. Eventually, he faded into the woodwork and someone else carried the torch.

Jimmy finished, got his degree, his golden ticket to teaching but not without consequences. In some teaching circles he was still recognized as being one of them. The old guard of teachers, those bleeding the red, white and blue, did not embrace practicing their profession with anti-American pacifist. His opportunities were non-existent. Word spreads. He was being blackballed. The haunting memory of that photograph would not simply disappear. Jimmy did his best to explain it away, but he was only met by those claiming he was lying just to get a job, fearing once he was hired, he would just try to spread his anti-American rhetoric. Bessy and I felt his pain but there were little we could do either. Shunned parents had no pull.

Clara Faye and Michael caught plenty of flack as well. It seemed odd given that Michael was serving in the Guard. Guilty by association and, in this case, blood kin. Bessy and I ached for our children and what they were going through. We prayed that this would blow over. The protests persisted. Jimmy finally reached his fill. He uprooted his family and moved north in hopes of starting over where no one knew him. He managed to get hired in a tiny boondock's town as History Teacher, of all things. He kept a low profile as he furthered his foothold at school and the small community. He even grew a beard to try to hide his identity. The school frowned on facial hair for their teachers, so he was forced to shave it off. Jimmy's students loved him. He was a natural in the teaching ranks. Being out of college allowed him to spend more valuable time with his family.

"Grandfather Nelson, sorry to interrupt but I never knew he had suffered so because of his accidental involvement in the war protests."

"You know your daddy; he always tries to focus on the positive things in life. But as those idiotic info commercials go, 'but wait there's more.' His hide and seek plan worked for a while until a seeker sought him out."

Jimmy had progressed nicely, almost four years in, and the school had taken note. The principle was retiring, and some were pushing him to be the replacement. As in any occupation, it isn't without politics and personal gain. Some feller, and I forget his name, wanted the head honcho job as well. He couldn't beat Jimmy purely on his academic accomplishments, so he took the down and dirty approach, determined to discredit him somehow. The weasel managed the uncover the article and photo of Jimmy protesting the war. You would have thought this would be no big deal years after the war, but some still viewed it as a sore spot, a disgraceful blemish against those that had fought in Viet Nam. The retiring principle was a decorated war hero and was held in high regard by the community. When word got out that Jimmy was one of those that had protested the war it was not taken lightly. How could they allow someone with such a disgraceful past follow in the footsteps of their beloved war hero? Those supporting Jimmy quickly fell by the wayside and refused to listen to his side of the story. To further make their point, Jimmy was let go. He was devastated as were many of his loyal students.

Jimmy up and moved his family again. He had a few months between the next school year to search for a new school. Uprooting his family was tough though. His past would not stay where it belonged, an innocent man, still perceived as guilty and disgraceful in the eyes of those unwilling to forget how solders were mistreated. Over the next few years, he moved about for one reason or another, mostly when there were links to his past on the brink of surfacing. It is difficult to understand how that generation took such hard stances on one side or the others. The folks in the military uniforms and those supporting them would not forget. Jimmy was almost a casualty of war himself. He had no way to clear his name. You would have thought that he was joined at the hip with that disgraceful actress, Hanoi Jane.

Ten or more years had passed, and he had finally found a spot where his past didn't seem so important any longer. He had even made it up the ladder to vice principle. Life for the Whiteside clan had hit a stretch of normalcy, something we weren't accustomed to. Never mistake the calm because there are always storm clouds threatening every surreal moment. My Bessy took sick. It was a gradual decline, so gradual that she didn't see to herself properly. She didn't even mention she was experiencing some health issues. Not one to complain, she just got by as best she could. By the time even I figured out that something was terribly wrong it was too late. The doctor diagnosed her with ovarian cancer, one of the worst kinds for a woman to have. She died within months. We had been married for forty-three years.

"David, I wish you could have known your grandmother. She passed before you were even born. No surprise to you, there is a large age gap between you and your siblings. That was not by design. Sometimes things just happen for reasons we can't explain."

"I always figured I was a mistake. Nobody made me feel like I was but how else could it be explained that I was born so late in their lives."

"Hush now, you were not a mistake. On the contrary you were a blessing. I reckon your parents have let you down by not filling you in on how you rewarded their lives. Well, I'm here to set the record straight."

Losing my Bessy was the worst hurt I had ever experienced, second closest when she suffered the miscarriages. That curse of tragedies, coming in threes, raised its ugly head again, the devil determined to test our faith. People find it so much easier to blame the Lord when bad things happen to them and forget that the evil prince of darkness likes having his hands in our lives, always looking for ways to skew our thinking. Brother Jeremy had gotten out of a prison a few years prior but as Jeremy always does, he quickly vanished. We were the closest thing to family he had left and he just up and went without so much as a goodbye or anything. One day after we buried my Bessy, he shows up out of the blue like he always does. He needed money but as usual he offered no explanation for where he had been and why he was dirt broke. One look at him and I could see he was in a bad way health wise.

So, what do you do, give him money or not? I offered him a bed and food but neither seemed that important to him. I thought about Keith and how he had hanged himself in the barn. And then there was Carol. Somehow, I had to manage this situation better and save my brother from himself. To hear his account, he didn't need saving. He just needed some cash. I knew if I forked over any he would be long gone yet again. The dark circles under his eyes, his gaunt frame and the persistent cough told me all I needed to know. If he left this time, I would never see him again, not alive anyway.

I was the youngest and the only one that had done my best to live a normal life. I had lost Bessy. I was not willing to chance losing Jeremy. Question though, how can you hold a person against their will even if it is for their protection. I used stall tactics telling him that I would not have cash until Friday when I got my paycheck. Today was Monday. I had four days as to scheme how I could derail his ill-fated plans. First things first, get him cleaned up, offer him a change of clothes and force feed him if I had to. He didn't fight me over the bath or change of clothes. Getting him to eat was another issue. By his shakes and slurred speech, I knew he thought he needed a drink in the worse way. Luckily, I did not have any. Not so lucky from his perspective. Someone with addictions will find a way to satisfy their need. Jeremy drank my aftershave then downed a quarter bottle of rubbing alcohol. I had not known he had consumed either until toxic behavior resulted and I pried out of him what he had done.

I rushed him to the hospital. He died there. I didn't know it until later that ingesting rubbing alcohol could lead to death within thirty to sixty minutes. I had no idea how long it had been since he had drunk it. Bessy, now Jeremy, my last brother, gone. Terrible things come in threes. Who could be next if the superstition held water? I tried not to dwell on it even though it was clinging somewhere in the back of my mind. Three days later I buried my brother, my last direct kin. I felt alone in the world even though Jimmy and his family, Clara Faye and Michael were there for the funeral. Jupiter called but couldn't make it. All of them left the next day. I couldn't blame them. They had their own lives and Uncle Jeremy had not been around them for most of his.

I returned to work and when Friday arrived, I was overcome with regrets, thinking how I had pushed back on Jeremy, stalling for time, time he did not have. Obviously, I had no way of knowing to what extremes he would go because of his addiction, or I may have handled it differently. Mulling over it now served no purpose. He was dead and would remain dead. I had not had time to mourn Bessy and now this. I had never felt so alone. God stood firmly by my side and lifted me up when I needed Him the most. I hadn't attended church as regularly as I should have. I was often off on jobs when Sunday rolled around. A man can always make excuses if he wants to. I was God fearing even if I didn't do right by Him on a daily basis. I didn't blame Him for losing Bessy or Jeremy. Blame gets you nowhere fast. I had plenty of wonderful years with my Bessy and a few scattered here and there with Jeremy. The carnival ordeal wasn't the best memory, but it was a memory just the same. We had bonded while on that across country excursion. I now recalled him shoplifting thinking was this the beginning of downward spiral or had it already begun while he was a carney.

It is tough to explain and understand how Keith, Carol and Jeremy had ventured down the dark paths they had taken and not me. None of us had been raised in a way that would push us in the directions they had chosen. I could almost understand Keith's life after being exposed to the horrors of war. Carol had gotten into one abusive relationship after another as if almost attracted to them. Jeremy, maybe he had just been destined to be freehearted roamer. Dwelling on their chosen lifestyles now would gain me no footing moving forward.

A week passed and the third shoe dropped if dropping a third shoe is even a possible analogy. This one was a humdinger. Thankfully it wasn't family that we lost but that didn't minimize the family impact. A murderous shooter had infiltrated Jimmy's school. With the principle out of town Jimmy being the vice principle had gotten caught in the crosshairs so to speak. He had been in the hallway when the gun toting scoundrel had entered the building. Shoots were fired and Jimmy ducked inside one of the classrooms. A teacher was mortally wounded as she tried to close her classroom door. The shooter moved down the hall room to room checking for one that had not been already locked. When he reached the one where Jimmy had entered, his patience had run thin. He opened fire on the door until he breached entry. Jimmy and the teacher had done their best helping children escape through the windows. Jimmy, Mrs. Reardon and three seven-year-olds had not been so lucky. The shooter opened fire with both Jimmy and Mrs. Reardon doing their best to use themselves as barriers to protect the children. She was killed as was the child she was protecting. Jimmy was shot too but the two children hunkered behind him had not been harmed. The shooter made a hasty retreat hearing the sirens approaching.

As it goes so often in situations like this, the lone gunman took his own life. A tenth grader, he had been expelled by the principle a month earlier for aggressively bullying others and verbally threatening another teacher. Jimmy had been shot twice, once in the abdomen and in the neck. Luckily neither had hit a main artery. The wounds were significant though.

He missed the remainder of the school year as he rehabbed from his injuries, both physical and emotionally.

"Your daddy never returned to teaching after that tragedy. Seeing Mrs. Reardon and that child murdered in cold blood as he tried his best to offer protection did a number on him. I call you a blessing and not a mistake because from death there came life. A year after that awful ordeal you were born. The timing could not have been more perfect. Bringing you into the world gave your daddy, your parents a purpose to move on with their lives. Your daddy focused on family and worked an office job, forfeiting what he had always desired to do, teach."

"I knew he had been a teacher, but he never said why he quit. Not ever seeing him in that role I had no reason to pursue the reasons. Thank you again, Grandfather Nelson, for clearing this up for me. After that anti-war fiasco he became a hero, didn't he?"

"That incident didn't make Jimmy a hero. In principle he fought hard for what he believed in and always wanted to be, a teacher. He overcame surmountable odds to fulfill his dream. Yes, maybe that ended earlier than he would have desired, but he found peace in being a father. He cherished what was most important, loving and protecting his family, being the best provider, he could be. I am proud of him and all my children. I think they were responsible for breaking the Whiteside family curse."

"Do you really believe our family was cursed?"

"If it weren't for bad luck, we wouldn't have had much luck at all in our world of forced family fun. Curse might be a bit harsh. No denying it, we were dogged by events unlike what most families went through. As you have heard, we had our share of skeletons in the family closet. We took crazy and quirky to new levels. I'm glad you got to know your grandmother Annie. I had never thought I would find love again. I reckon better said, love found me."

Chapter 22

"It's getting late, are you sure you want to continue David?"

"If you are tired, we can stop Grandfather Nelson."

"Takes more than something like this to wear me down. I'm a night owl by nature. It floats my boat talking about way back yonder times. Especially when I have someone like you that is interested in hearing it. How much juice you got left in that little recorder?"

"It's good. How much juice do you have left?"

"I reckon that thingamajig will wear out before I am apt to. What you say we test it? Me against the technological machine."

"Something tells me that my recorder doesn't have a dog in this hunt as you often say."

"Don't know about a dog in the hunt but I suspect it is going take more than that contraption to tree an old varmint like me. Mash the button and let's take it to the limit, David."

> Bessy was my heart. There is no replacing your one true love. Forty-three years is a long time to spend with one woman. We shared all the ups and downs and topsy turvy life tossed at us. None of it could be measured in wins or losses. They happened and we reacted and handled them for that better or worse part. Sometimes we came out on top and other times we got our butts kicked. Reckon our butts got kicked a plenty. One thing for sure, we never let anything knock us down that we couldn't get back up from. We might have beat a slow count a time or two, but nobody ever counted us out. Come hell or high water, we persevered. I can't say the same for kinfolk but that has already been established. One thing for sure, dying is part of living.
>
> One year blurs into the next and you just do your best to move forward and keep up with the flipping pages of the calendar. Travis had turned his construction business over to

his sons. I was still one of their foremen, but they kept me mostly involved in local jobs. I reckon they thought I was getting too old to travel. That was their opinion though. I could still run circles around any of the young whippersnappers. I could operate equipment better than most too, if need be. Truth be known, I would have preferred traveling some. It beat going home to that gosh awful empty house every afternoon.

Time at home led me to attending church a lot more than I ever had. No snake handlers in this one. It was a small rural one. Smaller was better in my opinion. You got to know the congregation on a first name basis. Some you got to know too well. Every church goer is not there to receive the Holy Ghost, let me tell you. There are a lot attending that make you scratch your head. I suspect plenty thought the same about me, given my rocky history of being absent more times than being present.

Being a widow can be a lonely existence. I still worked and that helped occupy my time but coming home to an empty house can sure put life in perspective. I had run short on family, and I wasn't much of a socialite. I mostly kept to myself. Too much of that is not good for anybody. I hadn't become one of those hermits or reclusive types but if not for church I might have become something close.

My children kept in touch as often as they could, phoning me or sometimes working in a visit. I loved spending time with the grands every chance I got. Those times were not nearly often enough. Some people told me I should get a dog for a companion. Some companion, you must feed and tend to critters. Plus, with me never knowing when I might be on the road it didn't make much sense, me having a dog. Excuse mostly, because I hardly ever was any further than same day driving distance from home. Others told me to get a hobby. If I didn't have time for a dog, I sure didn't have time to waste on a hobby.

Now that my Bessy was gone, I looked back, thinking I probably took her for granted. She was always there when I came home. She cooked and fed me, offered me backrubs and supported me unconditionally. She raised the children while I worked. What did I ever do for Bessy besides being a provider? I wasn't a drinker or rebel rouser. And I certainly wasn't unfaithful. A lot of the men in construction work that are away from home do fall into womanizing. I stayed clear of those types in my free time. I wasn't a gambler either. I worked too hard for my money and wasn't about to toss it away rolling dice or card playing. I kept to myself, kind of like how I was doing at home.

Nope, I was content as content can be, living the life I would rather not be living. Lonely can eat away at you no matter how much you try to convince yourself and others you're doing just fine. Forty-three years had worn me down and placed me slap dab in the middle of a comfort zone. Now I was quite uncomfortable not having that security blanket. People don't mean to be intrusive, but they just can't help themselves, always wanting to fix you up with somebody. I didn't need any matchmakers ruining my life with who they thought I should be hitched up with. It was always this one is a wonderful cook, that one was widowed too, the one over yonder has never been married and the one kin to somebody was just the perfect person for me. Good intentions, bad intentions, busybodies, mostly women with nothing better to do than mind my business. I did my best to be respectful and polite while turning down their offers. Some took it okay while others turned up their noses at me. Then there were the widows and spinsters that just wanted to fix me a meal for a price of course. My pigheadedness wore most of them down thankfully.

I had just gotten off a phone call with Jupiter and decided I wanted a root beer float from McSwain's Pharmacy in town. A storm was brewing to the west, not the best time for a drive but my sweet tooth won the argument. McSwain's was on the opposite side of town which meant a thirty-minute drive to satisfy my urge. It was Saturday afternoon and I had nothing else to do worth doing. Ten minutes into my drive the skies darkened, and the first huge drops hit my windshield. A flash of lightning and crack of thunder got my attention. I considered turning around but the storm would be there too. Another couple miles and the bottom let loose. Rounding the turn, I spotted a car in the ditch on the opposite side of the road. I didn't recognize the blue Chevy Impala, but I could make out a driver still sitting behind the wheel. It was terrible weather to be a good Samaritan. I pulled over anyway.

I could see the blown left rear that probably caused the car to swerve into the ditch, a ditch flooding with rainwater. Another bright flash of lightning told me that changing it was ill advised. I had left the house without my slicker not intending to fight Mother Nature but here I was faced with the torrent rain. I launched from my truck and ran across the road and tapped on the window. She rolled it down, a woman I still did not recognize. I told her who I was, where I lived and where I was heading adding that I would gladly change her tire but not recommended in the storm. She nodded saying she understood. It was then they I offered her a ride to town or home, wherever home was. She took me up on it saying she'd like to go home. I didn't have an umbrella, but she did. I advised her not opening an umbrella in lightning so had always said my mama. We ran back across the road, and I opened the driver's side door and she scooted across the seat.

"I'm Annie Donaldson. Thank you, Mister Whiteside, for assisting a lady in destress."

"Call me Nelson. Where do you live?"

"Take a right at the next intersection. My home is the old Craven place about eight miles further."

"Yeah, I know the place. I wondered what would happen to the homestead after Roy Craven passed last winter."

"Roy was my uncle on my mother's side. He left it to me saying I had always been his favorite niece. I was his only niece, and he had no nephews. I've been settling in the past week. Relocated from Chattanooga. I am opening a cloth store in town. That's where I had been before having the flat tire on my way back. Again, I do thank you Nelson. It was quite scary being stranded in that storm alone."

"You got any family here with you?"

"Just me. What about you?"

"Just me too. I mean I got family, but none live close by. Got two boys and a girl and three grandchildren. Had a wife but she died a spell back."

"Sorry to hear of your loss. I have no children and have never been married. Sometimes God's plan doesn't include what most take for granted."

"I reckon that's a mouthful. We'll get you out of this storm when it clears. I can see to it that your tire gets changed. You do have a spare, don't you?"

"I did but I had a flat during the move and never got around to getting it repaired or replaced. I apologize for being such a bother. I can call someone in town to come out and take care of it, that is, once they get my phone hooked up. Uncle Roy did not have one."

"Let's get you home first then we will figure out what needs to be done."

Well Annie was a nice Tennessee woman, born and raised there so she said. She even fixed me a root beer float for my troubles. Seemed she had a sweet tooth too and had root beer and vanilla ice cream on hand. It was her favorite. Imagine that. While we waited out the storm, I helped her hang some pictures and move some of the heavier furniture about. I was a regular handyman that afternoon and enjoyed every minute of it. Something to keep me busy on what might have been a lonely Saturday. When the storm finally passed it was too late to go to town to see about getting her another tire and nothing would be open Sunday either. She fixed homemade biscuits and fatback, washed down with a glass of buttermilk. It was a fine spread and hit the spot. I helped her with a few more chores before I figured it was time for me to head home and not wear out my welcome.

Annie invited me to join her for Sunday dinner and I invited her to join me at church. We spent pert near all Sunday together. I picked her up Monday morning and drove her to her cloth shop and then went to the construction site. After work I saw to fixing her tire and then followed her home and had supper with her. We had practically been joined at the hips since Saturday, a funny notion, me thinking of it that way. I enjoyed her company and likewise, she seemed to enjoy mine. My jaws hurt from all the talking and laughing we did. I had not enjoyed life so much since Bess had passed. Matter of fact, Bessy and I had gotten past this time spent together and rarely ever talked so much. I felt guilty thinking this way. It made me feel like I was cheating on her. I was no longer a grieving widower, but I don't know if grieving is supposed to have a time limit or expiration date. Bessy was dead and there was nothing I could do about her being dead. I meant no disrespect toward her or her memory, spending time with Annie. I had no intentions of getting involved with another woman. I had made that clear to all those matchmakers. Listen to me; thinking I might be getting involved. Was that what this was? Whatever it was and wherever it was headed I was caught in the current.

We began raising plenty of eyebrows showing up at church together every Sunday. Some of those widows and spinsters what had wanted to dig their claws into me hardly gave me the time of day. Suited me just fine. Nobody was trying that matchmaking anymore either. I had to pause and think on what I was thinking. Did this mean we were dating? I hadn't dated in over forty-five years so I could not decipher if we were or if we weren't. It felt natural whatever we were doing. Annie was three years younger than me, and I was sixty-seven. Neither of us was a spring chicken, not that it really mattered. She made me feel young and I think I had the same effect on her.

Two years we courted and then we decided it made sense that we get hitched to cut down on the wear and tear of having a long-distance relationship. Long distance being fifteen miles from my door to hers. I sold my place. We made her home ours. My family had taken up with Annie pretty quickly. She would never be Bessy, but she wasn't supposed to be. She said as much and let the children and grandchildren decide what they wanted to call her.

"She was Grandmother Annie to me, the only grandmother I had known on my father's side of the family. I remember her playing cowboys with me, calling herself Annie Oakley, the best sharpshooter in the whole Wild West."

"She was a pistol ball indeed, David. I can still see her smile, one that could melt you or open any door when greeting strangers. She filled the void, that big old hole left from the loss of Bessy. They were entirely different though. If I could have combined their qualities, I would have had the perfect soulmate. My Bessy never worked outside the home but dedicated her life to making our home.

Annie was everything but the homebody type. She could hold her own on the home front, but she loved working and meeting people. Annie was the ultimate people person, outgoing and even outrageous at times. One thing for sure, she was unpredictable. Spontaneity was her mantra while Bessy was, for the most part, calm and reserved, except for that one time when she challenged Livonia Barnhart defending Jupiter. That side didn't surface much, but when it did, Katy bar the door."

"I forget, Grandfather Nelson, how long were you and she married?"

"Not nearly long enough. Just ten years. She was seventy-three when she passed twenty years ago. I am glad you were old enough to remember her."

"Tell me more about her."

> She loved that cloth store and was a mighty fine seamstress to boot. She made everything frilly in our house. People practically lined up begging her to sew this and that or make them something special. She did well, combining her talents and selling cloth and whatnot. She encouraged me to give up the construction company but her persuasive tactics were not insulting. She never said I was too old, she just insisted that I should give up the daily grind and enjoy life more. Giving up anything was not in my DNA. Work kept me fit and alive. The sounds and smells of heavy machinery invigorated me to my very foundation. When she grasped what it meant to me, she backed off and let it be. I did sort of compromise eventually and cut back to three or four days a week. Travis and his sons cooperated with this little arrangement. Travis told me that a man knows when it is time to hang it up. He had hit that wall and turned it over to the youngsters. Sometimes one must be weaned off the hind tit like a mama dog does with her pups. My old boss and dear friend laughed saying I might be in the weaning stages.

I had not been one much for taking vacations. I regretted that Bessy and I had not seized the opportunity to travel and see other places. She never asked me to take her anywhere but that was just the way she was. I had a chance at redemption with Annie. I found out quickly that we were too much alike. She preferred working over traveling. Annie would say, 'What can the world offer us that we don't already have right here with each other.' I reckon redemption wasn't really in the cards, not that I really wanted to travel either. She would say things like, 'As we approach life's ending for us does it really matter what we bought or what we built, what we own and where we live? What's important is what we shared and not our successes that define us. Sure, they are a part of it but more importantly is that we live a life that matters and live a life of love.' She could say some profound things, a deep thinker she was.

Annie had no family to speak of. Like Jupiter, her mother had given her up too but at birth rather than deserting her later. She had never known her birth mom. Annie had been given up for adoption, her adopted parents footing all the medical expenses until she was born and then signed over so to speak. She was raised by wonderful parents. Her father had perished in a fire when she was seventeen. He was a fireman and while fighting a catastrophic high-rise fire the roof had collapsed on him while he attempted to rescue a dog trapped inside. Her mother had died of cancer, not the same kind that took Bessy. Hers was breast cancer. She was forty-six when she lost her battle. Annie had a lot of good years with her mother. Annie never desired to find her birth mother. She had perfect parents and didn't need finding the one that had given her up that might ruin what she had. She always said what could it accomplish. She had no more memory of her than the woman that forked her over had of a child she didn't keep.

I had always been healthy as horse. The only blemish on my health record was that dang accident I had on the construction site. Stupidity can be quite humbling. Annie had a unique outlook when it came to it as well. She would say stuff like, 'Good health doesn't necessarily come from medicine. It can come from something as simple as peace of mind, peace inside someone's heart, from laughter and life shared.' Annie could be quite the backyard philosopher. I reckon a lot of that rubbed off on me as well. She instilled in me new ways to look at situations, more of an eye open approach at viewing the world around us. She put to rest that saying that old dogs can't learn new tricks. This old dog was learning plenty under her stewardship.

We hardly ever had any bad times. She would not allow dark shadows in our lives. We were living and breathing and enjoying one another. She would point out that the Lord had already planned our destinies for us. Only we could derail those plans through careless actions. I can hear her saying, 'Embrace life. It is a circle of happiness, sadness sprinkled with hard times and good times. Don't let the hard times get the best of you. Keep the faith. Be patient. Good times are always just around the corner.' She would often tell me that we should never judge life as being difficult. If you do everything will always seem wrong. It is better to spend your energy focusing on what's right in your life and those good things to come. Be positive and you will always come out on top. Thinking better leads to feeling better about everything around you. That Annie knew how to spin it to make all gloom and doom disappear. We had some mighty fine years together.

Nothing made her happier than when the grandchildren were visiting or we were visiting them. She would tussle with the boys and have tea parties with the girls. I was in good shape, but she had energy tenfold. She was as natural playing cowboys as she was playing with dolls. Annie Oakley could transform to Barbie in a blink. I enjoyed watching her interact with them, never jealous but always envious of her relationship. She was just as comfortable threading a needle as skewing a red worm on a fishhook. I watched that woman climb trees with the best of them. She could throw a baseball or a football better than many of her male counterparts, present company included. She could be the perfect southern belle or a rowdy tomboy. God had blessed me with another good one.

Annie headed up the women's auxiliary at church and still had time to be a Boy Scout den mother, even though she didn't have children and no grandchildren lived in the area. She even worked the soup kitchen, recruiting yours truly to help too. She was the extrovert to Bessy's introvert. Oh, I loved them both. The Lord's plan had worked as perfectly as one with faith would expect it to work. Annie kept me on my toes, never knowing what charity we may be involved in next. She was indeed charitable to the core, saying that giving was always rewarded.

The church was breaking ground to build a new church to replace the old church. It was easier to start fresh than to continue patching up the old one. Annie volunteered my services, being that I could operate any of the construction equipment needed. Travis offered any of his equipment and some help from his crews to get the ball rolling; his donation even though he did not attend our church. I was almost slobbering, operating this and that as we laid out the foundation boundaries. In less than six months and under budget Preacher Douglas Powell was letting loose a sermon to christen the grand opening. Ours was a snake free zone but I did witness widow Celeste Davis feeling the Holy Ghost and speaking in tongues. I had not seen such a display since being a young'un when it scarred the tarnation out of me. I handled it better this time.

On to the next project. The grammar school needed a makeover. Yep, I was volunteered again. I was better in my element operating bulldozers and backhoes than brandishing a hammer and paint brush. At least I wasn't in charge of this one. I just followed orders even if it required me being a glorified gopher in some instances. Lucky for me I had a friendly face for support. Jupiter and his family were visiting for about a week, and I recruited him to help. It was better than wonderful, spending that extra time with him. Annie was beaming, too, relishing in the not so forced family fun. Like any project I throw myself into willingly or unwillingly, we completed it to the satisfaction of those who had recruited us. The only sad part, having to say goodbye to Jupiter and his family.

Shortly after they had departed Annie signed me up for another project. This is the same woman that had once asked me to retire, to take it easy and enjoy life. Still employed, I was working more vigorously away from work than I was at work. If retirement looked anything like I was experiencing, I would be more rested and content continuing to work. None of this fazed Annie, a perpetual ball of energy. She could perform cartwheels around me, and I was still feisty and energetic. I remained in awe of her, especially seeing the twinkle in her eyes when she was all in whatever we were doing…Scout's honor.

It was about then that Travis died. He suffered a widow maker heart attack. His sons were now fully running the show. While they respected me and my capabilities, they owed me nothing, lacked the loyalty of their father. That loyalty had gone both ways between me and Travis. I read the writing on the wall and instead of waiting for them to let me go, I decided to quit on my terms and timeline. I offered to work a notice, but they said it was not necessary, given how close their dad and I had been. Don't let the door hit me on the way out, in other words. I was now open for even more volunteering, no dust settling underneath my shoes, I suspected.

Annie supported my decision. Why wouldn't she, she had planted that seed years before. We even went to Gable's Diner to celebrate with a meat and three. Afterwards we had root beer floats over at the pharmacy. I was thinking I could get use to this lifestyle. We took the long way home and parked by the lake to watch the sunset. We held hands like two giddy high school teenagers parking on lover's lane. Sealing it with a long kiss we headed home for our first night of my retirement bliss. I asked her when she planned to call it quits too and she just smiled and rubbed my cheek, not exactly an answer or commitment.

I woke the next morning at my regular getting up time. Might not have to go to work but my work routine was still alive and well…alive and well! Annie was sleeping like a log, dead to the world, so I decided I would surprise her and cook breakfast. I wasn't the greatest cook, but I could whip up a mean breakfast. On the menu was scrambled eggs, bacon, grits and some of Annie's leftover biscuits open face, garnished with cheese and toasted inside the oven. I was beaming, admiring my spread. I poured Annie a cup of coffee, the perfect wakeup if she hadn't already caught a whiff of my cooking.

I set the coffee cup on her bedside table. She had her back to me, curled up. I sat down behind her, pushed her hair back and placed the back of my hand on her cheek. I jumped as if receiving an electric shock. She was cold as ice. The doctor said she had died peacefully in her sleep of natural causes. At the gravesite I spoke these words, "Good health doesn't necessarily come from medicine. It can come from something as simple as peace of mind, peace inside someone's heart, from laughter and life shared. We sure shared a life, didn't we Annie? I am reminded by something else that my dear Annie told me, 'It takes a lot of courage to push through the hard times. Never give up on anything no matter what obstacles are in your way. Good things are always coming sooner or later.' One of her favorite sayings, 'You can rely on the truth of only three things, a small child, a drunk or skintight britches.' Annie Oakley, shoot straight and I'll join you when His plan plays out."

Burying wives was getting no easier. I did my best not to question God's plan as to why I was still here, and they were gone. After all, He had blessed me twice, more than one man ever deserved. I almost allowed old lucifer to creep into my soul with thoughts of the Whiteside curse. I refused to let that red skinned devil ruin good memories with bad thoughts. If you let him get a hoof hold, he will dig in his claws. I figured the best way to fend him off, besides keeping the faith, was read some scripture. After the funeral I did just that and felt uplifted and burden free. I now faced the prospect of being in a lonely empty house once again. I was getting too old for this. The Lord had granted me a do-over with Annie. Now what? I was retired with too much free time on my hands. Annie had been the one orchestrating my volunteering. What now I wondered a second time, no closer to an answer than I was the first go round.

"I need a break, David, if that's all right with you. I promise we are not done. We will finish this even if we pull an all-nighter."

"I understand. Thank you again for sharing what must have been extremely difficult, Grandfather Nelson."

"On the contrary, treasures are meant to be cherished. Embrace life. It is a circle of happiness, sadness sprinkled with hard times and good times. Don't let the hard times get the best of you. Keep the faith. Be patient. Good times are always just around the corner. So a wise and wonderful wife once told me."

"Annie Oakley was a straight shooter."

"Deadeye to boot."

Chapter 23

"All right, refreshed and ready, David. I could spend into the wee hours telling you about your daddy, your aunt Clara and Uncle Mike and their families or even more about Jupiter but I wish to switch gears. At some point, if you are interested, we can go there but it is boring by comparison to what you have heard so far."

"You're driving. Tell it however you wish to share it, Grandfather Nelson."

"Very well, mash the button then."

> The blessing was born, and the past was set free. It is frowned on to show favoritism. I concur, it is wrong but not always without fault. I accept my role in this, but I will plead the fifth if cornered and asked. Don't even consider blackmailing me because of what I am about to confess on that little recorder. I am exercising grandfather-grandson confidentiality, lawful and biding. I will have some say on last editing rights where some of the next chapter in the Whiteside saga is concerned.

> Jimmy was in that bad place after the school shooter. The game changer and best medicine for starting the healing process weighed in at seven pounds, three ounces, a late life unexpected miracle birth. Robert Davidson Whiteside blessed our family with his arrival. Beet red face and a head full of jet-black hair, he was a sight to behold. This one had the Whiteside attitude from the get-go. You could tell by the nice pair of lungs on him commanding his parent's attention and those in surrounding counties. It was tough to decipher if he was unhappy or just the new mouthpiece of the family. When he bellowed, those around listened even if they didn't want to. There was no shutting out the joyful noise of the newcomer.

"Was I really that loud?"

"A banshee had nothing on you, David. Dogs howled and cats scatted when you took to bellowing. A bottle wouldn't satisfy you. Your mother could only quiet you by breast feeding you. Some say it is tougher to wean a young'un off the tit than a bottle. You proved it more right than wrong. Can't say I could blame you. My mama breast fed all of us, so she said. It was the natural thing to do."

"If you say so. She never told me that and I never thought it important to ask."

"It took some time, but they finally broke you, but not before you had started talking and walking."

"That sounds gross, Grandfather Nelson."

"I reckon some considered it so."

"Was I the modern-day shameful blemish for the Whiteside family?"

"Not hardly, David. If breast feeding was shameful, we would all be guilty as charged."

"Weaned, walking and talking, you were a little spitfire, a handful if ever there was one."

With the considerable age gap between you and your siblings I don't think Jimmy and Roselyn were quite prepared for rearing another. They had long fallen off that bicycle and getting it back up right posed some challenges. Riding a bicycle requires you to maintain your balance and keep peddling. Blessings come with responsibilities. A one-year-old isn't loaded with a lot of patience to break in parents, especially ones that are supposed to know what they are doing. Older doesn't always guarantee that you are wiser. I wished Bessy would have been around. She would have taken this little bullish situation by the horns.

Neither Jimmy nor Roselyn was suffering from any regrets. A bundle of joy can just pose challenges for those rusty on raising babies. God mostly gives children to folks when they are young and resilient. The Lord doesn't grant people a good life or a bad alternative. He just gives us life. It's left up to us what we make out of it. No, my son and his bride were not facing bad choices. The miracle given them had helped them heal and have purpose when all seemed lost and hopeless. David conquered Jimmy's Goliath, offering him a chance to put the horrors of that school tragedy in the past where it belonged.

I had almost forgotten what it meant to have a little one around. If they had lived nearby, I would have spoiled this one rotten. As it was, I missed too much of his time sprouting like a beanstalk. I wasn't around Jimmy, Clara or Mike as much as I should have been when they were growing up but one thing, I cherished was reading them the story of Jack and the Beanstalk. I read that a time or two to little David when the opportunity arose. It was in his pre-walking and talking days. I probably got more out of it than the little feller ever did. I sure liked that story, Jack learning his lesson, swapping the family cow for that handful of beans. Gold and giants in the clouds at the other end of a beanstalk, mighty fine writing for an Englishman. I loved reading and hearing those fairytales. Mama read them to us before bedtime.

Young David was about five when I took him fishing one summer while they were visiting. I wasn't much of a fisherman, learning a lot of what I knew from Uncle Rusty, the pond king. I had not fished in almost too many years to remember. Can't recall why I thought it was such a good idea taking my young grandson. I had to borrow the fishing rods and dig up some bait. Didn't have too many of those red wigglers but I wasn't intending to catch enough fish to feed the family. I really didn't care much if we caught anything or not. You catch it, you got to clean it. I was rusty on cleaning fish too.

I soon realized that wetting a hook held no fascination for David and very little for me as well. I spent my time with him teaching him how to skip rocks. We dangled our feet in the water watching as the little tadpoles used them for cover and tiny minnows darted about. A cork finally went under. I helped the little feller bring it in. There was no fish on the hook. Instead, it was a Cooter, a water turtle that we set loose after we landed it. Old grandpa still cherishes that day. It was short lived and a short stay, too short for my liking.

I remember taking David to his first county fair. Those traveling carnivals had not changed much over the years. Sure, the rides were different, but the concept and the ambiance were the same. There were none of those crazy side shows, wild boys eating live chickens, giants and dwarfs, sword swallowers or those scary pickled oddities. It was mostly just good ole fashion family fun, unforced and enjoyable. David was visiting for the weekend. Jimmy had dropped him off on the way to someplace. I forget where.

It was David and me. Annie called it the boy's night out. The wilder rides had height or age requirements. We did ride the Ferris wheel and merry-go-round several times. Those games of chance were money grabbers, but I did let David try the sure thing one, picking up ducks, a prize every time. We got our fingers all sticky with cotton candy and had a corndog. I gave in to going inside the House of Mirrors. There were no restrictions. I figured what harm could there be. I almost instantly regretted my decision when we became separated. Every time I thought I had found David, I ran into an optical illusion, smashing my face too many times until I learned to move forward with my hands out front. I was panic stricken yelling out his name. When I finally found my way to the exit, there sat the little booger on a bench chatting with a clown making him a balloon animal. I had been preparing my speech for explaining how I had lost him, thinking he would end up like my brother Jeremy, trapped as a carney.

"What happened that day remained a secret until now, David. I reckon your folks would get a hoot out of hearing it. Back then they would never have left you alone with me again though."

"I do remember bits and pieces of that fair. Maybe not to such detail but the house of mirrors does register with me. Now I know why I have always been afraid of going inside them. I think that clown was calming me down when you finally came out. I had already stifled my tears because I didn't want to upset you."

"Well, I reckon I learned something new as well. Thank you, David for sparing my feelings back then. I would have preferred that you not wandered off in the first place though. You were a gamer if ever there was one. One other story comes to mind. You were still a little sprig. It might have been before the county fair that it happened. I can't righty recall the sequence. I don't think it much matters. Just remembering it is good enough."

> It was during another visit. It was David's birthday. I wish I could remember which one. Annie was still with us. David was walking and talking to beat the band, old enough to be rambunctious but not in school yet. We had a birthday party at our place. Some of the neighbor's children had been invited, not many, just a handful. Henry Mercer was present. He was the grandpappy of one of the children in attendance and had brought the little chap, then hung around for the cake and ice cream. It had gotten dark, and the children were still in a playful mood, and so was Henry. He taught the four or five children still there a little song about 'There Ain't no boogers out tonight, grandpappy Henry killed them all last night.' Soon they were singing it left and right.
>
> Henry then posed a dare to them. In the almost pitch blackness, they were dared to go to the far side of the yard and circle the barn while singing the tune. He told them they had to walk, not run. Everyone that returned and touched the front porch would be rewarded with a quarter for their bravery. Each took their turn, Henry's grandboy going first.

There was one girl in the bunch. I got a little side story about her. My heart and soul, David was last to give it a try. Henry saved the best for last. He snuck through the house, out the backdoor and to the barn before David started his round trip.

David was singing as he vanished into the darkness and around the backside of the barn. The scream pierced the night and we saw David running full throttle, sliding and tumbling to a stop excluding the ceremonial touch of the front porch. Once he was able to catch his breath, he tried to explain what had happened.

"There was a growl coming from behind the barn. It was a bear crouched on all fours. It was going to eat me. I ran as fast as I could but not before giving that bear some 'what for.'

"What did you do, David?"

"He hit me with a pipe wrench, that's what the little snot nose did," said a bleeding, Henry Mercer."

"I stumbled over it and picked it up just in case I saw a boogeyman," explained little David.

"That boy walloped me with it good," added Henry, still wiping the blood from his noggin with his handkerchief.

"I 'bearly' remember that, Grandfather Nelson. I am glad I didn't kill my first bear."

"Henry was much obliged as well. Mash the stop button. It will save me that confidentially speech again. No recording, no evidence."

"Paused, you are in the clear."

"I would never say this in front of your brother and sister, but you were by far my favorite. I suspect your folks saw through it but if they did, they didn't let on. It was not intentional on my part. I reckon I had the chances to spend more time with you than I ever did

227

with them. Now, that doesn't mean I loved them any less. And if ever you try to get me to admit it in front of them, you are wasting your time. I will deny it and fall just shy of calling you a bald-faced lair. You wouldn't want to see an old man stoop so low, would you?"

"I'll just take it as gospel and let it stay between you and me. You were my favorite grandfather."

"Smooth talker…I am the only grandfather you ever knew."

"And only can be the best, right?"

"What you say we call this a done deal and get some sleep?"

"I thought you were a night owl."

"Even an old owl requires shuteye."

"Grandfather Nelson, I have enjoyed this day."

"Same here, David. More memories have been made, one for the books, you and me doing this."

Chapter 24

David showered and then dressed back in the same clothes. He smelled breakfast, his stomach already growling reminding him of Henry the bear. As he approached the kitchen, he could hear voices; well just one, his grandfather's. He spotted him and held up one finger while he finished the phone call. When he did, he sat heavily into one of the kitchen chairs.

"Are you all right Grandfather."

"I am more than all right, David. That was your Uncle Jupiter Whiteside. You are not going to believe this. His sister Rachel and brother Petey are alive and have reached out to him. It seems that Rachel launched an investigation and managed to locate Petey first then Jupiter. She started it almost ten years ago, trails getting hot then going cold. They have not yet met but are planning a reunion and want to do it here. You are going to meet your Uncle Petey and Aunt Rachel and will finally meet my nephew and niece. How about that? Jupiter had all but given up hope, but God stuck to His plan and performed another miracle. I am officially banding Daddy's saying of forced family fun as a family mantra. I might add, there is no such thing as a Whiteside curse. We are blessed not stressed. We have had the courage to bulldoze through the hard times while never giving up on the good times surely to eventually come our way."

"That is wonderful news and a fitting end to what we started yesterday. Uncle Jupiter must be cutting cartwheels."

"I suspect he is. He struggled so coming up empty handed so many times. Too often we can be hard on ourselves for circumstances we cannot control. Life is filled with plenty of chapters; some that we are fearful of sharing and reading out loud. We tend to forget it is much easier to take a deep breath, sit back and cherish what life we have been privileged to live. Mistakes often lead to greater wisdom, suffering giving us strength. Best we can do at the time is keep moving forward, endure and persevere. No matter how dark it seems the sun will rise another day and bless us with the rays of Almighty Lord."

"Powerful words, Grandfather Nelson."

"Powerful indeed as God intended them. David, sit and enjoy this delicious breakfast I have prepared. It is the most important meal of the day. I will let you know Jupiter's plans when he lets me know."

"I will relay the wonderful information to Father and Mother.'

"And it is your call as to what you share from those recordings."

****

The reunion went off without a hitch a couple of weeks later. We welcomed two more to the Whiteside fold. Rachel and Petey were accompanied by their spouses and children. I have never seen Jupiter happier than that day he reunited with his long-lost family. Family embraced and enjoyed the fellowship of family. There were more Whitesides present than you could shake a stick at. I noticed David recording much of the reunion, capturing those stories about where Rachel and Petey had ended up under the care of separate foster parents. They had the utmost respect and love for those they called mom and dad. Carol was no more than a blur, someone that had given them life in more ways than one. Jupiter, the oldest, told them what he remembered about their birth mother, purposely leaving out the bad memories. Not to steal David's thunder and his recordings, I filled them in on a few relatives they never met like cousins Jeremy, Keith and yes, Carol. I included Bessy and Annie as well as my parents just to let them know they came from a long line of wonderful kinfolk. Like Jupiter, I left out the ugly history purposely, my edited version.

It saddened me when everyone had to go their separate ways but before they did, we made plans for the best Christmas ever. Sadly, that was many months away. Everyone swapped personal information, addresses and phone numbers, vowing to stay in touch regularly. As the elder of the group, I made sure I tossed in a little guilt, saying I was not getting any younger and I counted on them to follow up with what they promised. I excluded telling them I was as healthy as a horse, given that I was just shy of turning ninety-eight. Families must start getting back together for Sunday dinner when possible and more so for family reunions and not funerals. FFF…Forever Family Fun.

****

A week later David's phone vibrated, and he retrieved it from his pocket. It was a text from his Grandfather Nelson. It read: *I renewed my driver's license then got me a new vehicle. A brand spanking new truck with a three-year lease. I plan to make it to a hundred and wave it in their face. It drives like a champ. Come over this weekend and we'll take it for a spin, maybe even wet a couple of hooks like old times.* David smiled and responded with an appropriate emoji, one with a wink and a kiss. His grandfather reciprocated with an emoji sporting a halo.

God had indeed blessed the Whitesides. Through tragedy and triumph, the family remained solid as a rock. The next generation would carry the torch. No one prouder than Nelson to turn over the reins. As for David, he would eventually transcript those recordings and publish a book, one as a keepsake for the family. Nostalgia preserved thanks to his grandfather. And as promised, he out lived the lease on the truck and then some, still holding his own at the ripe old age of a hundred and one.

About T. Allen Winn

Winn began writing in 2003 while being cooped up in hotels during business travel. Completing a 650 page so called novel he became hooked. The homegrown Abbeville, South Carolina boy embraced the experience completing one novel and then leaping into the next one, fun and therapy at the time. That changed in 2011 when a chance encounter brought stranger and new neighbor Bob O'Brien to his Pawley's Island doorsteps. Bob did not realize the neighborhood home had been sold and apologized when Tom greeted him instead of the man he had expected to see. Book in hand, Bob had just published his first novel, The Toppled Pawn and explained the previous neighbor had shown interest in writing. Tom remarked he dabbled in writing to which Bob asked, do you have a manuscript? Tom replied 'ten'. Bob had just started Prose Press, a publishing company and suggested publishing one. You cannot make this stuff up.

T. Allen Winn's first novel, Road Rage joined the ranks of the published a few months later, and he owes a special thanks to Bob O'Brien for making this possible. His first seven books were published by Prose Press. In 2016, T. Allen Winn established Buttermilk Books, his publishing company and has now published over thirty books. He and his wife reside in Myrtle Beach, South Carolina.

Ole 'T' does not write a specific genre. He writes what strikes his fancy. If you don't see something that fits your reading wheelhouse, just tell him what you like, and he might just write it for you.

Books are available on Amazon or online where books are sold. Select books are available at Southern Succotash on Washington Street in Abbeville, S.C., in Tabor City, N.C. at Grapefull Sisters Vineyard, and at Calabash Art and Curios in Calabash, S.C. Or *Message* T. Allen Winn on Facebook to arrange delivery of signed copies, or to schedule him to speak at an event or book club.

Fiction from T. Allen Winn

The Perfect Spook House

Dark Thirty

Lou Who

Raw Ride, a Wild West Zombie Apocalyptic Shoot'um Up

The Man Who Met the Mouse

Mister Twix Mystery, a Cat Scene Investigation

Come Here, Getouttahere, Tyler's Tail Wagging Tale

The Tenth Elemental

Last Stand on the Grand Strand

The Lord's Last Acres

Covert 19, 2020 A Devil of a Year

The Sot and The Savior

Outside the Clique

Guns and Ashes, Four Friends at a Fish Fry

Forced Family Fun, God Bless the Whiteside's

The Detective Trudy Wagner series

Road Rage

North of the Border

Tithes and Offerings

Trudy Wagner, Southern Belle, the Prequel to Road Rage

Bigfoot Trilogy

Book 1: Foot, Tree Knockers and Rock Throwers

Book 2: Another Foot,

What Really Happened to D.B. Cooper

Book 3: Final Foot, Willow Creek

Non-Fiction from T. Allen Winn

Being Bentley, A Dog Like No Other

December's Darkest Day, While I Breathe, I Hope

The Hardwood Walker of Port Harrelson Road

Cuz, My Brother, Life is Good, God is Good

Memoirs

The Caregiver's Son, Outside the Window Looking In

Vol 1: Cornbread and Buttermilk

Vol 2: Don't Sit Naked in a Grits Tree

Pushed Into The Pull, Thank You Cuz

The Endless Mulligan, Short Shots from the Golf Whomper

Books with Co-Author Benji Greeson

Abbeville, South Carolina Football

It's All About the 'A'

It's All About the Angels in the Backfield

Biographies

Clay Page, Somewhere In Between

Screw It, Let's Ride, The Legend Bub Lollis

www.ingramcontent.com/pod-product-compliance
Lightning Source LLC
Chambersburg PA
CBHW060154180626
46813CB00007B/2750